MW01075839

ROXANNE

The Italian Cartel #2

SHANDI BOYES

Edited by
NICKY @ SWISH DESIGN & EDITING

Illustrated by
SSB COVERS & DESIGN

Copyright

Written By: Shandi Boyes

Editing: Nicky at Swish Design & Editing

Proofreading: Kaylene at Swish Desigh & Editing

Beta Reading: Carolyn Wallace

Cover: SSB Covers & Design

Want to stay in touch?

Facebook: facebook.com/authorshandi

Instagram: instagram.com/authorshandi

Email: authorshandi@gmail.com

Reader's Group: bit.ly/ShandiBookBabes

Website: authorshandi.com

Newsletter: https://www.subscribepage.com/AuthorShandi

Also by Shandi Boyes

Perception Series

Saving Noah (Noah & Emily)

Fighting Jacob (Jacob & Lola)

Taming Nick (Nick & Jenni)

Redeeming Slater (Slater and Kylie)

Saving Emily (Noah & Emily - Novella)

Wrapped Up with Rise Up (Perception Novella - should be read after the Bound Series)

Enigma

Enigma (Isaac & Isabelle #1)

Unraveling an Enigma (Isaac & Isabelle #2)

Enigma The Mystery Unmasked (Isaac & Isabelle #3)

Enigma: The Final Chapter (Isaac & Isabelle #4)

Beneath The Secrets (Hugo & Ava #1)

Beneath The Sheets(Hugo & Ava #2)

Spy Thy Neighbor (Hunter & Paige)

The Opposite Effect (Brax & Clara)

I Married a Mob Boss(Rico & Blaire)

Second Shot(Hawke & Gemma)

The Way We Are(Ryan & Savannah #1)

The Way We Were(Ryan & Savannah #2)

Sugar and Spice (Cormack & Harlow)

Lady In Waiting (Regan & Alex #1)

Man in Queue (Regan & Alex #2)

Couple on Hold(Regan & Alex #3)

Enigma: The Wedding (Isaac and Isabelle)

Silent Vigilante (Brandon and Melody #1)

Hushed Guardian (Brandon & Melody #2)

Quiet Protector (Brandon & Melody #3)

Bound Series

Chains (Marcus & Cleo #1)

Links(Marcus & Cleo #2)

Bound(Marcus & Cleo #3)

Restrain(Marcus & Cleo #4)

Psycho (Dexter & ??)

Russian Mob Chronicles

Nikolai: A Mafia Prince Romance (Nikolai & Justine #1)

Nikolai: Taking Back What's Mine (Nikolai & Justine #2)

Nikolai: What's Left of Me(Nikolai & Justine #3)

Nikolai: Mine to Protect(Nikolai & Justine #4)

Asher: My Russian Revenge (Asher & Zariah)

Nikolai: Through the Devil's Eyes(Nikolai & Justine #5)

Trey (Trey & K)

The Italian Cartel

Dimitri

Roxanne

Reign

Maddox

Rocco

RomCom Standalones

Just Playin' (Elvis & Willow)

The Drop Zone (Colby & Jamie)

Ain't Happenin'(Lorenzo & Skylar)

Short Stories

Christmas Trio (Wesley, Andrew & Mallory -- short story)

Falling For A Stranger (Short Story)

K (A Trey Sequel)

Coming Soon

Skitzo

ONE

Roxanne

As Dimitri's eyes bounce between mine, I shake my head, denying the claims I see in his narrowed gaze. There's no doubt my face is visible in the image that's so zoomed in, the pixilation that should make me unrecognizable to anyone who doesn't intimately know me, but I'm not present in the physical sense. My face is being bounced off an industrial-size filing cabinet. The same filing cabinet I saw stacked behind my mother when she FaceTimed me the day after my failed meet-up to reconnect with my father.

She said she was sorry he had made me upset, and that she was determined to mend the rift between us. I told her not to worry. My father was the same cruel man he always was, so I wasn't interested in rebuilding bridges that had burned years earlier.

Our conversation barely lasted a minute, but if the anger teeming out of Dimitri is anything to go by, my last contact with my mother is more significant to him than it was to me. He's blistering mad. Our combined dispositions are enhanced beyond reproach.

"That isn't me," I hiccup through a sob.

When anger flares through his eyes, making them dark cesspools of annoyance, I realize my error. Denials won't get me anywhere. I need to prove to Dimitri I'm on his team. That's the only way I'll come out of this exchange with my life intact.

"It's me, but I wasn't there when they took Fien. You can see it's a reflection. Even a surveillance novice wouldn't be able to deny that..." My words trail off when Dimitri releases the first surveillance image from his death-tight grip to reveal a second, more terrifying one. It shows a tiny baby covered with white goop and blood being dangled mid-air by her feet. She's as still as a board, her only coloring coming from the cruel grip her captor has on her feet. He's clutching her so tightly, the blood that's supposed to pump around her feet pools in them instead. Their red hue matches the flames tattooed on the man's wrist—the same flame tattoo barely noticeable on my father's blood-smattered arm since he had it recently covered with a much bigger design.

If that isn't concerning enough, a tiny hand in the very far left of the image has an identifiable feature. It isn't a birthmark like Fien has on her stomach nor a tattoo. It's a ring—a ring that feels like it weighs a ton when Dimitri's eyes lower to take in its uniqueness firsthand. He glares at the custom jewelry piece I inherited from my grandmother, his blazing stare heating it up as effectively as his evidence makes my stomach flip.

I can't see the face of the man in the image, it's covered by a balaclava, but both his tattoo and his eyes are familiar to me. As are the hands of the woman reaching out to remove Dimitri's daughter from his clutch.

As tears flood my eyes, horrified I have any association with people capable of doing such a horrendous act, I blubber out a string of apologies. I'm sickened my parents would do something so inhumane, but I also don't want to be punished for something that wasn't my fault. They're my parents, but their actions don't lie on my shoulders.

When my apologies reach Dimitri's ears, he leans into me deeper, stealing both the words from my mouth and the air from my lungs. "They killed my wife. Your parents *killed my wife!*" He screams his last three words in my face.

"I know. I am so sorry. I had no idea they were capable of doing such an appalling act. I swear to God, I don't condone a single thing they've done. If I had any inkling they were involved, I would have told you."

"You're lying."

Tears fling off my face when I shake my head. "No. I had no clue. I swear I was in the dark as much as you." I am shocked I can talk. I'm not just stunned at the evidence he's presenting, I am also shocked we're holding this conversation in the room my father was murdered in. The anger emanating from him has vomit racing up my food pipe. It's seconds from being released. "I'm as angry as you."

Air traps in my throat when Dimitri interrupts, "Prove it."

"W-what?" I stare at him, utterly lost. How can I prove I'm as devastated as him? He killed my father. I can't display my anger as brutally as that. The person deserving of my wrath is dead. There's no one left for me to take my anger out on.

Oh no.

As the truth smacks into me, the door we walked through only minutes ago pops open, and a woman with reddish-blonde hair and arms scarred with track marks is thrust into the room. When my mother lands on the floor with a thud, first instincts have me wanting to race to her side. The only reason I don't is because I can't get the images Dimitri showed me out of my head. Although most of my focus was on Fien and my parents, no amount of shock could stop my eyes from drinking in the blurry person behind them. Dimitri's wife wasn't treated with any respect, so why should my mother be given any leeway?

An idealism on who our parents are supposed to be is embedded in us when we're kids. If you're lucky, your unfounded hopes might stack up. But for the most part, you'll be lucky to stumble out of childhood unscathed. Have you ever heard the saying, *Just because you can have kids doesn't mean you should?* That resonates well with my parents. I wouldn't be here if it weren't for them, but Fien would be. That, in itself, explains Dimitri's fury.

My heart tries to break out of my chest when Dimitri steps back, unpinning me from the wall. The anger radiating out of him isn't responsible for my heart's thuds, it's the angst he strikes it with when he digs his gun out of the back of his jeans and shoves it into my hand.

I could direct it at him as he did to me days ago, I could save my mother before saving myself, but for the life of me, I can't. I'm not a parent, but that doesn't mean I can't understand what Dimitri is going through. He was barely holding on last week, so I can only imagine how thin the thread is now. The images he showed me were horrific, and the pain in his eyes tells me they were just the beginning of the horrendous things he has seen.

"Please don't make me do this," I beg when he slides off the safety on his gun, so it's ready to maim. I'm shocked at how fast he moves. I am shuddering like I'm in an ice bath. The gun isn't close to stable—and neither am I. "I can make it up to you. I'll do anything you ask."

"You're already doing everything I ask." His words snap out of his mouth like venom, both vicious and maiming. They have nothing on the hate in his eyes, though.

"I'll do more—"

Dimitri whips around so fast, the waft of his quick movements blasts my face with the scent of a pricy aftershave. "More what, Roxanne? More trouble? More hurt?"

"Anything! I'll do anything you ask."

Tears roll down my cheeks unchecked when he says, "Kill the woman responsible for my wife's death. That's *all* I want you to do."

Ignoring the rapid shake of my head advising him I could never do that, he grips the scruff of my mother's shirt. His brutal strength forces her eyes from the floor. When they collide with mine, I almost become one with the wall. I don't recognize her in the slightest. She isn't close to the woman I remember. Her eyes aren't lit with life. They're shallow and lifeless, as bleak as my father's now are.

That doesn't mean I want to kill her, though.

"I can't," I whimper on a sob. "She's my mother."

"She's a kidnapper and a murderer. She deserves to die!" After dragging my mother to within an inch of my feet, Dimitri screams in her face. "Tell her what you told me." When the quick shake of her head grates on his last nerve, he backhands her so hard, my teeth feel the collision. "Tell her what you told me!"

I stare at my mother, begging for her to do as asked. If she wants to live, she must jump on cue, and even then, it may not be enough. Her death certificate was signed the instant she went against a man more powerful than she'll ever be, and no, I'm not solely referencing Dimitri.

While scratching at fresh needle marks in her arms, my mother stutters out, "We had to give them someone. W-w-we couldn't arrive empty-handed. We owed them money. *Lots* of money."

"So, instead of selling them your daughter as arranged, you convinced your husband to take my wife instead!" Even if we weren't in a small, concrete room, I'd still hear Dimitri's roar twice. That's how loud he's shouting.

"They wanted someone who could have children. They didn't care who they got. As long as she was fertile, they'd take anyone." My mother's cracked lips quiver as she locks her eyes with mine. "I just couldn't give them *my* child."

Dimitri is as unbelieving of the remorse in her tone as me. She was never overly motherly, so why would she start years after she abandoned me? "So, you gave them mine instead *after* cutting her out of my wife's stomach!"

"No." She adds to her denial of Dimitri's claim by shaking her head. "That was never the plan. They were only supposed to take your wife. T-t-they weren't supposed to take your daughter. I didn't know Ian's plan. He kept me in the dark." Against her better judgment, she slants her head to the side so she can peer at me past Dimitri's brimming-with-anger frame. "That's why I ended our call so fast that night. I heard screaming. I tried to stop him, Roxie, but I couldn't. You know what your father was like. He didn't listen to anyone, not even me."

She speaks about her husband as if his corpse isn't in the room with us, her disrespect as telling as the expression on her face. She once loved the man bound lifeless to the chair, however that was a very long time ago.

"Nothing I could have done would have changed anything. Once they realized who Audrey was, they were never going to listen to me."

I unconsciously shake my head, my body choosing its own response to the lies I see in her eyes. Audrey was eight months along. Her pregnancy was noticeable, so although she's pledging she had no part in what happened to Fien, she *is* responsible for her captivity—even more than me.

I try to make sense of the mess. "Why didn't you call the police? Or reach out for help? You can't live with a secret like this and not expect it to eventually come out, so why not come clean when it could have done some good?"

"I couldn't." When she shuffles closer to me, Dimitri raises his hand back into the air. It stops both the scuttles of my mother's knees and my heart. A slap is almost caring compared to how he could handle her stupidity, but I'd rather not witness her torture. She may not be the woman I once remembered, but she's still my mother.

With her hands clutched a mere inch from my bare feet, she locks her eyes with mine. "I haven't seen the sun in months. I don't even know what month it is, so how could I have sought help? Why do you think I didn't call you back that night, Roxie?"

I want to say because she abandoned me like she did when I was ten, but since that would swing the pendulum in Dimitri's favor, I keep my mouth shut. My stomach won't quit flipping from the smell emitting off my father. I don't want to see my mother killed the same way. I hate what she did, but turning into a monster to kill a monster won't stop the vicious cycle. It will continue circling until everyone is extinct—even the good monsters.

My queasiness takes on an entirely new meaning when Dimitri strikes my mother for the second time. "I told you to tell the truth, not the shit you tried to spurt earlier."

"Don't!" I shout when Dimitri raises his hand for the third time. His second hit split my mother's cheek. She won't come out of a third one without irreparable damage. Although she deserves his anger, a small part of me wonders if she's telling the truth. It's minute but undeniable.

When my words don't get through to Dimitri, I use the weapon he forced on me to my advantage. I fire one shot into the roof, squealing when it takes out the light hanging above my head.

It rains shards of glass down on me and has Dimitri's face the maddest I've ever seen. "You're going to shoot at *me*, the man who lost everything so *you* could continue living *your* miserable existence? They swapped *my* wife for *you*! They made her take your place!"

He grips the barrel of his gun like it isn't scorching hot from its recent firing, but instead of yanking it out of my grasp, he uses it to pull me in front of him.

With his hands curled around mine and his front squashed to my back, I can't garner the strength to stop him from aiming his gun at the pinched skin between my mother's brows. He isn't just stronger than me, his closeness has more hold on my wickedness than my morality.

"For once, give your daughter the decency she deserves. Tell. Her. The. Truth."

The reason for the extra thump in Dimitri's pulse is exposed when the quickest gleam darts through my mother's eyes when she spots the ring I inherited from my grandmother. For the first time tonight, I feel like siding with my family will place me on the wrong team.

Family members are supposed to be your go-to support network. They usually back you up in ways strangers can't.

I'm not getting that vibe from my mother.

All I'm feeling is devastation.

I've seen her wear this look before. It was when she raced out of my grandfather's barn, stating her eldest brother had been in an accident. When Nanna and I tried to race to Uncle Mike's side to offer assistance, my mother and father held us back, declaring it was too late. He was already gone.

That was mere days before my grandfather cut my parents out of his will. He didn't care about the tension it caused at Uncle Mike's funeral. He wanted it documented that in the event of his death, every possession he owned was to go to my grandmother. When she passed, it was to come to me. My parents were to get nothing.

That's how I inherited the antique Celtic ring Dimitri glared at earlier. Anything in my grandmother's possession at the time of her death was classified as mine—including the ring she gifted my mother when she birthed her first child.

My God, how could I not have put two and two together until now? My mother inherited my ring first. She never took it off, so why was it in the wreckage of my Nanna's accident?

"You were there. You…" I can't say it. The words won't come out of my mouth. Claudia's wrongful imprisonment proves traffic accidents aren't always as they seem, but still, this is too shocking to articulate.

Dimitri doesn't face the same issues as me. He has no trouble spelling things out as he sees them. "Not only did your mother attempt to sell you when her stash got low, she killed her only sibling *and* her mother with the hope of a big payout. It will take a few days for preliminary reports to come back, but I won't be shocked to discover your grandfather didn't die of natural causes."

I shake my head, too stunned by the honesty in Dimitri's tone to make sense of it.

"Killing my nanna wouldn't help my parents. If they wanted money, they would have needed to take me out as well."

When I say that to Dimitri, he presses his lips to the shell of my ear and growls, "They didn't want money…" His pause is the worst form of torture "They needed space. Space you gave them when you moved into a one-bedroom flat in the middle of the burbs."

I'm confused as to what he means until my wide-with-terror eyes collide with my mother's. She's wearing the same smug glare she wore when Uncle Mike's lawyer informed us he forgot to change his will when he married. When he died, all his assets went to my mother. Although he wasn't a wealthy man, he lived more comfortably than my parents. They thought they had hit the motherload when their bank balance rose by six digits.

"What did she need space for?" Although I'm asking questions, I don't need Dimitri to answer me to get the gist of what's happening. It's staring me straight in the face, eating away my morals as much as drugs stole the life of the woman kneeling in front of me.

"Was it for farming?" I don't mean to plant potatoes, tomatoes, or zucchini. I'm talking about the farms Dimitri mentioned during our talk before we came to the basement, the ones I can't forget no matter how hard my twisting stomach wishes I could.

If my intuition is true, if my parents are knee-deep in the industry responsible for Fien's captivity, this is worse than them switching a product mid-sale. They're selling babies for crying out loud—stolen-from-the-womb babies.

When I spot Dimitri's nod in the corner of my eye, I want to fold in two. The only reason I don't is because I have more pressing matters to attend to. It isn't just my mother's life at stake anymore. Mine is on the chopping block too.

"You need to tell him who you work with and *that I'm not involved.*" The last half of my sentence is voiced more punchily than the first half. I'm not just desperate to save my hide, I don't want *anyone* thinking I'm associated with such a callous, cruel world, much less Dimitri.

"Tell him!" I scream when my mother's silence works me

over as well as Dimitri's hand pummeled her face. "For once, protect me as you should have when I was a child. Put me first for a change!" Blinded by a rage too hot for me to think rationally, I curl my index finger around the gun Dimitri directed at her head. "Tell him! Tell him now!"

"I don't know who they are," she chokes out on a whimper, shocked I'm treating her as poorly as she treated me my entire life. "We didn't exchange names. We weren't a part of the production side. We were just... we..."

"Were a dumping site," Dimitri fills in when words allude her.

I never thought I would have a wish to kill someone, let alone the ability, but it's a close call when my mother bobs her head at Dimitri's claim. She isn't a victim like I believed during my childhood. She's as bad as my father and just as abusive, and once again, I'm done playing nice.

TWO

Dimitri

When I entered this room hours ago, my first thought was that I should crush Roxanne's windpipe as Smith's whispered words crushed my soul. I should destroy her as her parents destroyed me. At one stage, I even considered keeping her parents alive so they could witness me torture their child as they had mine.

None of my previous suggestions are being considered now.

Despite my intuition begging me to reconsider, I don't believe the anger blistering out of Roxanne is a ploy. Just like earlier tonight, she's prepared to slay for me by killing her own blood. If that can't convince me she's on my team, nothing will.

Audrey was taken as her replacement. She was kidnapped purely to fill the slot Roxanne's absence caused, but for the life of me, I can no longer place the blame for that on Roxanne's shoulders.

I looked away.

I fucked up.

This isn't Roxanne's fault.

In all honesty, Roxanne is so under my thumb, if she had the opportunity to switch places with Fien, she would in a heartbeat. I have no doubt about that. It isn't just men who are led by their libidos. Women are just as bad. The way Roxanne stared at me in the alleyway all those months ago is proof of this.

There's just one difference between her and women like my wife.

Some sit back and watch the shit unfold.

Others get into the nitty-gritty.

Roxanne is the latter.

The way she put her life on the line earlier tonight proves that as does the obvious twitch of her index finger. It's curled around the trigger of my gun, ready to be pulled back. She's just waiting for permission.

Permission I won't give since it would change her in an instant.

Your first kill never leaves you, and when it's your blood, it haunts you long after you've entered your grave. That's one of the reasons my father is so fucked up. He may not have killed my grandfather, but he was responsible for the bullet that pierced his brain.

I feel Roxanne's sigh more than I hear it when I lower the gun I'm forcing her to aim at her mother's head. She knows this isn't the end of her mother's punishment, she's just glad she isn't going to be her torturer.

I promised to protect Fien no matter what. Even with my

emotions not knowing which way to swing, I'll keep my promise. I just need to make sure the right people are being held accountable. I won't lie, it will be a hard road, but even a man bogged down with grief knows a child can't be held responsible for their parents' actions. I've never accepted culpability for my father's crimes, and Fien will never be at fault for mine, so why the fuck am I writing a new set of rules for Roxanne? I could blame grief, but in all honesty, I've worked that excuse to death the past twenty months. It's time for me to stand on my own two feet. I'm a man. I can admit my mistakes.

For the most part.

My heart stops harmonizing its beats with Roxanne's when she sinks to the far corner of the room to suck in some much-needed breaths. Her eyes reveal she's as mad as hell and ready to kill, but they also expose she wishes the outcome of her mother's poor judgment could be anything but death.

I'd be lying if I said I don't feel the same way. I hate killing women. Their punishments usually come with an automatic clause for mercy. However, this isn't something I can let slide. Not only did Sailor organize the kidnapping of my wife, she attempted to sell her daughter before killing the only person who gave a crap about her. That, in itself, deserves a much harsher punishment than death.

After sliding on the safety on my gun to ensure my teetering moods won't cause an accidental firing, I nudge my head to the door. "Head up with Rocco and pack. We need to be at the airstrip by eight. I'll meet you there."

Hearing the words I don't speak the loudest, Roxanne

strays her wide-with-fear eyes to my side of the room. "Dimi—"

"Go." I keep my tone stern, assuring she knows I'm not suggesting she leave. I'm telling her to go. "I'll only be a minute."

My reassurance that I won't torture her mother for hours on end does little to ease the heavy groove between her brows, but it does get her feet moving.

After glancing at Sailor for the quickest second, she makes a beeline for the door. Even with my pulse booming in my ears, I hear Rocco exhale when Roxanne breaks into the dimly lit corridor. He was waiting with three body bags, confident no amount of pleading would see Roxanne's family escape conviction for the second time.

Roxanne's gall ensures he will only need two.

Once the door closes with Roxanne on the other side, I devote all my attention to her mother. I want to maim, I want to kill, but more than any of that, I want to give Fien's mother the burial she deserves.

I'm not a religious man, but Audrey's family is. Until her body is returned to the ground, her soul won't rest. I'm happy to give them closure if it means they won't contest Fien's custody. They'd never win, but the less I have to worry about, the easier it will be for Fien to settle once she's returned.

"Where is Audrey buried?" My words are somewhat calm for how hot my veins feel. I'm seconds from blowing my top, but I am showing restraint, the shackle of my go-to emotion solely for Fien... and perhaps Roxanne.

When Sailor's eyes lift to mine, I realize just how fucked

she is, and for once, her undoing has nothing to do with me or my crew. She's been taken by demons way worse than a man's possessiveness. Drugs fuck you over in a way no man can. She's lost to it, completely fucking gone.

"I don't know——"

"*Where* did you bury *my wife*!"

She recoils at my shouted words, but they get her talking better than my fists ever could. "I took your daughter to get checked over. When I returned, your wife was gone."

I don't know her well enough to know if she's lying or not, but I do know one thing, pretending she gives a shit about Fien won't sit well with me. She didn't care about my daughter when she was forcefully removed from her mother's stomach weeks too early. She didn't care that her daughter was emotionally abused by her husband. She cares about no one but herself. The way she treated Roxanne her entire life is proof of this.

If Audrey hadn't arrived at Slice of Salt when she did, who's to say Sailor wouldn't have gone ahead with the original plan to sell Roxanne. She said it herself, Rimi wanted anyone. That anyone could have been Roxanne, and for some reason, that annoys me more than knowing she's responsible for Audrey's death. Don't ask me why. It's fucked for me even to think this way, but I'm merely being honest—for once.

Sailor's eyes shift from her dead husband to me when I drag a chair over from the side of the room. I balance one of the chair's legs onto her ring finger before taking a seat. Her tear-choked scream is similar to the one Roxanne's suitor released earlier tonight when I removed the finger he sneakily dragged up Roxanne's arm. He thought the severity of his punishment didn't fit his crime. I believed otherwise. He'll think twice before he ever touches something he doesn't own again.

If I truly believed Sailor had more information than a standard bottom-dweller in this industry, I'd torture her for the next several hours until she spilled the beans. Since I'm aware that isn't the case, I use her open mouth to my advantage.

When I ram the barrel of my gun down her throat, it shuts her up in an instant and has her paying careful attention to everything I say. Although I don't have a lot to say, it's best for her to listen. Paying attention is the highest form of respect. Without it, there will be no possibility of me offering her any leniency.

I don't mean from death, her expiration date is well past perished. I'm merely proposing a quick, clean death compared to letting Clover have his way with her. He won't rape her, that isn't his kink, but he'll be more than happy to add additional splits to her cheeks.

"This is your last chance, Sailor." I speak slow to ensure the hammering of her heart doesn't affect her ability to hear me. "Where did you bury my wife?"

THREE

Roxanne

_____

When the ricochet of a bullet being fired booms into my ears, I grip a designer dress so firmly, its pricy threads pop. I'm on the third level of Dimitri's New York compound, packing for a trip to God knows where. However, I still know the direction the noise came from. Not only did the devastating vibration tickle my toes, it also chipped away a piece of my soul like it did when my father carried Uncle Mike out of my grandparents' barn a decade ago.

I was barely ten, but the deathly swing of Uncle Mike's arm revealed he was gone. His skin was mottled like my father's. Even with my parents saying otherwise, I often wondered why he looked the way he did. He was run over by a tractor not placed into gear, but he was marked and nicked as if he had been in an underground cage fight.

Since I was so young, I never suspected my parents were

involved in his accident. Only after seeing the flare dart through my mother's eyes an hour ago did reality dawn. My parents didn't witness his accident. They killed him as they most likely did my grandparents.

My grandparents would never admit it, but everyone knew Uncle Mike was their favorite. He helped without being asked, never accepted a dime for his time, and agreed with their decision not to sell their little slice of heaven in the middle of a busy metropolis. His decision had nothing to do with money. Unlike my parents, he had done well for himself. He wasn't close to wealthy, but he had a humble, happy existence. He was married and expecting his first child in the spring.

Last I heard, Aunt Melissa was residing in Arizona. Her child was born three months after my uncle's death. I don't know if my cousin is a boy or a girl. When my uncle was laid to rest, it was as if his little family no longer existed.

After dumping my dress into a suitcase open on the floor, I drag the sleeve of my dressing gown under my nose, removing the mess pooled there. The past hour has flown by in a blur. I've been packing and guzzling down vodka like the man I willingly gave my virginity to isn't in the process of torturing my mother.

Estelle always says blood doesn't make you family, but still, I expected to feel some sort of grief at the thought I'm about to be an orphan. I feel a little empty and somewhat confused, but I also feel like the purge of my emotions will be good for me.

It's a sad reality, but by Dimitri wiping my slate clean, I'll have the chance to move forward without constantly looking over my shoulder. Although I never imagined it being this bad, I've always known there was something not quite right with my parents. It wasn't just the sex and drugs, there was a handful of other things that set alarm bells off in my head. I was just too young to understand what they meant.

I don't face that same issue now. My father didn't make me watch because he wanted to embarrass me. He was grooming me to take my mother's place, preparing to sell me as he had her. That's why some of his 'friends' gawked at me like they did my mother. They knew it was only a matter of time before I'd eventually be offered up as well.

With my stomach a twisted mess of confusion, I pace to the large window in my room to drink in the tranquil setting you wouldn't expect this close to a major city. The rugged terrain with a skyscraper backdrop has me recalling the time my mother dropped me off to live with my grandparents. For years, I thrived on the fact she cared enough about me not to let my father hurt me.

It was silly of me ever to believe.

While seeking financial aid for school, I discovered my grandparents had a significant mortgage on their estate. They had lived on their little ranch for over a decade before my mother was born, so it should have been paid off years earlier.

I initially blamed bad money management for their poor credit.

Even with my head blurred with alcohol, I'm not so stupid now.

"How fast can Smith look up transactions from closed bank accounts?"

Rocco cranks his neck to face me. He's been stationed at the corner of my room for the past hour. His unusual quiet has been off-putting, but considering the circumstances, it's also understandable.

Just as Rocco's lips move to speak, Smith's unique timber vibrates my ears. "About as quick as I can make a girl come. Why? What do you need?"

My eyes don't shoot around my room as they did hours ago, seeking the direction his voice came from. They hone straight in on the tiny camera in the far corner of the elaborate space. The lens appears to be a fault in the distressed wooden frame of a priceless piece of artwork above Dimitri's desk. Only those in the know are aware it's a state-of-the-art surveillance instrument. Smith disclosed not only can he see and hear me in every room, so can Dimitri. At the time, the thought intrigued me. Now it makes me worried. I don't want Dimitri to think I'm seeking excuses for my parents. I'm just trying to occupy my time before I go as crazy as drugs have made my mother.

While pacing closer to Dimitri's desk, I ask Smith, "My grandparents' accounts, can you see if there were any irregularities in their transactions?"

"Such as?"

My eyes rocket to Rocco when he answers Smith's question on my behalf, "She wants to know if her grandparents paid to keep her safe." As the thump of a keyboard being punished booms out of a hidden speaker above my head, Rocco pushes off the wall he's had his shoulder propped against the past hour. "Are you sure you want to go down this rabbit warren, Roxie? Knowing the reason for someone's fuck-ups don't make them any easier to swallow."

"I know that. I just..." I've got nothing but a heap of tension in my stomach and watering eyes. "What if it wasn't her fault? What if my father forced her like she said? He had a hold over her like Dimi..."

When my words are gobbled up by the shame raining down on me, Rocco takes up their slack. "Like Dimitri does you?"

I nod, too confused to continue acting like I'm fine. I held a gun to my mother's head in the room where my father was killed. I almost fired at her. If that isn't proof I'm already deep down the rabbit hole, nothing will convince you.

After watching me brush away a tear sitting high on my cheek, Rocco locks his murky green eyes with mine. They're still brimming with cheekiness, but there's a smart, noble gleam to them as well. "Even with taking out all the shit that happened when you were a kid, knowing what you know now, do you think your parents were or would have been upstanding, moral citizens?"

It should take me longer than two seconds to reach my decision. However, it doesn't. My parents have always been awful human beings, and that was before I discovered just how polluted their morals have become.

When I shake my head, air whizzes out of Rocco's nose. "Exactly! Don't get me wrong, I'm glad your parents couldn't resist the urge, I kinda like having you around, but if they weren't born—"

"Fien would still be here."

Confusion twists in my stomach when Rocco shakes his head. "This isn't just about Fien, Roxie. It's about you, and me, and a man who can't escape the demons of his past no matter how fast he runs." Acting as if his words don't have my heart racing a million miles an hour, he bridges the gap between us with two big strides. "No matter how fucked it is, we can't change the past… but we can stop it happening to someone else." After gripping my shoulders to lessen my unstable sways, he adds, "Your parents didn't just hit this scene once in desperation. They were shrouded in it. First, your aunt and uncle, then you and your grandparents before they moved onto Audrey and Fien. They weren't going to stop until someone stopped them. It sucks that the person has to be Dimitri, but trust me when I say it's better than it being you."

Even though I agree with him—I can see me forgiving Dimitri way sooner than I'd ever forgive myself—but I'm more confused than relieved. "What does my aunt have to do with this?"

Rocco curses under his breath before he sinks back to his makeshift station at the side of the room. No words escape his mouth for the next several seconds, but I see the truth in his remorseful gaze. Audrey wasn't the first pregnant woman my parents took. Even every day, decent Americans know criminals test the waters in their own backyard before playing with the big hitters.

"Hey, come on now, Roxie, breathe," Rocco says when the air in my lungs no longer feels adequate. It feels as if I'm drowning like I am being pulled into the abyss of my horrible life. My parents killed my family. All of them are dead, and I would have been next if it weren't for the man currently torturing my mother.

How fucked is that to even consider?

I can't comprehend it.

I also can't breathe.

When a high-pitch wheeze I'm certain didn't come from me breaks through the thud of my pulse in my ears, so does Rocco's clipped tone. "I'm just offering her comfort, dickwad. If you have a problem with me touching her, you're gonna need to tell me in person."

Rocco stops rubbing one of my arms in a nurturing manner, so he can give a one-finger salute to the camera in the corner of the room. With how tight my chest is, his shit-stirring grin shouldn't be comforting, but since it's full of mirth, it is. It allows my lungs to suck down the tiniest slither of air that's forced back out when a person bursts through the door on my left.

As Dimitri's narrowed gaze bounces between Rocco and me, his nostrils flare like his lungs are screaming as loudly as mine. He seems torn between wanting to punish me for accepting Rocco's comfort and taking me back to the dungeon responsible for making me an orphan.

He loses the ability to drive me to Hell's gates when I see the blood smattered on the collar of his dress shirt. It's so fresh, its putrid scent is stronger than the pricy aftershave he wears. It nosedives my hysteria in an instant and has me on the brink of a breakdown even quicker than that.

When a scream rips through me like a shard of glass, nicking my heart into hundreds of tiny pieces, I can't deny it's from me this time around. I hate what my parents did and agree they should be punished, but I still can't wrap my head around the fact it occurred without more fight.

I should have fought harder.

I should have pleaded for mercy.

And I should have done both those things long before my parents crossed paths with Dimitri's wife.

"I'm sorry," I force out through the despair clutching my throat. "For what they did. For choosing me over your wife. I'm so fucking sorry. They should have taken me. They should have hurt me. It's my fault. Everything happening to your daughter is my fault."

Dimitri appears shocked my regret centers around his daughter instead of my parents, but it has nothing on the surprise that hammers me when he replies, "You can be angry about what they did, you can hate them for how they treated you, but you are *not* to apologize for them. Do you understand me, Roxanne? You aren't to blame for a single thing they did."

Tears sting my eyes when I blubber out, "Fien would be here if it weren't for me."

I feel like he slaps me as hard as he did my mother when he shouts, "Fien would be here if I hadn't looked away. *I* fucked up. *I* made a mistake. This isn't on you."

I want to believe him, but I can't. "You said—"

"I made a mistake," he repeats, more forcefully. "And I'm trying to learn from it."

I'm so stunned by his grab of the culpability batten, I don't realize Rocco has left the room until I'm guided past the wall his brooding frame has been holding up the past hour.

As Dimitri walks me to the window I was peering out of earlier, the hammering of his heart is as audible as mine. I think it's because he noticed the half-empty bottle of vodka on his desk but am proven wrong when I notice a change to the scenic backdrop of his compound. The same city skyscrapers sparkle in the distance, and the same twelve SUVs line the cobbled driveway, however the lead SUV's taillights bounce red hues off locks not quite as vibrant as my hair's natural coloring, but undeniably similar.

After watching my mother be guided into the back seat of one of Dimitri's fleet cars, I raise my eyes to Dimitri's. I bombard him with an array of questions without a single word escaping my lips. I'm too stunned to talk, shocked my mother walked to her awaiting chariot instead of being slid into the back seat in a body bag. She's the reason Dimitri's wife is dead. There's only one punishment for that.

Seemingly wired to my inner monologue, Dimitri says, "She hurt you first. That means only you can sentence her." He drags the back of his finger down my wet cheek to gather up the tears there before adding, "I don't see you having the ability to make a rational decision tonight, so we'll wait."

The way he says 'we' makes me unsure which way is up. It was possessive and hot like I'm no longer his enemy.

Although I'm loving his changeup, something still doesn't make sense. "My father—"

"Was given a choice." Dimitri's interruption reveals he's still sitting on the edge of a very steep cliff. He's as confused as me, although not as emotional. "He either confessed to everything or took the easy way out. Although it was obvious he didn't give a crap about you, he couldn't shut down his feelings for your mother as easily. He thought he'd protect her by——"

"Taking the easy way out," I interrupt.

I hardly knew my father. Not even when I lived under the same roof as him did I understand him. He was different than my friends' fathers, and the older I became, the more I noticed that wasn't a good thing, but his love for my mother was undeniable. He became a monster to save her, and it's that monster that's slowly killing her.

Furthermore, the bullet entry point wound I've been endeavoring to wash out of my head the past hour with vodka was at an odd angle. It would have taken Dimitri distorting his wrist to replicate its oddness, but why would he bother faking his death? He's never hidden the fact he's a killer, so why would he start now?

Mistaking my quiet as deliberation on his honesty, Dimitri mutters, "If you don't believe me, Smith can show you footage."

Some may say I'm foolish to believe him, however, I do. "I believe you." Pretending the roaring buzz between us is from remorse instead of euphoria, I ask, "Where are they taking my mother?"

I feel cold when he breaks away from my side so he can commence undressing. It's been a long night in general, but he must be even more tired, considering he didn't sleep a wink last night. "To a rehabilitation center."

His reply comforts me in a way I can't explain. If he were planning to kill her, he wouldn't put steps in place to make her a better person. He would have let her go and waited for drugs to do what I'm not sure I am capable of. As

I said earlier, my parents are horrible people, but at the end of the day, I still wouldn't be here without them.

After placing his cufflinks into a dish on his desk, Dimitri pivots around to face me. "If it turns out what she said is untrue, her ruling will be taken out of your hands, do you understand?"

Even with my intuition dying to drill him on what she said, I nod my head instead. He looks as burned out as I feel. The lies my mother told with the hope of saving her hide isn't a conversation for today. I don't think there will ever be an appropriate day, but despite that, this question can't wait. "Did she tell you where Audrey's body is located?"

I'm not anticipating for him to answer me, he's not a fan of two-way interrogations, so you can imagine my shock when he shakes his head.

Willing to risk punishment for the greater good, I ask, "Do you believe she's at my grandparents' farm?"

My heart pains for him when he shrugs. "I don't know." His voice is the lowest it's ever been as are his shoulders. "We'll travel there in the morning. For now, I need sleep."

I nod, agreeing with him. He looks as tired as hell.

My head bob switches to a shake when he asks, "Have you showered?"

"No. Rocco stayed with me." My eyes widen when I realized my stupidity. "We didn't do anything. He stood by the door."

His cocky trademark half-smirk makes me hot all over. I'm too tipsy to determine if it's a good or bad heat. "I know. Smith isn't the only one with eyes and ears in this room."

Talking about Smith, he never got back to me about my earlier question.

I mentally book myself in for a scan to check for bugs when Dimitri reads my mind for the second time tonight. "Your queries into your grandparents' estate will have to wait. Until I know the full extent of what's happening, I instructed Smith not to give you half-ass assumptions."

Should my stomach gurgle at his confession or weaken its knot? If it were straight-up good, Smith would have given me an immediate answer. The fact it's in the unknown has me unsure which direction my mood should swing. I hate the murkiness of the unknown. Take now, for example, should I slide into the sheets Dimitri is folding down like he should be rewarded for issuing mercy to my underserving mother or take a stand about him torturing her? I know what my libido would prefer, but my morals should be an entirely different story, shouldn't they?

Needing time to deliberate on my wavering personalities, I wait for Dimitri to hop into bed before I hook my thumb to the bathroom. "I'm going to take a quick shower."

I barely pivot halfway around when Dimitri's deep timbre stops me. "No. No showering. You smell like me. If you wash that off, I'll have no choice but to replace it." Fighting the urge not to sprint to the bathroom, I crank my neck back to face him. His stare slicks my panties with moisture, but it also has my knees knocking together in a non-sexual way. "You don't want that, Roxanne. Not only are you drunk, I had three body bags to fill tonight. I didn't even manage one. Now is *not* the time to test my patience."

Hearing nothing but honesty in his tone, I slip between

the sheets, roll onto my side, then inconspicuously wiggle to his half of the mattress until the heat of his torso warms my back. I'm not close enough to be accused of spooning, however I do feel his battering breaths hitting the back of my neck for the next several minutes. He's as unhinged as me, and the irrefutable proof has me acting recklessly.

"Why do we sleep in the same bed every night? Your compound has heaps of rooms, but we always share the same one." I could pretend his low, shallow breaths are because he's sleeping, but I'm done playing stupid. "Is it because you want to protect me like you do Fien?" When his big inhale forces contact between us, my heart sinks into my stomach. "If you're here because you think I need saving, you're wrong."

"Stop it."

His warning growl does little to lessen the intensity of the fire brewing in my gut. Not even half a bottle of vodka could douse it, so I don't see anything working. "My father didn't hurt me. Well, not physically, so if you're thinking I'm your penance to get Fien back sooner, you're wrong."

"I'm not going to ask you again, Roxanne. Stop. It!"

I can't stop. Once my lips get flapping, there's no reeling them back in. "Most people assume I have daddy issues, and you'd be the best person to unkink them, but that isn't why I'm here."

"For fuck's sake, will you shut up!"

"I don't need saving. I was doing fine on my own. I was a little lonely and somewhat unsure what I was going to do next, but——"

"Goddammit, Roxanne." In less than a second, I'm

pulled onto my back, pinned on the mattress by Dimitri's large frame, and incredibly turned on. "You're not here because I want to save you with the hope a good deed will free my daughter. You're in my bed because I want to do the exact opposite. I want to devour you. Fuck you. Possess you so bad, the next time you have a gun pressed to your mother's head, you won't think about pulling the trigger, you'll do it. I want to mark every inch of you until the thoughts of what Rimi would have done to you if Audrey hadn't taken your place leave my head. Then I want to punish you some more for making me doubt who he should have taken."

His dangerous eyes dance between mine when he asks, "Do you have any idea the guilt associated with how you make me feel? The angst of wondering why I'm glad they took my wife instead of you. You were a fucking stranger, a goth standing on the corner undeserving of my time, but every single time I've prayed to go back and switch you with Audrey, I prayed just as quickly for that prayer not to be answered. She was carrying my daughter, my flesh and blood, yet I still couldn't put her first." It feels like my heart is torn out of my chest cavity when he adds, "So the next time you feel the need to ask why we sleep in the same bed, perhaps first consider the fact even someone as heartless as me can recognize that he doesn't deserve to get his daughter back, so he has no reason to save anyone, let alone someone who doesn't need saving."

With his jaw tight and words spoken he can never take back, he springs up from the bed without so much of a strain on his face before he stalks to the door.

His long strides are cut in half when I gabble out, "You

should have killed them, then I'd stop looking at you the way you hate, and you wouldn't feel guilty about something you can't control."

Nothing but my shocked breaths are heard when he replies, "Why do you think I held back?"

Stealing my chance to reply, he walks out the door, slamming it behind him.

FOUR

Roxanne

My blurry eyes lift to Rocco when he joins Smith and me in the lead SUV of Dimitri's fleet of four. The brutal slam of his door adds to the thunderous thump of my head, but it has nothing on the worry that bombards me when Dimitri fails to follow his trek.

We've been waiting almost twenty minutes, ten minutes over the time Dimitri demanded for everyone to be here this morning. We're not behind schedule because of Rocco. He only left the car in search of Dimitri.

"Where is he?" I ask, put off by the silence even with my hangover relishing it. Smith isn't much of a talker, but when he's paired up with Rocco, a girl can hardly get a word in. "I thought our flight left at eight?"

Rocco shrugs. "It does, but I don't know where he is."

I shoot my eyes to Smith. He can't brush off my inquisitiveness as easily as Rocco. He knows the insides of a monkey's butt.

When my glare becomes too much for Smith to bear, he gabbles out, "He told me he didn't want to be disturbed."

"So," I snap back with a grimace. "This isn't a standard day. It's important." From what I gathered from eavesdropping on Rocco and Smith's conversation the past forty minutes, our arrival at Hopeton this morning will be quickly followed by a trip to my family ranch. If it's the dumping ground Audrey was taken to, we'll know by the end of today.

"He only requests not to be disturbed when he needs a few hours away from the hell-hole he's been living in the past two years. If he doesn't take a breather, Roxie, he'll crack." Rocco intertwines his tattooed fingers. "This is only his second timeout since Fien was taken. The first was the night you wined and dined his guests."

"The night you took me to his office?" I'm not stupid, I can feel the nervy edge pumping out of Rocco, but I want to get my facts straight before I exert myself in a way I've never done before.

When Rocco lifts his chin, I lock my eyes with Smith's. "Find him." I hold my finger in the air when he attempts a rebuttal. "Did that sound like I was asking?"

He smiles a full-toothed grin, loving my gall. However, he doesn't give in. "If I disturb him when he asked not to be, there'll be hell to pay."

"Will it be worse than the hell he's been living in the past two years?" I don't wait for him to answer me. I can see the truth in his eyes, smell it slicking his skin. "If he cracks it, I'll take the blame. I'm the reason he's AWOL, aren't I?"

Their lack of denial stabs tiny knives into my chest. Mercifully, they don't cause me to bleed out before I see Rocco give Smith the go-ahead in the corner of my eye.

"All right," Smith breathes out as he grabs his laptop bag from the floor of the Range Rover. "But I'm denying any knowledge of this when the proverbial shit hits the fan."

Not even two seconds later, his face screws up in shock. "He's not on-site."

He isn't the only one surprised. This compound was designed to ensure Dimitri's guests have everything they could possibly want. They don't need to leave for anything, so what possible reason could Dimitri have to abscond these four walls?

Too inquisitive to listen to the warning gurgles of my stomach, I lean over to Smith and Rocco's half of the cab, so I can peer at the monitor of Smith's laptop. A state-of-the-art tracking software program reveals Dimitri's phone was last pinged in an industrial estate way too sleazy looking for a man with a lot of cash to burn.

Ignoring the pang in my chest warning me that this is a bad idea, I instruct the driver to take us to the location Smith honed in on. When he places the address into the GPS's mainframe, it advises us that Frosty Kinks is two point four miles from the airstrip we were supposed to arrive at ten minutes ago. It also highlights the services we could obtain once we arrive. They all point toward one field—the adult entertainment industry.

When the wheels on the SUV start churning over the miles, I sink back into my chair before connecting my eyes with Rocco's. "When did you last talk to him?"

He shakes his head at the accusation in my eyes, wordlessly advising me he had no clue Dimitri was at a strip club, much less the fight we had before he went there. "Last time I saw him, he was with you."

Smith raises his hands in the air like he's about to be arrested when my narrowed gaze snaps to him. "Same as Rocco. I had false admission papers to a rehab clinic to lodge. I didn't have time for snooping."

"So he went to a strip club by himself? Sure he did…"

My teeth grit when Rocco has the audacity to laugh. I don't know what the hell he thinks is funny. I'm anything but amused. "You're super cute when you are jealous, Princess P."

"Jealous? *Please.* I'm hungover and frustrated you dragged me out of bed for this." I'm such a liar. I could only be more jealous if I were green. Furthermore, I didn't sleep a wink last night. I was too busy pacing the room awaiting Dimitri's return. The only reason I stopped wearing a hole in the rug was because Rocco advised our transport was ready. I threw on clothes in under ten seconds and bolted outside, certain I was moments away from apologizing to Dimitri in person.

Alas, the only thing hearing my regrets this morning is my grumbling stomach.

Upon spotting the lie in my eyes, Rocco's grin doubles. "You still don't get it, do you?"

Too tired to lie, I shake my head.

My fast switchback to honesty doubles the smug grin on Rocco's face. "How many women do you think Dimitri slept with the week he found out Audrey was pregnant?"

"I don't want to know," I reply before I can stop myself. Just considering the many ways Fien could have been conceived has me all types of jealous. I don't need more insanity added to the mix.

Although Rocco's lips remain tightly locked, the gleam in his eyes tells me it's a number I don't want acknowledged. It makes my stomach swirl with more intensity than my wish to fall into a drunken stupor last night. I feel seconds from barfing.

Eager to test the durability of my stomach, Rocco asks, "How many women do you think he's slept with since you arrived on the scene?"

My words are barely audible through my clenched teeth. "If you say more than one, you better hope your gun isn't loaded, or I may blow someone's brains out."

I don't know whether to gleam or cry when Rocco's boisterous laugh vibrates through my chest. It doubles the thump in my head while adding to the twists of my vodka-sloshed stomach. "Chick, chick boom! That's *exactly* what I'm talking about. You're so fucking under, even with the blood of your mommy on the cuff of his shirt, you still wanted to take his dick between your lips."

His chuckled words are like a cold, hard slap to the face. They bring me back to reality even more than the jab my heart was just hit with. "He tortured my parents."

"To save you being buried in the same ditch his wife is most likely in." As quickly as Rocco's laughter arrived, it vanishes. "Why do you think he didn't kill them?"

Although I know the answer, I'd rather he spell it out for me, so instead of nodding, I shrug instead.

"Because the man is snowballing for you. You've got him so twisted up, he doesn't know which end is up and which end is down. He's got guilt by the bucketloads, remorse that won't quit even when he works to the bone for twenty-four hours a day, and a hard-on for you that stays firm no matter how much you piss him off... but he has no clue how to deal with any of it. He thinks that by giving you an hour, he's taking an hour from Fien, so imagine how fucked-up he feels when he realizes he wants to give you more than an hour." He scoots to the edge of his seat before tapping his tattooed index finger on my knee. "He wasn't like this with his wife. He didn't beat her father because he hurt her or offer mercy to her mother to save her from being hurt. He didn't care about her enough to even ask if she'd been hurt. That should say something, and it should have you playing on the same team."

Although I agree with him, there's one part of his statement I can't fix. "I can't ease his guilt, Rocco."

He brushes off the genuine concern in my voice as if it's fake. "Yeah, you can. You've just got to stop thinking you need to save him. He doesn't need saving. And neither do you." He lets out a chuckle. Even only knowing him for days, I know it isn't his real laugh. "You can't save someone who's drowning if you don't know how to swim."

My chance to reply is lost when the driver pulls in to the curb at the front of Frosty Kinks. As the 3D imagery on Smith's computer showed, it's a seedy, low-grade establishment that would have lost clientele when they stopped accepting pennies.

Rocco throws open his door before locking his eyes with mine. "Wait here with Smith, I'll be back in a minute."

"No," I reply while shaking my head. "I can't learn to swim if I'm not willing to jump into the deep end." After scooting across the bench seat and slipping out onto the sidewalk, I shift my focus to Smith. "Call the airstrip and advise them we're on our way. Offer them an incentive to ensure our time slot is held. If snow arrives early, our fastest transport home will take days. Dimitri will never forgive himself if his first slip-up in years delays the search for Fien for days, even if the weather is to blame."

"Now she gets it," Rocco says with a smile as he slings his arm around my shoulders. "Now bring that bat to the game, so we can knock some sense into this neanderthal before he crawls into his cave for another long hibernation."

FIVE

Dimitri

As I make my way through the dimly lit space that gets shadier for every tanked step I take, I scan my eyes over the flurry of women vying for my attention. I'm drugged-out on the good shit I usually reserve for 'guests,' too drunk to feel my legs, and I'm reasonably sure I look like a pimp since I switched out my suit for a pair of gray sweatpants and a black baseball jacket, but the women lining the walls of the back room at Frosty Kinks still look at me like I'm a god.

Although the outside of this establishment is as shoddy as hell, I'm reasonably sure I'm not the only high-end john they cater for. No one pays attention to the packaging when ordering a steak to devour. It's all about the quality. The women eyeing me with hungry, wanton gazes aren't as high-class as the ones who prance around my compounds, but they've definitely piqued the interest of my cock. He's almost at half-mast. Another line of coke should see him reluctantly joining the party.

He's pissed at me, frustrated I won't let him finish what he started two nights ago. He's not the only one annoyed, but since I'm miles from my compound, spaced out of my brain, I'll keep that story for another day.

Right now, nothing but forgetting my pathetic life for a few hours is on my mind. I've snorted the drugs and sculled the whiskey, now I just need a plump set of lips to seal the deal.

When I spot a woman who matches the one who won't leave my fucking head, I stumble to her half of the room. The bottle I chugged down in the dusty lot has finally reached my veins, meaning it isn't just my footing that's a little unsteady, so are my words. "How much?"

She bats her fake lashes, ignorant to the fact I'm already sold on what she's selling. "For you, I'll work for free."

"How much?" I repeat, shouting. I'm not seeking a relationship, commitment, or any of those other fucked-up things women seem to think they'll get from a casual hook-up. I want my dick sucked, and I'm willing to pay for the privilege.

When the blonde spots her competition hovering close, she pushes out, "Five hundred." Her fee is much less than I expected to pay. I would have forked out five thousand if that's what she requested.

After pulling my wallet out of the pocket in my sweats, I toss a handful of hundred-dollar bills onto the floor before pivoting on my feet and making my way to the room the manager of Frosty Kinks set up especially for me. I rarely branch outside of my industry for services like this. However, his respect won't go unnoticed. His girls will give my guests a pleasing array of new faces next month.

Because the blonde had to collect her earnings from the floor, it takes her a couple of seconds to join me in a pod similar to the one I spanked Roxanne in days ago. Just recalling the heat of her skin when my palm connected with her ass has my cock rising to the occasion. I'm almost as thick as I was when I stuck my dick in her for the first time, although nowhere near as firm.

Even fucked out of my head, my words still crack out of my mouth like a whip. "Close the door."

The blonde shudders from my roar before doing as instructed. My family name doesn't have the notoriety it once had, but my reputation is well known. I don't want my desperateness to get a feisty bleach-blonde with gleaming green eyes out of my head circulated amongst my enemies. Those fuckers are already riding my ass. I can't give them more fuel.

Pissed, my next lot of demands are almost abusive. "Remove your skirt and bra but leave your panties on." I don't want her for her cunt. I want her for her lush green eyes and fuckable lips. "Once you're done, get on your knees."

Disappointment makes itself known with my gut when the removal of her skirt reveals her sheer panties. I can see her cunt through the scant material. She's a natural blonde. The knowledge will make it harder for me to pull off my ruse, but I'm so desperate to lose myself for a couple of hours, I'm willing to give it a shot.

When she lowers herself onto her knees, I pull her hair back into a low ponytail, then wrap the glossy locks around my fist. She may be about to suck my dick, but I'll maintain all the control. One blonde has already caused me to lose my cool tonight. It won't happen again.

"Slower," I demand when she tugs on the waistband of my sweatpants with too much eagerness. I want her fumbling like she doesn't know what she's doing, somewhat naïve. I want to pretend she's Roxanne for just a minute.

"That's better," I growl on a moan when she lifts her eyes to mine while sliding the elastic waistband over the bulge in my pants with painstaking slowness. Her eyes are a shade darker than Roxanne's, but my coked-up head has a good imagination. "Take it out."

When her hands move to the waistband of my trunks, I scrub my thumb along her jaw, preparing it for the exhaustive activity it's about to undertake. This occasion has been on the backburner for months. It won't be a done-and-dusted event.

The hooker's submissiveness is hardening my cock, but it has nothing on the raging boner I get when the door of our private suite shoots open, and Roxanne steps into the sex-scented space.

SIX

Roxanne

Tension hisses in the air when my eyes bounce between Dimitri's naked backside propped against a sturdy desk and a virtually naked blonde on her knees in front of him. She has his erect cock in her hand, and her red-painted lips are narrowing in on the bead of precum on the top. Not even my unexpected interruption has the bitch taking her eyes off her target. Her mark is locked and loaded, and she isn't giving him up for anything.

Like fucking hell she isn't.

Acting as if I'm double my height and weight, I scoop up the blonde's clothes that are barely scraps of material from the floor, march across the room, then drag her away from Dimitri by the strands of her pretty little head. Her squeal at her hair being wretched out of her scalp has my heart falling from my chest, but it does little to slow me down. My anger arrived with barely a second to spare. Her mouth was a mere

45

hair's breadth from Dimitri's cock. She was a second from tasting him how I never have.

That's unacceptable.

"Get out." I thrust her clothes into her silicon-filled chest before nudging my head to the door, my orders delivered with a vicious glare.

"Rox—"

"Don't!" My nostrils flare as my squinted gaze shifts to Dimitri. Since the blonde is still on her knees, his erection is almost gouging her eyes out, and the blood of my father is still on his neck. Now is *not* the time for him to test me. And don't get me started on how intoxicated this man is. Dimitri isn't leaning against the desk for no reason. He can barely stand, for crying out loud. Payment or not, the blonde is more fucked in the head than my mother if she thinks this is acceptable.

"You have a plane to catch." I return my eyes to the blonde staring at me with a smidge of shock and a bucket-load of annoyance. "*We* have a plane to catch." My words are possessive and brimming with unwarranted jealousy. They rip the blonde's heart out of her chest as effectively as mine was removed when the horrendous thoughts bombarding me during my search of Frosty Kinks came true. Although I'm confident she only felt the weight of Dimitri's cock, who's to say that would have still been the case if my hunt was delayed by a measly two seconds.

The thought alone has me the most furious I've ever been.

"Leave before I show you what happens when you touch something you don't own."

Hearing my threat exactly how I intended, the blonde stammers out, "I didn't know he was take—"

"Go!" My roar kickstarts both her heart and her feet. She scampers up from her knees before making a dash for the door, her brisk exit faltered by Rocco entering from the other side.

He works his jaw side to side while taking in Dimitri's slouched frame. He's so far down the rabbit warren, he can barely hold up his head.

"Help me." My tone is lower than the one I used on the hooker, but Rocco acts as if it was just as stabby. He steps back with his hands held in the air and an arrogant grin on his face.

I discover the reason behind his lack of assistance when he chuckles out, "I ain't helping you while his dick is hanging out. We're tight, but we're not *that* tight."

Before I can issue a single scold bubbling in my chest, a much more dangerous situation unfolds. Dimitri hasn't noticed we have company. While his cock thickens to the point it must be painful, he scrubs the back of his fingers across my ruddy lips. "I bet your mouth tastes like candy." Only now does it dawn on me that we've never kissed. He's gone down on me, blew his load on my chest, and been inside of me like no other man ever has, but we've never kissed. "Your cunt is as sweet as candy, so I bet your lips are too."

While dropping one hand to his cock to squeeze it, he weaves the other one through my hair. It feels like time stands still when he drags my lips to within an inch of his. The man I can't stop thinking about is right here, directly in front of me, but for the life of me, I can't act on the impulses burning me alive.

I'd give anything to forget everything that has happened the past few days, but I can't. If I do that, I not only break a pledge I made to Dimitri about not taking more time than he can give me, I'll also break the promise I made to Fien in the wee hours of this morning.

Dimitri is all she has.

I can't steal the focus away from her for even one second.

With my mind made up, I tug on Dimitri's sweats as roughly as I did the blonde's hair to guide them back up his thighs.

"Don't put my cock away." As he struggles to hold back his grin, he drags his teeth over his lower lip. The strong scent of whiskey exuding from his mouth shouldn't make it seem sexy, but it does. "He's been dying for this for months. Don't leave him hanging."

I'm unsure if it's lust or anger deepening my voice when I reply, "We have company."

I assume my confession will have him falling in line. I soon discover I have a lot to learn about this man.

With two clicks of his fingers, Rocco slips out the door, closing it behind him. "Now, we don't. We have all the time and privacy we need."

Dimitri's growl when I step back doubles the damp slickness between my legs, but like many times in the past, I don't put myself first. "If we don't leave now, our flight will be rescheduled. I don't know about you, but I have a heap of questions I need answered. Answers I can only get in Erkinsvale."

That seems to sober him up a bit. "Erkinsvale?"

I nod before stepping back into the ring, gloved-up and hopeful the drugs running through his system will only last as long as our flight home. "I know you're tired, and you are probably sick to death of playing with the hand you've been dealt, but we're so close, Dimitri, the end is right there. It would be ludicrous for us to give up now."

Once again, my voice is more possessive than it should be, but then again, I don't care. So many of Dimitri's actions make sense now. The shift of the blame. His inability to give himself a single moment of reprieve. The remorse in his eyes when I stepped into this room. He's holding on by a thread, and my presence the past week made it the thinnest it's ever been.

That has to stop. I'm already responsible for him losing his daughter. I refuse to be the reason he loses everything.

"Let me help you, Dimitri. Please."

The crackling of energy that forever teems between us doubles its output when he runs his fingers across my mouth for the second time. His eyes are as bleak as my father's when he went on a bender. I'm not even sure he's entirely here, but it feels as if the world shifts beneath my feet when he dips his chin for the quickest second.

Stealing his chance to change his mind, I dart for the locked door to let Rocco back in. He has his back braced on the outer wall of the room Dimitri was found in, either disinterested in the theatrics of a strip club or more concerned about Dimitri than he's letting on.

I realize it's the latter when his eyes swing my way. He's quick to shut down the concern in them, but not quick enough for this sly fox. "Done already? I'll have to show the old guy some new tricks."

He laughs when I roll my eyes before he joins me inside the room reeking of desperation for a second chance. The humor on his face vanishes when his eyes follow mine to Dimitri. He's no longer balancing on the desk. He's slumped on the floor, out cold.

I didn't realize Dimitri's team followed us to Frosty Kinks until Rocco says, "Send Clover in." Past incidents advise me he's talking to Smith. The knowledge our every move is being monitored doesn't lessen the knot in my gut when Rocco checks Dimitri for a pulse, though. "It's weak but there. Trace back footage so we can get a better idea of what he's taken." Rocco lifts his eyes to mine. "Did he mention anything to you?"

I shake my head, too stunned to talk.

Clover barrels into the room just as Rocco rips up the sleeves of Dimitri's jacket. He's checking for track marks. How do I know this? My mother did the same thing to my father anytime he returned home from an all-night bender. "There are no needle marks to indicate he shot up, so I'd say his drug of choice was coke."

"Is this how he usually responds to drugs?" With fear clutching my throat, my words are as weak as the vein fluttering through the tattoos on Dimitri's neck.

Air whizzes out of Rocco's nose before he shakes his head. "But it's been a while since he's used." He drifts his eyes to Clover. "Help me get him up. We'll take him back to the compound so Ollie can take a look at him."

"No." Rocco responds to the snapped command in my

tone. Clover acts as if I'm not in the room. "Take him to the airstrip as planned."

The strain of holding up a man as large as Dimitri is heard in Rocco's voice when he says, "If he's ODing, we can't help him thirty thousand feet in the air."

"We can't, but Ollie can. Make him come with us."

Rocco takes a minute to consider my suggestion. It adds even more tension to his face. "I know you're trying to help, Roxie—"

"This isn't about helping. It's about doing what Dimitri would want us to do. If you go back to the compound, we won't be able to fly out until tomorrow at the earliest, and that's only if forecasters are wrong. Take him to the airstrip, have Ollie meet us there. I'll pay him with my maxed-out credit card if you're worried about the fucking bill." I grit my teeth when my last four words come out with a sob. I'm panicked out of my mind for Dimitri, but I also know this is the right thing to do. "Please, Rocco. You want me in the deep end, but you're refusing to let me jump." When his eyes stray to Clover, my panic is showcased in the worst light. "Don't ask his opinion. He's paid to be here. We're not."

Although Clover *tsks* me, my scorn rolls straight off his back. He knows I'm no better than him as only days ago he heard me offer myself to Dimitri for a little bit of coin.

I don't have a tiny bead-like device in my ear like Rocco, but it's clear Smith is on my side when the strain on Rocco's face clears in an instant. "If this backfires—"

"It won't," I reply, issuing him a promise I have no right to issue. "I swear to God, everything will work out."

With his brows hanging as low as Dimitri's head, Rocco

jerks up his chin before shifting half of Dimitri's lifeless weight onto Clover's shoulders. "Tell Ollie I'll pay him double if he beats us to the jet."

SEVEN

Dimitri

W hile swishing my tongue around my bone-dry mouth, I hesitantly open my eyes. The dream I was having was intoxicating until Roxanne was ripped from my grasp as cruelly as Fien was removed from her mother's stomach. Being thrust out of a nightmare so brutally has me feeling like death warmed over, although I'm skeptical not all the thump of my pulse is compliments to my rude awakening. My head is thumping as if I drowned in a bath of whiskey. My skin is patchy and dry, and my cock is acting as if the first half of my dream is all that matters.

I shouldn't be shocked. He doesn't give a fuck if it will riddle me with guilt for eternity. If he wants it, he's there with bells on—no matter the consequence. He's the sole reason I sought solace outside of my compound last night. If I didn't do something to calm the beast, he would have had me taking my anger out on Roxanne.

Although she's deserving of the wrath, for some fucked-up reason, I can't hurt her any more than she's already been hurt. I couldn't even pop a bullet between her mother's brows, for fuck's sake. Her eyes are too similar to Roxanne's. They seared through me until my fried brain had me confusing her for Roxanne. It's lucky in a way. If she hadn't issued her mercy, I doubt anything I could have said would have brought Roxanne out of her panic attack last night. She was drowning in filth years in the making, being suffocated by the very people who should have kept her safe.

She was Fien twenty years from now.

Ignoring the begs of my throbbing head, I raise to a half-seated position. I'm stunned when my awakening occurs without the grumbles of a needy redhead who accepts money for the privilege of occupying my bed, though it has nothing on my surprise when the familiarity of the room smacks into me. I'm not at a seedy strip club hidden away, so townies won't get busted by their preacher attending a show, nor am I at my New York compound. I'm home, in my bed, and the faintest trickle of a shower is heard in the distance.

"Smith…" My voice is swallowed by a husky cough. I'm so fucking dry you wouldn't think there's an IV line inserted in my arm.

What the fuck?

"Smith."

My eyes shoot to the side when Smith's grumbly tone booms through my ears. "I heard you the first time. There's no need to shout." Instead of his voice projecting from the speakers implanted throughout every room of my house, it comes from the reading nook in the corner of the large space. From his setup, anyone would swear he works out of the office in my room instead of his computerized hub.

After shutting his laptop screen, he paces around his desk. Worry is seen all over his face when he whispers, "I'll tell him."

Confident his words aren't for me, I wait for him to join me at my beside before asking the obvious. "What happened?"

"You—"

"If you're about to say I overdosed, you need to go back to the fucking drawing board and start again. I snorted a few lines of coke and drunk a little too much whiskey, but that's nowhere near enough to make me pass out for hours on end."

"Days." He angles his watch so I can see the date stamped on the top. If he isn't messing with my head, which would be very unlike him, I've been out cold for three days— three whole motherfucking days. "Although Ollie believes part of your condition was from exhaustion, blood work-ups showed you had GHB in your system. The high reading indicated whoever slipped it in your drink didn't do it to maim. They wanted you dead."

With my blood hot and my wish to kill the highest it's ever been, I rip out the IV tubing from my arm and stand from my bed. I'm mortified when I realize the tubing in my arm isn't the only one attached to my body. There's another one near my cock. Mercifully, it's taped over my manhood instead of being shoved inside of it.

After ripping off the second tubing more gently than I did the IV, I snatch a pair of gray sweatpants from the floor next to my bed, then shove my feet inside of them. "I'm going to kill the fucker who messed with me, and I'm going to do it slowly."

I stop considering the many ways I can kill a man when Smith says, "You're too late. Most of the culprits are already dead." He tosses a manilla folder onto my bed. When it bounces off the springy mattress, several glossy photographs fall out. They show Frosty Kinks was burned to the ground. Not even its trademark red Louboutin billboard remains. It's as black as ash.

My eyes float up to Smith's when he says, "When Rocco found you passed out, he asked me to trace your movements. Frosty's surveillance was shit, but I worked it for all its worth." He shuffles through the still images until he finds one of a man with a round stomach and a bald head. Although my head is still a little hazy, I think he's the bartender who served me most of the night. "That's Jake Warsaw, co-owner of Frosty's. He has no priors and isn't up to his ears in debt like most people in his field, leading us to believe this wasn't the first time he's done something like this." His groan is as loud as mine. "Clover and Rocco worked him over good, but he didn't give up any juice."

His smirk tells me he would have unearthed his mark even without the force Rocco and Clover love to utilize. I do too, but that's a story for when I'm not stunned like a mullet.

"Who paid him?"

The crunch of my teeth is heard over my growl when he tosses a second photograph onto the stack. Even with us only meeting once, I know this man very well. He wanted Roxanne so badly, he was willing to pay more than triple what his competitors were offering. He also called on the hour every hour for the twelve hours following her auction, demanding to be updated on when bids would be finalized.

"I went through reams of footage obtained since the auction. Dr. Bates spent more time in his car outside the compound than he did his hotel room the days following Roxie's auction." Smith locks his eyes with mine. For a guy who's usually as cool as ice, he looks extremely worked up. "He only left when he followed you to Frosty's."

Although jealousy is a perfect motive, I feel there's something more at play here than a man being pipped at the post. I'm just praying Rocco and Smith felt the same vibe as me, or I'll be left with more questions than answers.

After working my throat through a stern swallow, I ask, "Is Bates dead?"

For the first time in a long time, I feel lucky when Smith shakes his head. It grows tenfold when he adds words to his confirmation. "Roxie asked us to hold back on his punishment. She wants to discuss an idea with you before bringing him before the courts."

"Roxanne?" I could add to my query, but I don't need to. Smith can see my shock. He doesn't need it voiced.

"She's been running things around here." His smile is way too fucking blinding for my thumping skull. "With guidance from Rocco and me, of course."

He walks to my desk to gather up his laptop. Once he has it fired up, he shows me the many angles they've been working the past three days. The reports are so impressive, they have me worried I've been out a lot longer. Not only is

Dr. Bates's office wired to the hilt with state-of-the-art equipment, he has a month's worth of work on display.

"For now, Roxie's grandparents' estate is a dead end. There were a handful of biochemicals there, but it was mainly placentas, fetal matter, and the occasional soiled mattress. No bodies were located." He sounds as disappointed as I feel. "Some good came from the search, though. We unearthed a set of records in the rubble. They date back years before Audrey was taken. I'm not sure of their significance yet, but I'm working a few angles." He waits for me to jerk up my chin before he hits me with the motherlode. "We also found Roberto."

"Dead or alive?" I don't know why I asked my question. If he's not dead, he will soon be wishing he was. I had barely gotten over Ophelia's death when he disappeared, and his vanishing act sliced my siblings from four to nothing in an instant.

I take a step back when Smith says, "Alive." When he clicks on the keyboard of his laptop two times, an image of a much older and rounder Roberto fills the screen. If you exclude the dirty apron stretched across his midsection and his unnoteworthy strut, his identity could never be discounted. The Petretti genes are strong.

"Il Lido," I stammer out, testing the name on my lips. "I swear I've heard of that restaurant."

Smith nods before he opens up a secondary screen. It reveals that Il Lido is an Italian restaurant in New York. It's owned by none other than Mr. Isaac Holt.

My next question is barely heard since my words are

ground through my clenched jaw. "Why is Roberto working as a dish hand for Isaac?"

The worry blazing through Smith's eyes tells me I won't like the answer to his question, but he gives it to me anyway.

I'm an unforgiving, malicious man, however even I have a hard time stomaching the image of my eldest brother huddled on the floor, tearing his hair out as efficiently as the tears streaming down his face tear my heart out. He's completely undone, wholly destroyed by the horrid world we were born into.

Once the footage ends, Smith brings up several news clippings on the death of a Rochdale woman. She was struck by a drunk driver, killing both her and her unborn son. Although the reports don't say Roberto is responsible, my heart knows that's the case. He was a drunk longer than he was a man.

Can you blame him? He was our father's firstborn son. He didn't just have the world on his shoulders. He had our entire legacy as I do now.

"How is he living?"

Smith gives me a halfhearted shrug. "It's not close to luxurious, but he's comfortable."

"Like CJ?"

His second shrug is nowhere near as willy-nilly as his first one. "Similar. He just works for what he has instead of his little brother handing it to him." His underhanded ribbing isn't to maim, he's just stating things as he sees them. CJ does nothing for his money. He merely waits for me to deposit a check every month. "We can fix that if you want?"

I take a moment to deliberate before shaking my head.

"If Roberto stayed hidden this long, he wants to remain hidden." My brows join when an ill-timed grin crosses Smith's face. Unlike Rocco, he knows the right time to express himself. Now isn't the right time. "What?"

"Nothing." He places down his laptop and fiddles with some papers on my desk like he can't feel my scorning wrath burning a hole in the back of his head.

"Smith—"

"It's nothing, I swear." When I growl, he squawks like a canary. "Roxanne said the same thing. It's kinda cute how you two are synced like that." He steals my chance to respond to his ridiculous statement by gathering up his stuff and making a beeline for the door.

Since he believes he's seconds from safety, he gets on my last nerve. "Rocco wanted me to tell you he only kept Roxanne's sheets warm for two out of the three nights you were out cold."

Not thinking, I pick up the stapler on my desk and peg it at his head. It smacks into the drywall a mere second after his head darts past it. Although he's sprinting down the corridor like I'm hot on his tail, I hear his chuckles as if he's standing next to me. He isn't laughing loudly. His voice is being projected through the speakers above my head.

He should count his lucky stars his breathless chuckles remind me that I'm anal about security, or my next aim would have included a bullet.

After ensuring my door is closed, I grab my tablet off my desk and log into the security app Smith installed months ago. With Smith's disclosure at the forefront of my mind, I drag the timeline back to three days ago. I still feel like shit, and my brain is pounding like drummers are going to war between my ears, but this can't wait. I haven't been out of the loop this long in years. I'd hate to think about what I've missed.

Yeah, right. If you believe that, you need therapy even more than me. All I care about is discounting Rocco's claim he kept Roxanne occupied the past three nights. Considering everything that's happened, it should be the last thing on my mind. Regretfully, the unknown can send the most stable man insane. Why do you think I went off the rails? Staying one step ahead of the game is exhausting, but it has nothing on the tiredness you feel when you're forever chasing your tail.

I stop the footage just as Ollie requests privacy to make sure I don't piss the bed. His demand sees Rocco dragging Roxanne to the far corner of the somber space for a chat. It's clear from the strain on their faces that their conversation isn't flirty, much less what Roxanne says next, "If that's what Dimitri would do, do that. Burn it down." Although Rocco's voice is too low for me to pick up, Roxanne keeps me in the gist. "I won't let anything happen to him. Ollie agreed to stay until he's awake, and I won't leave this room. I swear, Rocco, I won't cause any trouble." After a few seconds of deliberation, Rocco agrees to her request with the slightest lift of his chin. "Thank you."

My jaw tightens when Roxanne rubs her hand down Rocco's arm in a comforting manner, but it clears when her return to my side of the room sees Rocco requesting a minute with Smith. "Keep this place on tight lockdown. As far as anyone is concerned, Dimitri and Roxie are still in

New York. We don't want any unexpected visitors." He doesn't say my father's name, but I know that's who he's referencing because nothing but disgust is seen on his face whenever he talks about my father.

They discuss protocol for a few more minutes before Rocco leaves the room. Within minutes of him doing so, Smith sets up a command station on my desk, where he stays for the next three days. Roxanne also doesn't move from this spot. She floats between the couch across from my desk and my bed during the day before spending the entire night in bed, with me, where she belongs.

It's the fight of my life not to jump out of my skin when Smith's voice suddenly booms through the speaker of my tablet. "She's real smart, you know. She organized the search of her grandparents' estate, unearthed Roberto's where-abouts, and coordinated the events for your guests Friday night all from the room you're standing in." The creak of his office chair sounds down the line a second before his snarky comment, "Imagine what she could achieve if you'd let go of the reins just a little?"

Either panicked he's about to be hit with my wrath, or confident he has no reason to fret since he smacked the nail on the head, he disconnects our feed just as the shower faucet in the bathroom switches off.

EIGHT

Roxanne

A fter sliding my drenched arms into my dressing gown, I twist my hair until it's held off my face by a low-riding knot, then pace to the vanity mirror. I'm still not a diva, but the gold-leaf framed mirror is housing more condensation than usual. I had the faucet at the highest setting, hopeful a good dose of scorching water would conceal the red marks my cheeks have been wearing the past three days.

I understand Dimitri is exhausted and am aware he had enough drugs in his system to kill him, but I wish he'd wake up. There's so much going on right now, I feel like my head is about to explode. Someone tried to end Dimitri's life, the brother he believes is dead isn't, and I've lost the ability to look at my grandparents' property with anything but disgust.

Although the hundreds of men who scoured every inch of the mostly unused land didn't find any bodies, there was enough evidence to expose my parents were a part of the baby-farming industry.

Just the thought they'd stoop that low makes me sick to my stomach. The terror is holding on firmly, and there's no end in sight. I don't know how much longer I can continue like this. Good deeds are meant to be rewarded. That doesn't seem to be the case with the Cartel. The more you try to better yourself, the harder your competitors work to drag you down.

Just like me, Dimitri can't even rely on his family. Smith guards his secrets as if his life depends on them, but it doesn't take a genius to realize Dimitri's father is being as closely monitored as Dimitri's enemies. I doubt Rocco would have gone back to New York with Clover to persecute the men who drugged Dimitri if Col's whereabouts weren't being constantly scrutinized. The fact Col is far from here is the *only* reason Rocco has riled Dimitri via the speaker above his head instead of in person.

My sly grin doubles when I catch sight of it in the mirror. I shouldn't like the way Dimitri stirred every time Rocco picked on him, but I did. Only a heartless man fails to respond when teased. Dimitri isn't one of them. He's paying for my mother's rehabilitation out of his own pocket, and he didn't hold back on the purse strings, either. She's surrounded by celebrities and beginning to feel as remorseful as me.

I'm honestly unsure where we'll go from here. Sorrow can't take back all the horrendous things she's done, but with how far down the rabbit hole she is, I won't need to consider the next step for a while.

Once I have my game face back on, I make my way into the main part of the room. "Have you had any word from Rocco this afternoon? His silence is a little off-putting..." My words trail off, gobbled up by the shock roaring through me. Smith isn't seated behind Dimitri's desk. Dimitri is. He looks as dark and deadly as ever, but very much alive.

I've been accused of being a ditz a handful of times in my life. Today is the first time I'll agree with their assessment. I don't stand back and watch in awe that the man who was on his death bed only days ago is standing in front of me, appearing as strong as an ox. I race across the room as fast as my quivering legs will take me before throwing myself into his arms.

"Dimitri."

He startles from my unexpected affection, but as quickly as his shock arrives, it leaves. With his heart beating as erratically as mine, he pulls me into his chest as he did almost two weeks ago. This time, his shirt doesn't catch my tears, his tattooed chest does. I hate myself for blubbering like a baby, but boy, it feels good to finally release the hurt that's been eating me alive the past three days. I wasn't just upset someone tried to claim Dimitri's life, I was frustrated I was left alone to deal with feelings I've never handled before.

I jumped into the deep end as Rocco suggested, then I was left treading water for over seventy-two hours. Even an Olympic swimmer would struggle in those conditions. Since I was in waters way too deep, I should have drowned days ago. I probably would have if anger wasn't also keeping me afloat.

I've never wanted to hurt and comfort someone as much

as I do right now. My emotions honestly don't know which way to swing. The last time they were this erratic, I fell asleep in Dimitri's arms, and he didn't speak to me for days.

I refuse to let that happen again. I don't care if he punishes me. I'd rather his punishment over another three days of painful silence.

After scrubbing my face to ensure I don't look like a total wreck, I peel my wet cheek off Dimitri's pec, then align my eyes with his. I startle when our eyes collide not even a second later. He's staring straight at me. His watch is heart-stuttering, but it's without an ounce of malice. His unusual mischievous gawk liberates me from the worry I'm about to overstep the mark. It allows me to talk freely for the first time in a long time. "I was worried you were never coming back. I thought I'd never see you again. Do you have any idea how panicked you made me?"

He's humored by my worry, but deep down inside, I also believe he appreciates it. "It'll take more than a little GHB to bring me down."

When he laughs, it's the fight of my life not to whack him in the stomach. I wouldn't hold back if I believed it was the only abuse he's endured in his life. "It's not funny. You could have been seriously hurt, then what would happen to Fien?"

That wipes the smile right off his face. He's as stunned now as he was when I threw myself in his arms. Even staying by his side twenty-four-seven the past three days doesn't have him believing I'm on his side. In his eyes, I'm still the enemy.

"I held a gun to my mother's head, then left her with you even on the belief you were going to kill her, yet you still think I'm the enemy. What can I do to prove I'm on your side, Dimitri? Sentence my mother to death for her crimes? Sell my virginity to the highest bidder? Take the place of your daughter? I'll do anything you want. Anything at all—"

My words are stopped in the most beautifully tormented way. Dimitri doesn't demand me to be quiet like he did when I went on a rant on how I'm not with him because I have daddy issues or cut me off with a cruel scorn.

He kisses me.

It isn't an all-encompassing kiss with teeth, lips, and tongues. He holds back a beat, so I have time to react to how I feel about being kissed by him. He isn't a nice man nor is he gentle, and he wants to ensure I know what I'm signing up for.

Even with his embrace being as innocent as a schoolyard peck, it sends fireworks exploding through me. It's sweet and blistering, and ten times better than I could have ever imagined.

When I moan into Dimitri's mouth, my body choosing its own response to the fiery blaze smoldering between us, he weaves his fingers through my hair like he did at Frosty Kinks before he adds a stack of wood to the fire in my gut. He explores my mouth with teasing bites, long licks, and breathy growls that have my temperature rising to a dangerous level.

I'm naked beneath my dressing gown, and Dimitri is only wearing a pair of sweatpants, but within seconds, it seems as if there are too many articles of clothing between us.

After uncinching the cord of my dressing gown, I shimmy my shoulders, aiding the static-loving material's fall to the floor. The waistband of Dimitri's pants come away just as easily.

His grunt when I circle my hand around his thick cock is desperate and loud. He wasn't lying when he said his cock has been waiting for this day for months. The heaviness of his impressive shaft is a sure-fire sign he was telling the truth, much less the sticky droplet of goodness on the tip.

I whine like a child when he pulls back a few seconds later. My fret is unfounded. He isn't ending our exchange before it truly begins, he's ensuring he is the sole investigator on if the light in my eyes changes like it did for my mother. He's keeping this exclusively between us.

He hits a button on the edge of his desk, curls my legs around his waist, then walks us across the room. His lips don't leave mine until the softness of bedding caresses my curves. After wedging his knee between my thighs that I'm trying in vain not to squeeze together, he drags his eyes up my body in a slow and dedicated sweep. When his eyes land on my face, the earth shifts beneath my feet. Just like his earlier watch, this one doesn't have an ounce of spite to it either. It's brimming with way too much yearning ever to be confused with a hatred response.

"Are you sure?"

His chivalry catches me by surprise, but it makes the nod of my head even more convincing. He could have taken what he wanted like he was raised to or tried to profit from me as my father did. Instead, he made it my choice. That makes the claws of his almost deceit nowhere near as painful to my heart.

"It will hurt, Roxanne." His comment seems to panic him more than me. "You're tiny—"

I cut him off by pulling him on top of me so I can reattach our lips. I kiss him how I've dreamed of kissing him since I saw him standing in the rain outside the alleyway. It's an urgent, hurried kiss, as impatient as the hand slithering between us to join our bodies in a way that's both personal and intimate.

"Fuck," Dimitri moans on a growl when he lines up his cock before he drives home, sheathing me with one quick thrust.

He was right. It does hurt, but it also feels right. I've always felt a little lost like I don't quite belong. I'm not experiencing that now. Fien is the cure to unlocking Dimitri's misery, but I could very well be the key to the cabinet holding the potion.

My hips jerk upward when our exchange goes further than our previous attempt. With his feet splayed to the width of his shoulders and his eyes locked on my overstuffed pussy, Dimitri circles the bundle of nerves between my legs with his thumb, bringing the pain ripping through me down from a ten to a seven.

"I need you wet for me, Roxie. If I pull out now, I'll fucking tear you. You're clutching me too tightly."

His unusual use of my nickname shocks me for a second. Not enough to stop me from hatching a wickedly intense plan, but enough to add a quiver to my voice. "Kiss me."

When his eyes lift to mine, certain he heard me wrong, the pain lowers by another notch. "What?"

"Kiss me," I repeat, smiling at the shock in his tone. "If you want me wet enough not to hurt me, kiss me."

I grunt in pain when my request causes him to notch another inch of his cock inside of me. I doubt he's all the way in, but I'm too in awe at how skillfully he kisses to worry about him never fully entering me.

Within ten seconds, I'm so caught up in our kiss, my clenched muscles relax.

Within twenty seconds, I'm kissing him as intensely as he's kissing me.

Within thirty seconds, the rock of our conjoined hips sees his cock moving in and out of me in rhythm with his explorative tongue. We're not close to fucking, but for how fast we got to this stage, I can see us reaching that peak remarkably quick.

"That's better," Dimitri says as he slants back so he can take in the sight of his cock pumping in and out of me. I don't need to peer down to know the evidence of my excitement is tinged with blood. The tangy scent in the air is evidence enough, much less Dimitri's increase in breaths. "But it could be better."

I feel excruciatingly empty when he suddenly withdraws before he requests my eyes to his. It's a void that's filled by a blinding climax when the collision of our eyes causes cum to erupt from Dimitri's cock. As my name tears from his throat, he coats my pussy with his spawn before he uses his still-erect cock to push the murky white substance inside of me.

He stuffs in two inches, pulls back out, swipes his engorged knot across my clit, then reenters with an extra inch. He continues doing this until the shudders making it seem as if I'm possessed, weakened to a shiver, and almost every inch of his impressive cock is inside of me.

As he rocks in and out of me, his speed increasing along with my moans, the ache of taking a man his size is notable. Although it's painful, it is a good ache, one I'm certain I'll crave time and time again.

"Lock your ankles around my back."

I immediately jump to his command. He's more experienced than me, and for now, I'm happy to use his skills to my advantage.

"Now, give me your eyes."

Pleasure overwhelms me when his cock throbs from the collision of our eyes. I'm being stretched beyond repair and am certain I'll be in pain for days after this, but the sensation roaring through me is unbelievable. My orgasm is coming hard and fast, but I want it right now. I'm barely grasping reality. I am too far down the rabbit hole to think about anything but my raging libido.

"More."

Dimitri spreads my thighs wider before he drives into me on repeat.

"Faster."

He grunts and hisses as he pushes me to the very brink of despair.

"Harder."

He fucks me like he's possessed. Pumping, grinding, and stroking every inch of me. His hands are swamping my tits, his pelvis is grinding into my clit, and his cock is commanding every inch of my pussy.

This is better than I could have ever imagined. Our fuck

is raw and primal, but it's also brimming with emotions. We should be enemies who hate everything about each other. He hurt people I loved, killed others I didn't, and spanked me in a room full of spectators, yet, our bodies come together as if they've intimately known each other for years.

A sensation I've never experienced before gathers inside of me. It builds with every thrust of Dimitri's hips and each lively glint in his eyes. No one could accuse him of being dark and dangerous right now. There's too much light in his eyes—too much life.

When realization sinks in, a climax slams into me.

I'm responsible for the shift of color in his eyes.

Me.

As I grip the bedsheets in a white-knuckled hold, pleasure rolls through me unchecked. It hits me everywhere—my trembling thighs, my thrusting chest, my aching sex. It even hits my heart that's almost as full as my pussy.

Before I can put my ego in check, Dimitri withdraws, flips me over, then reenters me from behind. All I can do is scream. His change-up in position means he's more deeply seated than he was only minutes ago, and his thumb is pressing against a region of my body I'm unsure I want claimed by any man.

Within a few strokes, it dawns on me how unfamiliar I am with my body. Instead of repelling away from the thumb hovering above what I thought was a no-go zone, I'm arching up to it, wordlessly encouraging Dimitri to increase the pressure on my back entrance.

"Not yet." Dimitri moves his hand away from my puckered hole so he can spank my butt cheek instead. "You're too tight to take both my fingers and my cock." I'm already burning up everywhere from the fiery burn his hand caused to my ass, much less what he says next, "I can't wait to claim every inch of you, but we need to build you up to that. Once I've got your snug cunt customized to my dick, we'll switch to other parts of your body." His comment doesn't sound like he means tonight. He's talking days away, perhaps even weeks.

My muscles clench with greedy need, excited about the possibility of this lasting more than a night. The tight clasp of my vaginal walls around Dimitri's cock almost sets him off. The veins feeding his magnificent manhood throb as his poundings turn punishing. He fucks me with everything he has, not stopping until another blinding orgasm convinces my limbs that they're broken.

Even with my body refusing to play the game well, I ride my orgasm out, shuddering and shivering while screaming Dimitri's name on repeat. His wondrously fat cock and multiple orgasms have created the perfect blend of pain and pleasure. I'm sore, delirious, and certain I'm on the brink of a coma, yet my body still craves more.

Defying legs that feel like Jell-O, I return to a kneeling position, roll my shoulders back, then meet Dimitri's pumps grind for grind. We go at it for several long minutes, pounding, grunting, and fucking like our intimate act isn't being shared with Dimitri's neighbors. I'm moaning loud enough for all of Hopeton to hear, but I don't care. This is too glorious for a half-assed response.

Dimitri demands my eyes to his when another orgasm creeps up on me. When he gets them, his hips still a mere second before his cock pulsates inside of me. The heat of his cum spurting out of his cock sends me spiraling again.

His name falls from my lips over and over as my orgasm zaps the last of my energy.

When I collapse into a heap, this time around, Dimitri comes with me. His large frame almost crushes me to death, but the rhythmic beat of his heart and the exhaustion overwhelming every inch of me soon lulls me to sleep.

I'm dead on my feet—figuratively.

Thank God.

NINE

Dimitri

My eyes lift to Smith when he has the audacity to snicker at me for the third time tonight. He isn't laughing because sleeping for seventy-two hours straight didn't stop me from catching a couple of hours of shut-eye with Roxanne after our romp. He's amused about the shock on my face.

He was as honest as a saint when he said Roxanne was smart. Not only did she keep my operation afloat when I was flat on my back, she improved it. She tidied up the books, found a discrepancy that will cost someone their life, then made a handful of tweaks to the Arabian events that will improve my profit margin by six percent if not more.

I'm fucking astonished, and my surprise has nothing to do with how well she fucks. I killed her boyfriend, taunted her father until he blew his brains out, then tortured her mother, yet instead of plotting my demise when I was at my weakest, she made me stronger.

The knowledge has my cock thickening like I'm not sitting across from key members of my crew, strategizing our next move. Rules were broken, and although most of the rule-breakers have been brought before the court, the main players are still roaming free—most notably, Dr. Bates.

After adjusting my cock so my zipper stops biting it, I ask, "When is the good doctor expected back at the office?"

Even with him only returning from New York an hour ago, Rocco jumps into the conversation like he's kept tabs on proceedings while busting noses. "He was originally sched-uled to return last Tuesday. However, Princess P piqued his interest too much for him to consider leaving."

He smirks when my teeth grit over his nickname. I don't need him to spell out who he's referencing. We've been friends for two decades, but we've been rivals even longer than that. It started with a video game every kid on our block played, and it continued long after Mario saved Princess Peach from the Mushroom Kingdom.

Rocco, along with nearly every other *Super Mario* fan, doesn't understand Bowser's character. He doesn't constantly attack the Mushroom Kingdom because he's evil. He wants to show Princess Peach she isn't a damsel in distress. She can kick ass as much as the rest of the characters. You've just got to push her buttons right.

Kind of like Roxanne.

My scowl switches to a smirk before I get back to busi-ness. "Now he's been told his bid was unsuccessful, did he readjust his schedule?"

I scrape my hand across my cropped beard when silence falls over the room. I didn't fully shave because even with my mouth going nowhere near Roxanne's intoxicating cunt, I can still smell it on my skin. It made showering before my meeting really fucking hard—both mentally and physically.

"We agreed to announce the failed bids within twenty-four hours of the auction, stating the winner wished to remain anonymous." The shit I'm spurting isn't unusual. Almost every man at the auction last week was married. They don't want their spouses knowing they're bidding for a virgin any more than I want to consider what would have happened if I had lost my cool a few hours earlier. I wouldn't have covered Roxanne with a bedspread before sneaking out of our room an hour ago. I would have been tossing dirt on her.

"That was the plan—"

"Was? What do you mean *was*?" I stray my eyes to Smith, the deserver of my wrath. "I gave an order. It should have been followed."

"Jesus, for a man who's blown his load more the past week than he has the past year, you've certainly got your panties in a twist. Calm down, D. We're not your enemy."

As my eyes shoot to Rocco, my nostrils flare. "If we haven't announced that the bids have ended, Roxanne's virginity is still up for sale. If her virginity is for sale, she's for sale. Point fucking blank. Can I explain it any simpler for you, Rocco?"

I balk like the bruises on his knuckles are from punching me in the gut when he replies, "That's the point. She wants her sale to remain open."

"That's what I was referencing earlier." Smith scoots closer to the table before balancing his elbows on a stack of paperwork he brings to every meeting. "Roxanne is willing to take our ruse one step further—"

"No."

"At least hear the man out, D."

"No!" I repeat more forcefully this time. "Bates didn't bid three times that of his competitors for no reason. He wants Roxanne for more than her virginity." Before Rocco can interject again, I continue talking, foiling his endeavors. "Furthermore, the ruse will no longer be effective."

I'm not peacocking that I pinched Roxanne's virginity, I am being straight-up honest. Roxanne said it herself. No one would believe our connection is fake because it's never been made up. She fooled them last week because she was innocent. It won't work this time around.

I stop considering a workaround when Smith says, "That's why she wants to go in as a patient instead of a purchase. If the farmers are picking up clients from Dr. Bates's office, we have another way of infiltrating their operation. Faking a pregnancy will delay things by a couple of weeks considering Roxanne was just auctioned as a virgin, but the hold-up will give me plenty of time to make sure we won't face any hiccups."

I want to immediately say no again, but for the life of me, I can't. Although her plan is dangerous, it's also smart. I've been chasing Rimi for over twenty months. The closest I've come to catching him was the night I stopped to help Roxanne. This type of ruse could increase the odds of finding him, but something isn't sitting right with my stomach.

This kills me to admit, but I'm not sure I can guarantee

Roxanne's safety. If she had suggested this before she proved she's on my side by offering to switch places with Fien, I wouldn't have cared she was at risk. Now... now I don't know which way is up.

A collective sigh bounces around my downstairs office when I mutter, "Let me think about it." To the men who know me, that's a straight-up no. To those still out of the loop, it's a possibility. "But for now, I want eyes on Dr. Bates at all hours of the day and night. His name wasn't mentioned during interrogations..." —*by interrogations, I mean torture*— "... but that doesn't mean anything. People only keep quiet when they have something to hide." When another joint hum trickles into my ears, I stand to my feet, eager to get our meeting over. I loathe the political side of my job as much as I hate my father. "Is there anything else?"

I'm halfway out the door when Rocco's deep timbre stops me. "One last thing."

I work my jaw through a tight grind when he requests for everyone but Smith to leave. I understand his distrust. The longer Fien's captivity continues, the more certain I become that I have a rat in my crew. Furthermore, the tension on Rocco's face tells me I won't like what he has to say next.

Once only three bodies remain in my office, Rocco joins me partway to the door. "Theresa Veneto has made numerous requests to meet with you the past week. I assured her as derogatively as I could that you're not interested in anything she's selling, then she gave me this." He digs out a folded-up piece of paper from his pocket. Although the image is dated, I'm relatively sure it's the brunette who was on Isaac's arm last week.

My eyes lift from the college snapshot when Smith says, "Roxie was right. She did see Isabelle in a documentary. Well, kind of." He swivels his laptop around to face me. It has a poorly made video playing on the screen. It's amateur at best, even with Smith cleaning it up. "She thought this lady was Isabelle." He points to a brunette at the side of the footage that has an uncanny resemblance to the photograph of the woman I'm clutching. "Where in reality, this is Isabelle." He highlights a toddler just left of the woman he pointed out. "The documentary was filmed years ago, but the doco remembered the female. Her name was Felicia. She was Vladimir Popov's favorite whore."

I don't know which fact to work first, so I go for the easiest. "Was?"

Smith jerks up his chin. "Coroner said she overdosed. The head doco had a different recollection of events. He swears she was murdered."

"By Vladimir?"

Smith shrugs. "Rumors circulated that he choked her in a jealous rage, but that never held much credit. Felicia was never seen with anyone, and strangulation isn't Vladimir's kink. He prefers—"

"Long, painful deaths," I fill in. "Unlike my father. He loves nothing more than to see the light fade from a woman's eyes."

Could that be the cause of the rift between the Petrettis and the Popovs? There's never comradery between opposing cartel groups, but things have been strained between the above-mentioned families for decades. Vladimir has the power my father wants but will never have. Like a spoiled child, instead of striving to outdo Vladimir, he set out to destroy him. His tactics the past few years have barely created a ripple in Vladimir's armor, although the same can't be said for his offspring.

Rico, Vladimir's eldest son, is a hothead, but he's got nothing on his younger brother, Nikolai. Nikolai has a massive chip on his shoulder and a beef with everyone. I'll be shocked if he makes it to his thirties. I've been tempted to order his hit numerous times, and I've never met the guy. He rubs me the wrong way. I have no clue why. It could be jealousy, but it feels more than that. His family's name might be more powerful than mine and his pockets lined with more money, but I'd rather suffer the injustice of being born into my family than have my fire-breathing father breathing down my neck for every hour of every day like Vladimir does to Nikolai.

Perhaps that's it? Maybe I feel sorry for the guy? I'm also the youngest of my family, but I don't have to knock down my siblings to reach the top rung. Their knighthood fell long before I picked up my sword.

I freeze when snippets of the clues Smith handed me slowly slot into place. "If Felicia was Vladimir's favorite whore, who's Isabelle's father?" Smith doesn't need to answer me. The truth is all over his face. "Isabelle is Vladimir's daughter, and now she's working for the Feds. How the fuck did that happen?"

Naysayers say I'm working for the Feds as well, but only you and I know that isn't true. Those fuckers work for me more than I work for them.

"Felicia died when Isabelle was a child. She was sold a couple of months later."

I shouldn't smile at Rocco's admission, but I can't help it. I often forget I'm not the only mafia kid with an asshole for a father. In a way, depending on who purchased her, Isabelle could have gotten lucky.

Seeing an array of questions in my eyes, Rocco says, "She was bought by none other than Mr. Fed himself."

"Tobias?" I query, certain Rocco is mixing up his nicknames. Most of my exchanges with Tobias occurred while Rocco was in jail, so a slip-up is understandable.

When Rocco lifts his chin, air whizzes out of my mouth. Tobias was a little shady, but he usually still followed protocol by the book. This isn't close to any legislations I've seen in the Feds' handbook for agents.

Although I'm somewhat shocked, and a smidge proud of Tobias's bend of the rules, I don't understand what any of this has to do with Theresa's request to meet with me.

When I say that to Rocco, his grin turns blinding. "Maybe it isn't just you and Roxie that have a sixth sense around each other. Perhaps we have one, too?" Smith coughs to cover his chuckle when Rocco puckers up his lips for an air kiss. "Who said Mario was chasing Princess P? He might have liked hairy Italians."

His words become as windless as Smith's chuckles when I sock him in the stomach. I understand the reason for his riling, it's how he handles things when he feels out of his element, but I've got too many theories swirling around in my head to add his antics into the mix.

"What was Theresa's response to your question?"

Rocco rubs his stomach, feigning injury while replying, "That you'll lose more than a couple of bricks of coke if you don't meet with her."

My brow cocks, shocked she had the audacity to threaten me. If my thoughts hadn't shifted to Fien after she stole from me, she'd be lying on the bottom of the ocean with Eduardo, feeding the fish.

Rocco's grin reveals he responded to Theresa's threat with the same malice tracing through my veins. "My gun got real friendly with her head, but you know bitches, they don't lay down even when they're in heat."

I take a moment to deliberate a response. Although it could be a waste of my time, discovering the reason Theresa met with my father last week should swallow the injustice. Theresa is like India. She only sniffs around when there's a carcass ready to be boned. If my family is carving it up, I want to know about it.

"Set up a meeting for the AM." Smith appears shocked about my offer, but his lips remain locked. "But warn her if she wastes my time, she'll need to clear her schedule for the remainder of her life."

Believing all is said and done, Smith grabs his paperwork and laptop off the desk and makes a beeline for the door. He doubles back when I add, "Also announce that Roxanne's auction was finalized and that her winning bidder was me." When a fretful mask slips over Rocco's face, I do my best to shut it down. "The auction was conducted under my father's branch of our entity. I could have been in attendance as a bidder. Furthermore, if you want the people Dr. Bates is working for to be tempted by the lure we're considering dangling in front of them, we need to make it as appetizing as possible. If this is personal, as we believe it is, making the mark associated with me will work in our favor." Before relief can cross Smith's features, pleased I'm considering his tactic, I continue, "*If* I go through with this, there will be no holds barred. I won't be fucked in the ass by Rimi for another two years."

"I agree with what you're saying." Rocco's words are more at ease than his facial expression. "But by going down this road, you'll place Roxie on your father's radar."

He looks torn between wanting to pat me on the back and punch me in the face when I reply, "Isn't that the point?"

TEN

Roxanne

I stretch out lazily, loving that a solid few hours of sleep hasn't fully unwound my tired muscles. I slept through dinner, dessert, and the midnight cap Smith forced on me every night the past three days to encourage me to sleep, but I feel refreshed. Calm, even.

It's amazing what back-to-back orgasms can do. My hang-ups from the past week have vanished, and nothing but optimism appears on the horizon. It's a nice feeling after years of worry.

"You better quit moaning before I come over and take care of them."

The bedding falls away from my naked chest when I prop myself on my elbows so I can stray my eyes in the direction the voice came from. If it were twanged with anything but an Italian accent, I'd cover up, but since I want to entice my greeter into following through with his threat, I don't bother.

"Good morning."

My eyes shift to the only window in the room, truly unsure if it's morning or not. I feel like I've been asleep for weeks but am untrusting of my delirious head.

My lips twist when not a ray of sun shines through the pleats of the drapes. It's early enough for the slightest bit of gray to mottle the sky, but it isn't close to the time I usually wake up.

A hunger unlike anything I've ever felt before smacks into me when Dimitri says, "Rosa left a club sandwich on the nightstand. You should eat. You'll need the energy."

His voice is as seductive as the lust roaring through my veins, however I can't act on it. He isn't seated behind his desk at this late hour for no reason. He's working through the files Smith and I collated while endeavoring not to make it seem as if we were holding a candlelight vigil at his bedside.

After placing on my dressing gown Rosa must have gathered from the floor, I snatch up the sandwich Dimitri mentioned before pacing to his half of the room. I won't lie, lust thickens my veins when I notice his inconspicuous watch. He stares at me through hooded eyelids, acting as if my frumpy dressing gown is made from the finest silk.

The indecent swing of my hips tapers when I notice which articles he's perusing. He has 3D printouts of my grandparents' farm spread across his desk. Smith took my knowledge of burial sites up a notch when he showed me how ground-penetrating radars and electromagnetic tests can narrow down the search area when seeking unmarked graves. It was fascinating to watch, but the circumstances for our search sucked.

Once I've swallowed down my unease, I say, "No significant increase in conductivity was found during electromagnetic testing, leading us to believe there were no bodies buried on-site."

Dimitri raises his eyes to mine, either shocked at the extent of my knowledge or turned on by the lack of disgust in my voice. He should count his lucky stars he was out cold the first three days of my internship, or he would have witnessed me heaving more than once. I have a morbid curiosity for crime shows and the scientific side of hunting for murderers, but having a personal connection with the people involved was a bitter pill to swallow.

After a quick breather, I continue updating Dimitri on our findings. "Smith organized ground-penetrating searches for a handful of smaller sites that had increased conductivity. Nothing came from it. Most were stock animals or farming equipment."

"Did they dig below the animal carcasses?"

I shake my head. I wasn't on-site during testing, but I kept a close watch on proceedings from my station in Dimitri's room with Smith. "Why would they dig deeper?"

I'm reasonably sure I won't eat for a week when Dimitri asks, "When searching for a body, what's the most obvious shape examiners seek?" Although he's asking a question, he continues talking as if he didn't. "If you don't want a body found, instead of burying it horizontally, dig a vertical gravesite. It makes the disturbance to the land less noticeable and often has conductivity results overlooked by examiners." He snickers about my whitening gills before adding, "The smart criminals might even add a dead animal on top of the corpse to ward off suspicion."

"That's disturbing."

He smiles at the gag my reply was delivered with before muttering, "It's actually smart depending on which side of the law you're on. If you were digging up a square burial site, and you stumbled upon a family pet, would you keep digging?"

"Uh, no," I force out through a gag. "And I'm reasonably sure ninety-nine percent of the population wouldn't, either."

I wish he'd quit smiling. They're making me all types of hot. "That's my point. We're not seeking an upstanding member of society, Roxanne. We want that one percent."

Considering what we're discussing, I shouldn't relish how he says 'we.' However, I do.

After standing to his feet, Dimitri says, "We need to take another look at your grandparents' farm." Ignoring the loud gurgle of my stomach that has nothing to do with hunger, he gets straight down to business. "Smith… Smith…"

Before his third call for Smith can rumble out of his mouth, I place my hand over his balled one resting on his desk. "He's probably sleeping."

My reply was meant to calm him down, not rile him up. He's more frustrated now than he was when I placed on my dressing gown. He's pissed Smith isn't at his beck and call, having no clue he'd be dead if he continued walking down the path he has the past eighty-plus hours.

"He barely slept the past three days, Dimi. He was a walking zombie." When Dimitri's eyes snap to mine, shocked at my unusual use of his nickname, I forcefully swallow the brick in my throat. "We'll get the search done, but it will have to wait until the morning. You won't find anything but raccoons at this hour."

The jest in my tone adds the slightest furl to his top lip. It's not a smile, but it isn't a scowl either.

"Have you eaten?" When he jerks up his chin, I ask, "Was it better than this?"

His eyes stray in the direction my head is nudging. After drinking in my soggy sandwich I'm sure was super fresh six hours ago, he shakes his head.

"Do you want to risk death?" The unease I see in his eyes makes me smile. "I can whip up a mean batch of pancakes... I just have a bad habit of burning them."

I can tell he wants to smile, he's just riddled with too much guilt to allow himself to be happy. I can't say I don't understand his objection. I still haven't laid my eyes on Fien, and I feel bad I'm standing across from her father instead of her.

"Come on. I'm sure your insurance will cover a kitchen fire. If not, I'm just as confident you have the dough to cover my mishaps."

My thumping heart from barging him out of his comfort zone could be to blame for my poor hearing, but I swear he grumbles, "If only money could keep you safe."

Two dozen burned pancakes and six salvable ones later, I prop my backside onto the counter Dimitri is seated behind before blurting out a question that hasn't stopped bugging me the past hour. "Can I see a photo of Fien?" When Dimitri's fork drops onto his plate with a clang, I talk faster. "I'm just curious if I'm picturing her right. Like you know how when you read a book, and you imagine the character one way, but when you jump onto the author's Facebook page, you realize they look completely different than you were picturing. It's like that for me with Fien." I stop for a much-needed breath before raising my eyes to Dimitri's. He's as shocked by my ramble as I am. He has been inside of me. I should no longer be nervous around him, but for some reason, I am. "I just want to know if she looks like you."

There he goes with his infamous half-smirk again. "The Petretti genes are strong."

"I'm sure they are," I say with a smile as blinding as his. "But I'm still curious. Does she have curly hair or straight? Blue eyes or brown? Dimples in her top lip like her daddy when he smiles, or did she inherit his elf ears instead?"

With the sentiment in the air thicker than lust, I'm anticipating for him to shut down my inquisitiveness with the cruelness he was raised by, so you can envision the dramatic drop of my jaw when he says, "Her eyes are blue, her hair is as straight as an arrow, and she got both my dimples and my elf ears."

Tension cracks between us when he slips off his barstool to gather something out of the drawer next to my thigh. His fridge and fire mantel aren't adorned with family snapshots and heirlooms. This is more a business premise than a home, so the last thing I anticipate for him to remove from a drawer full of cutlery is a palm-size photograph.

Upon spotting my shock, Dimitri mutters, "I have a photo in every drawer and cupboard as a reminder of why I'm here."

After a quick breather, he hands me Fien's photograph. It's the fight of my life not to coo like an imbecile. She isn't just cute, she's downright adorable. Her nose is tiny, her eyes are wide, and she has the rosiest lips I've ever seen. And Dimitri was right, she did get both his elf ears and his dimple-blemished grin.

"She's adorable." I sound like a ditz, but it's the most honest I've ever been. Seeing Fien's chubby cheeks has brought everything into perspective. It's also made me super mad. If it weren't for me, she'd be standing across from her father instead of me.

I'd hate to think what my life would be like now if my mother hadn't convinced my father to swap me with Audrey, but it's just as horrid realizing you're the cause of someone else's unhappiness. I'm not solely referencing Fien, either. My pain centers around Dimitri and Audrey as well.

"Can I be a part of the search today?"

Dimitri doesn't consider my offer for even a second. He immediately shakes his head.

"I lived there half of my life. I could see something important, stuff others may have missed."

"No, Roxanne." He snatches Fien's photograph out of my hand before he places it back into the drawer. "Shit like that changes you."

I don't pause to consider the protectiveness in his tone. "Shit like this *has* changed me, Dimitri. I'm not the same woman I was when I walked into this house, and I won't be the same when I walk out."

He's up in my face in an instant, his clutch on my face anything but kind. "I said no."

His reply is stern and to the point, but it doesn't weaken my determination in the slightest because it isn't anger in his eyes, it's worry. "You said I could help."

"Fixing your parents' fuck-ups isn't your job."

With every ounce of my self-control lost, I shout, "It isn't yours either, but you're still doing it!"

I don't solely mean my parents. From what I've over-heard the past few days before Dr. Bates was seen following Dimitri to Frosty Kinks, Dimitri's father was suspect number one. As far as I'm concerned, he still deserves to be watched. Dr. Bates isn't operating alone. Our one-on-one talk included the words 'our' and 'we' much too often to believe he's the sole operator of a baby-making franchise.

Before I can announce that to Dimitri, I'm yanked off the kitchen cabinet by my wrist, bent over the island bench I made a mess of while preparing an early breakfast, exposed by the high lift of my dressing gown, then spanked like I'm a naughty child.

I fight his first three spanks, but by the fourth, I'm nothing but putty in the hands of a madman. Just like the public punishment he issued me in a room many miles from here, his spanking offers the perfect amount of pleasure and pain. The heat racing across my backside is enough to have my back molars gritting together, but the slap of his finger-tips against an area that hasn't stopped buzzing the past twelve hours is unbelievably divine.

I'm hot all over in an instant and doing everything in my power not to beg for more. I love how he towers over me. It's like he's a big brooding giant, and I'm a naughty little fairy who loves pushing his buttons.

The lust roaring through my veins doubles when Dimitri growls, "Tell me again how you're planning to walk out on me?" I thought his anger centered around my request to be a part of the search today. I had no clue it was from me mentioning an upcoming departure.

I want to answer him, to tell him I'd stay a lifetime if he'd let me, but lose the chance when his spanking hand switches to nurturing. He rubs my butt cheeks that are clenched in pain before he lowers his hand to a wetness more prominent than the pancake batter. His fingertips barely caress the aching flesh, but it feels like he's tugging at my clit with his teeth.

I discover the reason for his unusual gentleness when he says, "You're still swollen from taking me last night."

His breaths quiver as much as my thighs when I reply, "I don't care."

"You may not care, but I do." His voice is so low, I'm reasonably sure his words weren't for me.

I almost whine when he lowers my dressing gown until its hem floats above the marble floors of his kitchen, but it's gobbled up by a moan when he growls out, "Ass on the countertop. I'm about ready for a second helping of breakfast."

Not waiting for my shock to sink in, he twists me around, throws off the dishware stained with remnants of our shared breakfast, then lifts me onto the kitchen counter as if I'm weightless. A moan unlike anything I've ever heard before rolls up my chest when my backside's collision with the gleaming counter is closely chased by him lowering his head between my legs. He doesn't wait for permission, nor does he remove my dressing gown. He merely uses the slit in the static-loving material to his advantage, so he can devour his second sickly sweet meal of the day. I don't care. I'm too in awe about him lapping up the slickness his dominance caused between my legs to worry about him gaining permission to do so.

As my fingers weave through his dark locks, he slips two fingers inside of me. They enter without effort, made easy by the wetness of his hearty licks. Within a minute of his magic fingers taking control, I'm grunting, moaning, and cursing as if I'm being tortured instead of pleasured. The sensation is almost too much. I've never felt more unhinged —even more so when Dimitri lifts his eyes to mine. His stare rings the words he spoke to me days ago through my ears. *"You don't want a man. You want a monster, a bastard, a man who'd rather destroy you than ever have you believe you deserve more than him."*

This is his way of destroying me. He will spoil me so much in the bedroom, just the thought of being with another man will feel disturbing.

I don't mind. There could be worse things to be dependent on.

My parents' addictions are proof of this.

Like everything else in life, Dimitri doesn't follow the rules in the bedroom any more than he does outside of them. He licks, finger fucks, and devours me until anyone but him is far from my thoughts. He brings me to the very brink of orgasm, tonguing me and tugging at my clit until I'm writhing against his face, then he withdraws all contact.

I can't hold back my wail this time around. It roars out of me just as frantically as a husky moan when Dimitri lowers his trousers as if they're sweats. He fists his erect cock in his hand before giving it a long and slow tug. "What was our agreement, Roxanne?" He sounds angry, but I don't pay the angst in his tone any attention.

I can't fear a man I crave more than my next breath.

My eyes snap to Dimitri's when he strangles out my name as forcefully as he fists his cock. His eyes demand my focus as much as the stimulating visual bombarding me, but I'm not strong enough to listen to both my libido and my head. It's either one or the other, which has me wondering if that's why he asked his question while stroking his cock. I'm already on the back foot for most of our exchanges, but when his impressive manhood is on the table, I'm as submissive as it comes.

Evidence of this is submitted without prejudice when I mumble, "That I'm to do as you ask when you ask..." I wet my lips, hopeful a bit of moisture will ease my next set of words past the lust clutching my throat, "... for precisely how long you ask."

"And what have you been doing?" He strokes his cock faster when he spots a witty comeback in my eyes. The way a handful of pumps alters the direction of my reply reveals I'm worse than a man. I'm not being led astray by my pussy, I am being wholly controlled by it. He has me by the throat, and he's milking it for all its worth.

It's a pity for him I saw the light in his eyes change when

he went down on me. He's more powerful than me, a million times richer, and undeniably more dangerous, but there's one thing we have in common that social status will never change.

He craves me as much as I do him.

"I'm doing as requested. Answering your every whim." The bangs fanned across my forehead rustle in the frantic breaths that pump out of Dimitri's nose when I lower myself onto my knees in front of him. "Even the pleas you're not willing to voice just yet."

After replacing his fist with mine, my tongue darts out to lap up the sticky bead on the end of his impressive cock. The bunching of his thigh muscles exposes he's trying to act unaffected by my switch-up, but the growl I hear rumbling in his chest weakens his endeavor. He's dreamed about me sucking his dick as often as me, if not as long.

"This changes nothing between—"

I steal his words by taking him as deeply into my throat as I can. My impatience wasn't just to stop him saying something he couldn't take back, it was also because I couldn't wait a second longer to have his beautifully thick cock between my lips. My mouth is watering at the thought of tasting his cum, and I won't mention the slick wetness between my legs.

The pain I experienced last night makes sense when my lips burn from being stretched beyond what's comfortable. His eyewatering girth and length also explain why he's lax on protection. The condoms my nanna shoved into my hand not long after my sixteenth birthday will never get close to covering him up. He's too thick. Too long. Too delicious for the threat of a little STI to stop me from devouring him.

There's also the thought of bringing a man as powerful as him to his knees. I've barely strived for a single thing in my life, but I want this more than anything. I don't want to take his power, I merely want him to share it with me for just a second.

An orgasm builds like a tornado in the lower half of my stomach when Dimitri's wish to clutch my hair sees him licking the fingers he had inside of me. He cleans them as if my juices are tastier than the breakfast we shared.

Once all the evidence of my arousal is cleared away, he rakes his fingers through my hair as if his hand is a comb before he secures it in a tight ponytail at the back of my head. I anticipate for him to steal all the control from here, so you can imagine my surprise when his grip on my hair doesn't alter the speed of my sucks. He just drinks it all in, loving that not even a strand of over-bleached hair blocks his view.

Stroke after stroke, I take him deeper. I'm greedy, so much so, every suck has the head of his cock bottoming out at the back of my throat. I gag but continue, more than happy to suffer the injustice if it keeps him moaning the way he is.

When his dick jerks several long minutes later, I swivel my tongue around the rim circling his knob, moaning when my eagerness to taste his precum produces more of the sticky substance.

"You like this, don't you? You've wanted my cock between your lips for months."

I don't deny the cockiness in his tone because everything he said is true. I wanted this even while in the room he tortured my father in.

After flattening my tongue to ensure his impressive manhood sinks to the very back of my throat, I raise my eyes to Dimitri's. His are showcasing his triumph, smug as fuck I didn't deny his claim.

"Finish me." This isn't a command. It's a beg. He's as undone as me and just as desperate. "Then, perhaps if you've shown you can follow orders, I'll let you come with us today."

Although his response has me all types of excited, it has nothing to do with him bending the rules. I love how on edge his voice is. Anyone would think this has been in his dreams as often as mine the past few weeks.

"It'll be my pleasure."

My husky words draw his balls in close to his body. He's on the brink, and the realization that I'm going to push him over the edge has me hollowing my cheeks to the point it's painful.

"Fuck, Roxie," Dimitri growls on a moan, his hips rocking. "You're such a wildcat, a dirty, filthy fucking minx." I love his use of my nickname, not to mention the dirty words that followed it. The way he loses control is as intoxicating as the taste of his mouthwatering cock. "I'm going to come down your throat, then I'll give you everything you want." His arrogant smirk should be one of his less stellar features. It isn't, especially when it's directed straight at me. "Well, as much as you can take. I don't want to ruin your sweet little pussy before customizing it to my cock."

My moans whizz out of my nose, forced there by Dimitri's dick commanding every inch of my throat. He pumps in and out of me, burying himself deeper with every thrust. He face-fucks me until I forget this is supposed to be about getting him off. His dirty words, the taste of his scrumptious cock, and the tight grip he has on my hair has me right there with him, on the very peak of the cliff, ready to fall, but I hold back, remembering he needs this as much as me. Keeping your head above water is exhausting in general, let alone when you're dealing with all the shit Dimitri is. I doubt he's let go of the reins like this in months, if not years.

"Look at me."

My hands fly out to get a grip on Dimitri's thighs when the collision of our eyes sees him losing control. With his head thrown back and his hand holding my mouth hostage to his cock, he pumps into me two more times before the saltiness of his cum floods my tongue.

Giving head isn't supposed to have this level of fireworks associated with it. I never enjoyed doing it to my college boyfriends and usually spat out evidence of their excitement within a second of their bodies expelling it, but this time around, I suck it down as if it's liquid gold, moaning when its slipperiness soothes the burn of my throat from my hearty screams.

I've hardly mollified the blister when I'm plucked from the ground, spun around, then curled over the kitchen counter. My knees knock when the lowering of Dimitri's hand to my pussy is quickly chased by a growl. "You're still swollen. If I take you now, you'll be all types of fucked by sunrise." My knees join for any entirely different reason when he adds, "Perhaps that's the solution to your disobedience? Maybe I should hurt you so bad, the only thing you'll consider doing today is soaking in a tub for hours on end."

My worry he's reneging on his offer doesn't linger for long. His fingers are too wondrous to instigate any emotions not fueled by need. He drags them through the folds of my clenching sex before circling them around the nub dying for his attention. "You're so fucking wet for me. You are dripping like my head didn't leave your cunt the past hour."

I don't respond. I can't. He's barely touching me, and I'm on the cusp of a climax.

"You better get a heap louder than that if you want me to give you permission to come."

He doesn't need to ask me twice. I moan like I'm possessed while grinding down on his hand as if it's as ribbed as his cock.

"Please," I beg a short time later. "I need…"

"Me," Dimitri fills in like anyone else is on my mind. "Because that's all you're going to get from here on out. Me and only me. Do you hear me, Roxanne?"

Sweat rolls down my cheeks when I frantically nod. It's more submissive than when I was on my knees being fed his cock one marvelous inch at a time, but he still wants more.

"Say it."

"You," I squawk like a canary, my fantasies shattered by a reality better than any dream. "I'll only ever want you."

Dimitri pinches my clit until my every sense is being held captive by a madman. "And the walking out part? What about that?"

He's still worried about that?

Before I can answer my unvoiced question, Dimitri asks one of his own, "Has that left your head yet, or do I need to be more persuasive?"

I'm torn on how to answer. I want to say no, hoping I'll discover exactly how alpha he is, but I also want to come. It's blistering inside me, burning as effectively as the burn my lips endured while sucking him off.

With my libido overriding all my senses, I take the coward's route. "It's left my head——"

My pathetic show of womanhood is cut off by a gravelly, accented voice. Although it's oddly similar to the one towering over me with the command of a caveman, it sends a chill scattering through me. It isn't a good shudder. I've only heard this voice once before. It was when he instructed me to turn around so he could see my eyes while he killed me.

Hell has been left unoccupied again. Except this time, the imp isn't walking the corridors of a hospital seeking new recruits, he's visiting his son.

"Eyes to the floor." When my eyes instinctively lift to Dimitri, panicked by the fury in his gruff tone, his jaw tightens. "Eyes to the fucking floor!"

Their fast drop fills my hazy head with dizziness, but the cloud isn't thick enough to miss me watching Dimitri raise his hand in the air in threat. He's seconds from striking me, and I'm at a complete loss as to why.

With my submissiveness on display for all to see, Dimitri grunts something about how frustrating it is for him to put the help in their place before he demands me to clean up the mess I made.

Confident I won't defy him for the second time, he yanks up his trousers huddled around his ankles, then hightails it in the direction his father's voice came from.

ELEVEN

Dimitri

"If that's your idea of a punishment, I'm disappointed. If the help isn't smelling of blood by the time you've showed her the ropes, you let her off easy." My father jerks his chin to the kitchen I'm in the process of forcefully removing him from. "I can smell her cunt from here." The frantic pump of his nostrils makes me want to gut him where he stands. "I guess I can understand your change-up. Even I may be tempted to offer leniency for a smell that sweet."

When he pivots back around, I grip his arm with enough force, I'm certain he'll be wearing my marks as long as Roxanne's ass. "She isn't close to repaying her debt, and I'm not willing to share her until she has." When my father's brows bow, I realize my error. By admitting I want her, his interest in Roxanne tripled in an instant. "She cooks like Ma. Even with her cunt being greedy for a pounding, I'm considering sending her to Petrettis to show them how it's done before shipping her to her buyer."

For a man his age, my father should have more wrinkles on his face than he does when he cocks his brow. "Good cooking skills are to blame for your pants being wrapped around your ankles?"

It takes everything I have not to retaliate to the mirth in his tone. "She fucked up. I wanted my dick sucked. I took advantage of the situation. Sue me."

He laughs in a way that makes my skin crawl, though it has nothing on my reaction when he says, "What can I say? You take after me with more than looks."

The Petretti genes are strong, but this is the last fucking thing I want to hear.

After guiding him into my downstairs office, I gesture to him to take a seat in the chair opposite my desk. Forever willing to test the boundaries, he opts to sit in my chair, instead. He thinks he's smart. In reality, he's an idiot. I use this office for nothing but fucking, purely because of him. He can snoop all he likes down here because he'll never find a single shred of evidence about either my operation or my daughter.

As he scans the fake business documents on my desk, he slouches low into my chair. He doesn't even try to hide his snooping. To him, this is his realm. I merely live in it.

Confident the articles aren't of interest to him, he locks his eyes with mine. "I have some very dissatisfied customers." I assume he's referencing Theresa Veneto's numerous requests to meet with me. Although she was scarce with details when Rocco organized our meeting for later today, she did hint that it was concerning an unfavorable purchase she made from the Petretti entity but am proven wrong when he nudges his head to the hall we just walked. "She created quite the kerfuffle, only for her sale to be canceled because her seller couldn't keep his dick in his pants."

"As far as the buyers are concerned, her sale was umbrellaed under your entity of our family. That means I was entitled to bid as a buyer." With my tone much too possessive for my liking, I try another tactic. "You said it yourself. Her cunt smells like candy. I wanted to see if it tasted the same."

Imagine a perverted old guy grabbing his dick while watching kids play in a playground. That will give you an idea of the sleazy look on my father's face when he asks, "Does it?"

The egotistical side of my head wants to say Roxanne's cunt is the tastiest dish I've ever sampled, but my business side shuts it down. Acting as if I can't stand Roxanne won't just favor me, it will keep her safe as well.

"If it were, do you think she'd be cooking me breakfast?"

He doesn't want to believe me, but I've given him no reason not to. "If it's that bad, ship her to the next candidate. Dr. Bates will be more than happy to wade through your slops."

The mentioned name pisses me off to no end. "As I said earlier, until her debt is paid in full, she's not going anywhere."

Not even a man as arrogant as my father could deny the ownership in my voice this time around. It has his lips begging to hitch into a smirk, but for some reason, he holds it back.

"Very well. Do with her as you wish."

He stands from my seat before buttoning the middle

button of his business suit jacket. Considering the hour, I'm going to assume he's about to turn in for the night. Most of the load in this industry is done at night. It's why I rarely sleep.

"But I'll expect your check on my desk by close of business today. If she were mine to sell, I expect dividends from her sale."

I want to believe the swift end of our conversation is because money comes before anything to my father. However, my gut is advising me not to be stupid. He knows as well as I do that Roxanne's auction was only the tip of the iceberg in her earnings. If this were purely about profit, he'd milk her for all she's worth.

As confident I'll jump to his command as rapidly as Roxanne does mine, he dips his chin before exiting my office via a concealed entrance. It isn't an entrance many people know about, but it's the only clue I need as to why the scent of Roxanne's juices on my hand is being overridden by an emasculating perfume.

"Entering a man's house uninvited warrants him permission to shoot you."

The shadow I'm glaring at switches on the lamp next to the single chair she's seated in before she strays her eyes to mine. "I'm an invited guest."

I shoot Theresa a stern look, warning her I'm not in the mood for her games. "You were instructed to arrive at ten o'clock, not enter my house at an ungodly hour."

I'm tempted to gouge her eyes out when she drinks in my shirtless form with a prolonged gawk. It's clear what she's here for, so I make it just as clear I'm not interested.

"You stole thirty thousand dollars' worth of uncut coke from me. Even if I could forget that, we'll never mess the sheets." I lock our eyes, ensuring she can see the truth in mine when I say, "I don't fuck women I plan to kill."

She smiles like her life isn't on the line. "That isn't what I hear. Supposedly, that's your thing now."

Aware of her attractiveness, she rakes her teeth over her lower lip. I won't lie, she could give half the whores in my arsenal a run for their money. She just needs to thaw out her icy insides first. Not even hard-ass men like me want to bed a heartless woman.

"I wonder if you'll change your mind when I share the information I've unearthed about your father the past month?"

My lips tuck in the corner. I should have known her early visit isn't purely about whetting her sexual appetite. If the law can't catch my father, they side with him. When they get burned, they come running to me.

"I'm done fixing my father's mistakes…" My words trail off when Theresa holds a photograph into the light. It's the same image she handed Rocco earlier this week. "The bad can turn good just as easily as the good can turn bad." I don't hold back my arrogant smirk this time around. "You should know that better than anyone."

Theresa is as corrupt as they come. The only reason she hasn't done time is because she has one of those golden pussies Clover mentioned weeks ago. It's got nothing on Roxanne's, but I can see how it could make some men do whatever she asks.

"Your father is cashing in favors he'll never repay, and here you are, acting ignorant to a Russian invasion."

My laugh echoes around my office. "A Russian invasion, my ass. The last time that happened, Vladimir—"

"Found out his wife birthed a child with your father."

I take an involuntary step back. I hate that I allowed my shock to be seen, but there was too much honesty in her tone for a nonchalant response.

Theresa soaks up my surprise as if it's whiskey, and she's an alcoholic. "This can't be the first time you've heard about illegitimate siblings, surely. I know of at least three."

She's right. My family has faced rumors about my father's infidelities for decades—baby mamas included—but this is the first time the rumblings included someone who could possibly steal my crown before I've sat on my throne.

"Male or female?" I don't know why the fuck I'm contemplating this. If he or she wants to contest my position, bring it on. I'll take them down as well as I did their predecessors. I guess a part of my curiosity can be blamed on the fact the last time the Petrettis and Popovs went to war was the year before I was born. If an extramarital affair is the cause of this, there are rules not even I can break because this time around, a coup won't just get me killed, it will take down my daughter as well.

I want to pretend I don't recognize the face of the man Theresa brings up on her phone, but unfortunately, you'd have to be dead the past decade not to know him. The Popovs are loud, proud, and Vladimir's second eldest son soaks up the attention for all it's worth.

Nikolai Popov is a media whore.

He's also four months older than me.

Fuck it!

After working my jaw side to side, I play it cool. "Unfounded rumors like this will get you killed quicker than theft."

Theresa paces my way, her hips extra swingy. The fact she thinks I can be led by my cock pisses me off more than her presumption I'd want to get freaky with her. "Who said it's unfounded?"

When she's within touching distance, I grip her throat with everything I have. Like the dumb fuck she is, she gets turned on by my hold instead of fearing it. That's why we played well when we did. She's as kinky as she is corrupt.

A liar would tap out within seconds, a woman seeking a cheap thrill would have tears springing down her eyes shortly after that. Only someone with nothing to fear would return my glare without the slightest bit of sheen in her eyes.

Regretfully, that someone is Theresa.

She gives it her all not to answer the screaming protests of her lungs when I loosen my grip on her throat before tossing her to the other side of my office. She loses her fight when she lands on her backside with a thud. She won't stay down. She will quietly lick her wounds before kicking me in the gut with the three-inch heels she's wearing. That's her way.

Before her pumps can get anywhere near my stomach, I mutter, "Tell me what you want before I add visible wounds to your hidden ones."

For once, she pays attention to the angst in my tone. It's for the best. I wasn't joking. I hate killing women, but I'll make an exception for her. "I want the same thing you do, Dimi. Revenge."

Even having no knowledge of the inner-workings of women whatsoever doesn't spare me from knowing who her comment refers to. Women get their panties in a real twist when their baby daddies don't come to the party for child support, much less when they deny paternity all together.

As a smirk curls my lips, I prop my backside onto my desk and fold my arms in front of my chest. I can't believe it took me this long to slot the pieces of the puzzle together. This isn't a turf war. It's a law enforcement officer learning she can't always have things her way. I only fucked her to have her looking past illegal shipments, yet she still responded to her deputy's wish to deepthroat my cock with the contempt of a scorned woman, so I can only imagine how she feels knowing her baby daddy is moving on.

"As I told you years ago, the Petrettis don't meddle with custody disputes." Before she can call me out as a liar, I add, "Unless you want Isaac Holt to go on an extended vacation, we have no business."

"His girlfriend is Russian. She has Popov blood running through her veins. How can you not be worried about this?"

I give her a look, warning her she better keep herself in check. I'm already pissed I left Roxanne hanging mid-orgasm. I don't need more annoyances heating my blood. "Because if I thought she was a threat, I would have held back her transfer the instant you forced it through the system."

Now Theresa is the one balking. If she thinks I'm so stupid not to look a little deeper into her sudden return to my state, the act I worked on her was as legitimate as the one I hit Audrey with when she stated she didn't want to date someone in my 'lifestyle.'

"You brought Isabelle here for a reason… what was it?"

Theresa strives to shut down the jealousy blazing through her eyes, but she's not quite quick enough. "She was supposed to go undercover—"

"Not fall for the mark?" Her lack of denial reveals I hit the nail on the head.

My next set of words are barely audible since they're cloaked with laughter. "I'm sorry you got thrown out on your ass, but a bruised ego isn't something I can help you with."

I'm also not eager to go against Isaac again. It isn't that I'm afraid of him. I just learned that karma can gnaw the wrong ass when you attempt to get out of a fucked-up situation in a half-assed way. CJ hasn't been the same since their rigged fight, Ophelia is dead, and Roberto's hiding out as Isaac's dish hand. Those fucked-up set of circumstances would keep the deadliest man on the straight and narrow.

My last comment holds my attention a little longer than it should. I can't be accused of fucking with karma if Isaac stirred the pot first. Alas, I've got enough on my plate, so I'm not interested in anything Theresa is selling. Wasn't years ago. Certainly am not now.

"If you want my help, you'll need to come back with over thirty thousand in uncut coke and a less bitchy attitude."

Theresa attempts to fire something back, but I'm out the door before a syllable leaves her mouth, and even quicker than that, I make my next move. "Call Mikhail. If a Russian so much as schedules a flight out of Vegas, I want to know about it."

Confident Smith is always listening, I make my way to the room I share with Roxanne, eager to award her earlier submissiveness in a way that will have her eating out of the palm of my hand even quicker than Theresa organizes a raid of Ravenshoe PD's evidence vault.

TWELVE

Roxanne

I curse at the soap as if it's my whining libido when it slips from my grip for the second time the past two minutes. It's acting as if Dimitri's threatened slap hours ago would get me off as well as his teeth tugging on my clit. I should have been scared he was acting so violent. However, all I felt was excitement.

In a weird way, it felt like he was protecting me, like his shift in personality was solely reliant on the unexpected arrival of his father. I even got that vibe from Smith when he guided me through Dimitri's residence, so I'd avoid walking down the hallway Dimitri dragged his father down only seconds earlier.

I stop seeking snippets of clarity in an insane world when the faintest hum of multiple engines warming up breaks through the madness swamping me. Before his father interrupted us, Dimitri gave me permission to attend the second search of my grandparents' ranch today. Wailing libido or not, I'm not going to miss it for anything.

After shutting off the faucet, I scrub my skin dry with a towel, twist another around my midsection, then race into the main part of my room. My pace slows to that of a snail when a gleaming device catches my eye. It isn't the prototype laptop Smith loaned me when I offered to help him keep things afloat while Dimitri recovered from having his drink spiked. Nor is it the ring I tossed at my mother when I realized she was responsible for my unexpected inheritance. It's my cell phone.

My heart launches into my throat when it suddenly commences ringing. It vibrates across the nightstand to the ringtone I set for Estelle's number, wordlessly urging me to pick it up.

I almost fall for his trick until I realize what's happening. I'm proud of how well I sucked Dimitri's cock, but even if I had sucked the marrow from his bones, I don't believe he'd award me two offerings in one day. This is a test, I'm certain of it. If I answer Estelle's call, the SUVs I hear idling at the front of his compound will leave without me. If I leave her call unanswered, I further my proof I'm on Dimitri's side.

It sucks that he needs to be constantly reassured, but it's also understandable. I heard the tone Dimitri's father used on him in the hallway. He doesn't love his son. I'm not even sure if he likes him.

With that in mind, I send a telepathic message to Estelle that I'll buzz her as soon as possible before I continue my sprint for the walk-in closet. Since my time is limited, I throw on the first dress I see. It's more suitable for a nightclub crawl than a daytime hike through overgrown fields, but I act ignorant to the fact.

Once I have on a pair of shoes and have thrown my hair into a messy bun, I hotfoot it to the door.

"Smith?" I query when my attempt to open my door is thwarted by a trusty lock.

"Smith," I try again after unsuccessfully rattling the lock three times.

It feels like I'm thrust into a mean, demoralizing game I'll never win when a churlish voice asks, "Aren't you going to answer your phone?"

I peer at the camera in the corner of the room before shaking my head. I can't testify that Dimitri is watching me, but it feels as if he is.

It dawns on me that I'm on the money when his thick Italian voice asks, "Why not? Estelle hasn't heard from you in almost two weeks. I'm sure she's getting worried."

Air whooshes out of the speakers when I say, "I'm sure she is, but I don't want to fail your test."

"Who said I'm testing you?" The way Dimitri speaks freely down the line assures me he's the only one listening in. He is close with Rocco and Smith, but I doubt even they truly know how many layers he has. "Perhaps I'm trying to stop you from getting hurt."

"You can protect me better in person than you ever could locking me away."

I'm hoping my confession will have him deliberating for a minute.

He doesn't even give it a second.

"Although I appreciate your confidence, I disagree, and

that's why I'm going back on my earlier offer. You're to stay in your room until I permit you to leave. Do you understand?"

"No," I say with a brutal shake of my head. "I did as you asked. I proved I'm on your side."

I push down on the door handle for the fifth time. It fails to budge just as much as Dimitri's domineering personality.

"Dimitri!"

I bang on the door three times, confident the lack of static above my head means he's no longer listening to me but unwilling to give up. He's not being fair, and I'm about ready to call him out on it.

"You're not thinking rationally! I passed your test. I'm on your side!"

I continue screaming until the hum of a fleet of top-of-the-line SUVs stops buzzing in my ears, and the debilitating silence surrounding me stretches to days.

THIRTEEN

Dimitri

I glare at Rocco as if he's standing directly in front of me instead of peering at me through the camera propped above Roxanne's door. "Make her eat."

He places down Roxanne's untouched breakfast onto a side table in the hallway before asking, "And exactly how would you like me to do that, D? Ram the bacon down her throat."

"If that's the only way you can get her to fucking eat, then yeah, ram it down her throat." I lower my voice a few decibels when my roar gains me the attention of a handful of staff at Petretti's restaurant. I'm hiding out like a coward, pretending its business as usual even with it feeling anything but.

Our second search of Roxanne's grandparents' estate found bodies. No, you didn't hear me wrong. I said bodies as in multiple victims. Although preliminary findings lead us to believe the decomposition of the female bodies points to them being buried quite a few years ago, I know for a fact you can alter the decay of a corpse to make aliases more concrete.

It's a little hard to pin a murder on someone when the victim supposedly died while you were in another country. Add that knowledge to the fact several victims were in their final months of pregnancy, and Fien's ransom request arriving a week earlier than usual, for triple the amount, and you've got me with a ton of attitude I could easily take it out on the wrong person. Since I don't want that person to be Roxanne, I need to maintain distance between us.

I said her mother's verdict would be her choice, that I wouldn't kill her until she gave me permission. I don't see me keeping my word if I discover her mother buried my wife on her family ranch, then lied about it. I gave Sailor plenty of chances to come clean, so she will lose more than an ability to lie if I find out she has played me for a fool.

As if the above matters aren't enough to make my mood the sourest it's ever been, I looked into Theresa's claim my father got friendly with a Russian enemy's wife. I want to report that her claims are as bogus as my oath she gives good head, but that would make me as deceitful as her.

Nikolai isn't Vladimir Popov's son. That doesn't automatically make him a Petretti, but his markings most certainly do.

He has icy blue eyes—just like me.

He has the makings of a madman—just like me.

And he hates his father with every fiber of his being— just. Like. Me.

If traits replicated genes, our similarities would automatically make us comrades. Alas, the fact we could be related won't do Nikolai any favors. If anything, it will make matters worse. I'm not giving up my throne for anyone, much less a Russian. I'd send every member of my family to the grave before I'd ever let our sanction be run by a Russian. The Petretti name isn't what it once was, but that doesn't mean it's worthless. Honor comes in many forms. The past is just one of them.

While scrubbing at the scruffy beard I haven't trimmed in almost a week, I recall the reason for the extra heat in my veins. It has nothing to do with a hotheaded Russian and everything to do with a mixed-bred American who pushes my buttons like no one else.

Roxanne hasn't eaten in days. If she doesn't soon, there won't be anything left of her. Usually, I don't give a fuck about anyone but Fien and myself. This, however, is rubbing me the wrong way. Roxanne is tiny. Her body isn't built to withstand a weeklong hunger strike. She's already looking sick, and it has me taking drastic measures—measures I usually wouldn't hesitate to use.

"Threaten her."

Rocco's eyes snap to the camera before he shakes his head. He wouldn't be standing outside Roxanne's room unattended if I weren't desperate, so I don't know why he's acting surprised by my request.

"Do you want her to eat?"

He makes a 'duh' face before rolling his eyes like he isn't tatted to the hilt.

"Then threaten her."

"I'm not fucking threatening her, D. That shit is above my paygrade." I'm about to remind him exactly how well-off he is because of me. Sadly, I don't just recall he doesn't give a fuck about money, he reminds me that he isn't here solely for his hip pocket. "If you want to hold a woman captive *like your daughter*, you gonna need to do that shit yourself."

Stealing my chance to reply, he tosses Roxanne's breakfast into the camera before hot-footing it down the corridor. I could let his temper tantrum slide, but as I said earlier, I've got too much anger bubbling in my veins. If I don't release some of it soon, I'm going to explode.

"Smith…"

His instant reply reveals he witnessed the exchange between Rocco and me. "You know he wouldn't be so hard on you if you told him the truth."

I scoff like I don't have a dick between my legs. "If you believe that, you don't know Rocco."

Air whizzes out of his nose, but he fails to cite an objection, proving I'm right. Rocco might back down for a second or two, but the instant his head is screwed back on straight, he'd be right back up in my face causing trouble like he always does.

With that in mind, I say to Smith, "I need you to send Clover on an errand for me…"

My words trail off when a disturbance in the main part of the restaurant captures my attention. Considering we're still a few hours from the lunch rush, I'm shocked when it sounds like someone getting into a scuffle. The clientele get feisty when someone takes the last dish of risotto, but it's never had this edge of excitement attached to it before.

"I'll send you the deets. Make it quick. This is a matter of utmost importance." Smith gasps like he's insulted I insinuated he'd ever slack off, but before he can voice his annoyance, I add, "Buzz me when Clover is ready. I want to be in charge of comms."

He hums out an agreeing noise before disconnecting our feed. Just as quickly, I punch out the details on the errand I want Clover to run.

I've only just hit send on my email app when the raised voice of one of my father's goons booms into my ears, "I'm his exterminator."

I make it to the entrance of the kitchen in just enough time to see a fool make a costly mistake. Brandon James, one of Tobias's highest-ranked foot soldiers, mutters out a string of unintelligible words before he jabs the edge of his palm into Don's throat.

His maneuverer is effective, but it would have been more impressive if he disarmed Don's sidekick first. He's up in Brandon's business in an instant, aiming his gun at the crease between his blond brows as if Brandon doesn't have a direct kill lined up.

With my mitts needing to remain off Roxanne, and my every move monitored by my father, my wish to kill is the strongest it's been. I should step back and watch the carnage unfold with a smile. Regrettably, I owe Tobias a heap of favors he can never cash in, so it sees me offering leniency —just.

"Standdown." Disappointment echoes in my low tone. I don't know Brandon, but that doesn't mean I can't hate him. He and his gun-toting law enforcement friends are what's wrong with society these days. Rules make everything worse —starting at my inability to kill my father because that pathetic, insolent man is the rule-maker of my realm.

When my direct order is ignored, I get inventive. "Should I remind you what happened to the last man who ignored me? Or would you like me to show you, instead?"

Since my threat was delivered in Italian, Brandon does nothing but smile when my father's goons immediately lower their guns. After assisting a third passed-out man off the floor, they race for the safety of the parking lot.

While watching their dash for freedom, Brandon unclips the magazine from the gun he yanked out of the back of Don's pants, unloads the bullets onto the floor, places the disarmed weapon onto the hostess's podium, then wipes it clean. Although I'm impressed he's distrusting enough to remove his fingerprints from a gun the Feds would love to get their hands on, the brainless blonde manning the hostess section of the restaurant reveals why blondes are given so much shit.

She stares at the gun Brandon placed down, too feared to touch it, yet somehow turned on by the thought. Her mixed emotions have my thoughts immediately shifting to Roxanne. I want to say it's a good shift, but like anything the past few days, I couldn't be so lucky.

"Go!" My shouted word scarcely reaches the other side of the restaurant when the blonde sprints for the exit even quicker than her big, burly counterparts.

Once she's out of eyesight, I drift my eyes to Brandon. He looks smug. Shows how fucking stupid he is. "You're an idiot showing up like this unannounced. You could have gotten yourself killed."

"By whom?" He follows me into the kitchen, his strut way too haughty for my liking. I discover the reason behind his peacock walk when he jabs me with a below-the-belt hit. "By you? Or the man you're sheltering after sending every one of your siblings to their deaths?"

Fighting the urge not to slit his throat with the ladle in my hand, I spoon a helping of Malloreddus into the bowl on my left before gesturing with my head for him to sit in the chair across from me. Although my father has returned from New York, I'm not worried about him walking in on our conversation. He uses the Feds to his advantage—just like me.

With the knowledge I'm more like my father than hoped, I drag the ladle across the bottom of the saucepan as if I'm scraping out my father's insides while saying, "I don't protect my father. You're well aware of that."

Brandon dips his chin, mindful I'd kill him for anything less than an agreeing gesture. "Have you been back long?"

My lips itch to lift into a smile, but I hold back the urge. I had wondered how closely I was being monitored by the Bureau after Tobias's death. Now I know it's more than an occasional glance. The months I spent in Italy weren't widely broadcasted. The family didn't want to risk an attack if our enemies became aware one of the main players were abroad, so we kept it on the down-low.

After setting down a bowl of Malloreddus in front of Brandon, I give him a stern look. "I flew in early last month.

The Bureau is unaware of my return. I'd like to keep it that way." My tone reveals I'm not suggesting for this to happen, I am warning him it better occur.

Even being close to a second bender in under a month, my glare has the effect I'm aiming for. "Your secret is safe with me, although I have a few questions I'd like to ask."

I'm not a fan of being interrogated, especially when the questions are being asked by a federal agent, but I jerk up my chin, mindful of how these things work. The more I scratch Brandon's back, the less itchy mine will be.

Unless I get hives, which is what hits me when Brandon asks, "Were you aware CJ was participating in your father's underground fighting circuit?"

After stabbing my fork into my meal with enough aggression for his throat to work hard to swallow, I answer, "I had a feeling a few months before I discovered it the hard way." Brandon isn't the only one shocked by the honesty in my tone. I'm blown away by it as well. "CJ was a good fighter. He was also willing to do anything to get into our father's good graces, so I shouldn't have been surprised."

Once again, I'm being straight-up honest. CJ had world-class skills. He just wasn't in charge of his battles. That day, Isaac walked away with the champion's belt. If CJ hadn't given up on life, he could have claimed victory on their next bout.

Brandon gives me a sympathetic look. It makes me hate him even more. I loathe people who feel sorry for me without having the faintest clue my biggest battle is also my most unknown. It's kind of like depression. Just because you can't see the illness eating you away doesn't mean it doesn't exist. It's there, gnawing at you for every second of every day. You've just got to be stronger than it.

My thoughts shift from the present to the past when Brandon asks, "Were you aware Isaac Holt fought under your father?"

It's the fight of his life not to scowl when I say, "Who?" I could add more authenticity to my lie, but I can't be fucked. I've hardly slept the past four days, and I don't have the energy for theatrics.

"Isaac Holt." Brandon shovels a forkful of food into his mouth like he's been on a hunger strike as long as Roxanne before he pulls a photograph out of the pocket of his swanky trousers. The shoddy pixilation from being zoomed in reveals it's an image from an FBI file, much less its markings. It has 'confidential' stamped all over it. "This was obtained at an event your father organized."

When Brandon's eyes lift to gauge my response to his inaccurate statement, I stray my eyes away, acting disinterested. "Isaac didn't fight for my father." I shrug before giving him a tidbit of information on my family's inner workings, hopeful it will see him offering leniency when I cash in a future favor. "Col wanted him to, but Isaac wasn't budging. We put steps in place to make it happen."

"We?" His one word is choked through a clump of tomato goop lodged halfway down his throat.

Just like earlier, I could sit back and watch the carnage unfold. Unfortunately, I've got enough issues keeping the Feds off my ass while waiting for the bodies at Roxanne's family ranch to be identified. I don't want another corpse added to the mix.

After pouring Brandon a glass of water, I hand it to him. He chugs down half of it before he almost chokes for the second time from me explaining, "We, as in Ophelia and me."

His fork hits the edge of his bowl with a clatter. "Your sister helped you? How *exactly*?"

Needing to hide my smirk, I dab at my lips with a stained napkin before placing the bowl I used earlier into the sink. "Our father wanted Ophelia to coerce Isaac into fighting for him—"

"So she dated him to deceive him?"

I arch my brow, wordlessly warning him he better not interrupt me again.

Confident he's got the gist of my annoyance, I say, "No. Ophelia was never with him for that. She truly loved him." I pause for a beat, shocked by my confession. That's the first time I've admitted Ophelia loved Isaac. Up until now, I always pretended it was puppy love. "Ophelia wanted a way out—"

"Of?"

My nostrils flare as my glare picks up. I fucking warned him only seconds ago what would happen if he interrupted me again and look what he goes and does. He interrupts me —again!

"Sorry." He tugs at the collar of his dress shirt before gesturing for me to continue.

I give him a few seconds to authenticate the level of my threat before continuing with my purge. "She wanted out of the family. If you think my father was cruel to his sons, you should have seen how he treated his daughters. Monster is too kind of a word." The room cools drastically fast. "We knew how desperate Col was to have Isaac fight under him. We were also aware of how good of a fighter Isaac was, so we plotted for them to meet, knowing Col would use Ophelia as a bargaining chip." I work my jaw side to side, struggling to hide the tick my confession caused. "We had no clue CJ was fighting for our father that night until it was too late. They fought. CJ lost, and Ophelia went into a blackened rage." Eager to display our conversation won't last long, I snatch up Brandon's scarcely eaten meal and throw it into the sink. "That was the night of their accident."

Although he's disappointed his meal is ruined, Brandon's inquisitiveness is too high to discount. "Ophelia and CJ's?"

I jerk up my chin. "CJ spent weeks in the hospital before he vanished." You have no idea how hard it was for me not to add, 'to the bush' to the end of my comment. The only reason I didn't was my recollection that Brandon isn't my friend. Only a handful of people know CJ's location. My father and the Feds aren't on that list. "Ophelia was buried with only one member of her family in attendance, and I never told a soul about the ruse we attempted to pull. I'll take it to the grave." *As will you if this ever leaves this room.*

I have no reason to voice my threat. The shudder rolling up Brandon's back reveals he'll take it to his grave along with me.

Curious, I ask, "What does this have to do with anything? I get you're after Isaac, but the fight circuit you're talking about has been running for decades. The Feds are well aware of its existence. They're not disbanding it for a reason. For intel…" My words trail off when Brandon echoes my confession. "So why are you bringing up old ghosts?"

It dawns on me that my purge worked in my favor when nothing but honesty rings in Brandon's tone when he says, "I'm seeking connections between Col, Isaac, Henry, and Kirill Bobrov."

The first three names I've heard a hundred times before. The latter is fairly new in my inquiries. It has only come up a handful of times the past year or two.

Although curiosity is burning me alive, I play it cool, conscious the best secrets aren't immediately unveiled. "Vladimir will be disappointed he didn't make the cut."

"He's still there." Brandon's short response exposes he's endeavoring to keep more than a handful of secrets hidden. "Have you heard of Kirill before?"

I hesitate, untrusting of anyone. "It's been a while…" What? I'm not so stupid to link myself with a current investigation, much less one as perverse as baby trafficking. "… but his name rings a bell. What's his kink?"

Brandon shrugs. "Your guess would be as good as mine. We have an inkling perhaps he's in the sex trafficking trade, but we're only sitting on that theory because of one reason."

Since he's being honest, I do the same. "Katie Bryne?" When he lifts his chin without hesitation, I let him see a small selection of the cards I'm holding. "I knew I had heard the name before."

I can't hold back my smile when I gesture for Brandon to join me in an office at the back of the kitchen. He's carrying a weapon, yet he's still afraid of what I might do to him in a room without a camera. He isn't any safer in the kitchen. The cameras planted throughout the restaurant are solely for looks. If it's electronic, Smith has proven it can be hacked, so there's no fucking chance we'd encourage for the hub of our entity to be placed under unwanted scrutiny.

With that in mind, I come to a dead stop just inside my office. Air whizzes out of Brandon's nose when I halt his entrance by splaying my hand across his chest. He can see the demand in my eyes without a word needing to seep from my lips. It makes me wish he wasn't so anal about following procedures. If he was a little more like his former trainer, we could have an interesting collaboration.

I wolf-whistle when he raises his shirt to show me he isn't wired. I don't give a fuck if he thinks I'm a freak. I just want him on the back foot, so he doesn't reach for his gun when I run the edge of my knife down the front of his pricy outfit. I've been caught out by this preppy boy's love of camera buttons once before. It won't happen again.

"Learned my lesson the hard way," I mutter while dumping the buttons from his business shirt and coat into a half-empty glass of whiskey on my desk. Confident they're broadcasting nothing but the grumbles of my stomach from downing one too many whiskeys last night, I take a seat behind my desk before motioning for Brandon to sit. "If word of this gets out to anyone outside of these walls, my guests will dine on freshly minced veal this evening."

After a quick swallow, Brandon nods, wordlessly sealing our deal. I won't lie. My heart beats a million miles an hour when I place the eight-digit code into the safe bolted to the floor under my desk. I hate giving the Feds anything to work with, but since hardly anyone knows of Fien's existence, I don't see them having any luck working out the combination. It's Fien's birthday followed by her name, an easy combination for me to remember but almost impossible for anyone who doesn't know me to crack. Not even my father has worked it out.

I yank out the multiple cross-references to Fien's case from the leather-bound document before placing it onto my desk. Although Katie's sale has nothing to do with my daughter's captivity, I earmarked her page. Rumors were rife years ago about a rogue Russian sanction kidnapping a local girl, so when her name showed up on a Petretti ledger years after her abduction, I took notice.

I always take notice when Russians are involved.

After pushing across a handful of catering receipts, I set the handwritten ledger down in front of Brandon. "Katie Bryne…" I drag my index finger under her name in the ledger, "… was sold to K Bobrov for three hundred and eighty-five thousand dollars." From what I've discovered the past couple of weeks before Dr. Bates bid on Roxanne, Katie's sale was a record-breaking amount. Kirill wanted her no matter what, and he was willing to pay for the privilege.

Brandon raises his confused eyes to mine. "The date shows her sale was a little under five years ago. Katie was abducted nine years ago."

While grumbling about his inability to do the legwork himself, I slap the ledger shut, then store it back into my safe. Once it's locked away, I take a moment to deliberate whether I should give him the long answer or the short answer.

Not even five seconds into my pondering, Brandon tries to cut it short. "Tobias's arrangement is still in effect, Dimitri. You're immune from prosecution. Within reason, of course."

Air hisses out of my nose as I balance my elbows on my desk. "It's the men picking the reason that I'm wary of." That was my pleasant way of saying I don't trust him. He doesn't want to hear my unkind response. "Hypothetically speaking..." I wait for conformation to register in his eyes before continuing, "... each sanction runs their operations differently. Some prefer underage girls. Others prefer more mature ones. Then there are ones who aren't specifically looking for a whore. They want a wife, someone to raise children with, but they don't have the time to seek her in a crowd of millions, so they look to someone who can give them what they're seeking without additional training."

Brandon's blond brow pops up high on his face. "Training?"

Over the game, and too fucking tired to care about the ripple on effect my father's shady dealings could cause our family name, I answer, "On being the ideal wife. They're taught how to cook, clean, raise children, and anything else their procurer wants of them. Some take months to learn their role. Others take years." I lower my eyes to the floor to hide the gleam they forever get when Roxanne's feistiness pops into my head. "Some never learn."

My eyes return front and center when Brandon stands to his feet. His eagerness isn't shocking, but what he says next most certainly is. "IRS is planning to raid this restaurant on the eighteenth. I suggest you do some in-house cleaning before then."

Not speaking another word, he makes a beeline for the door, scarcely missing Clover's entrance. It's barely noon, but he's gloved up and ready to kill, unaware the only slaughtering he will do this afternoon is to Roxanne's ego.

FOURTEEN

Roxanne

I roll onto my opposite hip, saving my stomach the torture of my eyes drinking in the overloaded burger and fries taking up a majority of the nightstand. My ruse is stupid, and I'm doing more harm to myself than anyone, but for the life of me, I can't give in. I'm being held against my will and persecuted for crimes I didn't commit. A hunger-strike is the low end of the scale for how I could protest to Dimitri's unfair ruling.

I've had plenty of time to contemplate other methods, but for now, I'll continue with this one. It's the safest of the three I thought up, and the least likely to shed blood. Even with my head delusional with hunger, I'm reasonably sure my other two ploys would kill more than my anger. Dimitri doesn't handle his jealousy well. It makes him as unhinged as his distrust makes me.

My brows draw together when a frantic buzz overtakes the grumbles of my hungry stomach a few seconds later. It isn't the drone of an electronic lock opening, nor the static that comes out of the speakers a second before Smith's voice. It's foreign yet familiar like it entered my room along with the eleventh meal I've refused to eat.

Too curious for my own good, I roll onto my back, prop myself onto my elbows, then stray my eyes in the direction the buzz came from. Although the black device nestled on the serving dish a scrumptious-smelling burger is resting on doesn't appear to be a cell phone, it rings as if it is one. It vibrates and bounces across the antique wood serving tray, its shriek growing louder the longer I stare at it.

A normal captive would gobble up the first sign of life outside of these walls as if it's the key to their captivity. As I've said before, I'm nothing close to ordinary. Just like each meal has become more and more enticing the longer I refuse to eat them, this is another trick in Dimitri's vault-load of arsenal. I'm certain of it.

When the device halts ringing a few seconds later, I lock my eyes with the camera in the corner of my room, glare at it as if the only meal I'll ever agree to eat is Dimitri's balls when I rip them off with my bare teeth, then I roll back onto my side.

I've barely sucked in two body-cooling breaths when the annoying buzz starts up all over again. It rings and rings and rings until my temper gets the better of me.

Imagine a robot malfunctioning after you take to it with a baseball bat. That's the noise the little black device makes when I send it hurtling across the room. It smacks into the door that only unlocks when I'm using the bathroom before it crumbles to the floor.

Feeling somewhat victorious—and a whole heap hungry—I squash my back to the bedpost that has handcuff marks notched into the wood before curling my arms around my knees. This position makes the gnawing pangs of my stomach less noticeable. We won't mention my jealousy, though, or you'll book me in for a psych workup.

I quit contemplating sneaking into the bathroom to guzzle down stomach-filling gulps of tap water when a third buzz for the morning trickles into my ears. My eyes shoot to the remnants of the device splayed across the floor, shocked as hell it still works. It's a mangled wreck—almost as twisted as my emotions when I discover the noise isn't coming from the homemade device, it's being projected through the speakers planted throughout the room.

If that isn't shocking enough, the sweet voice that drowns out the annoying hum is downright controversial. "Roxie? Are you there?" Estelle breathes noisily out of her nose, a sign she's pissed. "If you ignore my call one more time, I'm going to scream! What's the go with you lately? Are you too good for your friends now?"

I almost reply with a resounding 'no' but lose the chance when a thick Arabian accent sounds down the line. "Less talk. More looking. I haven't got all day."

I hear Estelle shoo away Clover's snappy tone as if he doesn't kill thousands of people a year. "Don't push your luck, mister. After the way she left me high and dry the past few days, she should be grateful I took her call. I'm pissed, and it's that time of the month, so you better watch yourself."

"Estelle—"

"Oh, so you do remember my name. How kind of you." Her tone is bitchy, but I know deep down inside she's more upset than angry. "Now tell me what I'm searching for so I can get on with my day." When I balk, shocked she thinks I need something from her, she reads my mind like she always does. "Mr. Cranky Pants said he was ordered here to collect a package, and that he isn't leaving until he gets it. Considering he handed me your boss's business card, I'm assuming the mysterious package has something to do with you."

The frantic scream of my pulse drowns out her last four words. I'm panicked out of my mind, suddenly clued on as to why Dimitri would send Clover to my apartment instead of Rocco.

This isn't an endeavor to have me seeing sense through the madness.

This is a shakedown.

"Don't do this," I beg, staring straight at the camera. I can't see Dimitri, but I know he's watching me. I can feel it in my bones. "She has nothing to do with this."

"Nothing to do with what?"

I pretend not to hear the panicked gasps following Estelle's question. "I've done as you asked. I followed your rules."

When the camera swivels to my right, I follow the direction of its gaze. Although I could pretend it's staring at anything, I know its focus is on the only bit of power I have left. Dimitri is eyeing the overloaded burger as efficiently as my hungry eyes did when Rocco delivered it, his gaze as demanding as ever even with it being projected through electronic waves.

I scarcely shake my head for half a second when the panic in Estelle's voice steals my attention. "Excuse me, I asked you to wait in the foyer."

Through my raging pulse, I hear the shuffles she takes away from an unusually quiet Clover. The slosh in the bottom of my stomach threatens to spill when the terrifying noise of Estelle's knee smudging the rim of our bathtub sounds down the line. She's backed into a corner. She has nowhere to run. Her very existence hinges on me coercing Dimitri off the ledge.

"Please, Dimitri," I beg again, my eyes watering. "She's all I have. I won't cope without her."

"Roxie..." Estelle sounds on the verge of tears. She's as rattled as me. "What's going on? I thought you were working for some old geezer who can't wipe his ass."

I want to laugh at her ability always to find humor in any situation, but I'm too petrified Dimitri will use it against me to set it free. "I am. I'm just—"

"Not following the terms she agreed upon." I hate how my body responds to hearing Dimitri's voice for the first time in days. It prickles with excitement instead of repelling in disgust. "And since she's too stubborn for her own good, I had to get inventive."

"So, you sent a member of your staff to collect her belongings?" Estelle's low tone reveals she's lost as to what's happening, but she's also curious. Even being a love-sick idiot wouldn't stop her from hearing the innuendo in Dimitri's tone. It's brimming with possessiveness and a nasty side dish of arrogance. "If you want Roxie to fall into line, you should have threatened her family…" Her voice trails off when the penny finally drops. "Oh, shit."

A second later, glass smashing against tiles sounds down the line. It launches me to my feet as quickly as Estelle's breaths batter the speakers. She's endeavoring to run even with her having no place to hide.

"Please!" I scream, panicked out of my mind. "I'll do anything you want."

Dimitri's demand is stern and to the point. "Eat!"

Tears roll down my cheeks unchecked when I nod my head. The seeded bun of the burger soaks them up when I shakily lift it to my mouth and take the biggest bite I can. I don't chew. I just bite and swallow, bite and swallow until the greasy meat sits in the bottom of my stomach along with my heart.

After wiping at the slosh drooling down my chin, I lock my eyes with the camera above my head. I'm bawling, shaking uncontrollably, and on the verge of being sick, but it feels like I hit the jackpot when Dimitri says, "Enough."

He isn't approving of my grotesque eating skills. He's telling Clover to back off, halting the horrific noises of a woman fighting for her life from sounding over the speakers. He's sparing the life of my best friend all because he was handed the last bit of power I had left.

"Go," I push out breathlessly, hopeful Estelle can still hear me.

My prayers are answered when she asks, "Where?"

I wipe at the tears streaming down my face while answering, "Anywhere. I'll find you. I promise."

"Roxie—"

"I'm fine. I promise you I'm okay. I just need you to go."

Her snivels break my heart. "Okay. I love you."

"I love you too."

I wait for the creak of the safety gate on the elevator of our building to sound down the line before locking my eyes with the camera above my head. I stare straight at the blinking contraption as if not an ounce of fear is bombarding me. I don't know if my strength stems from my determination not to have my entire world stripped out from beneath my feet or the wary churns of Estelle's motor when she cranks the ignition on her shit box. Whatever it is, it shifts my protest from peaceful to anarchy in less than a nanosecond, and even quicker than that, it sees me shredding off my clothes as brutally as Dimitri did weeks ago.

Once they sit in tatters on the floor, I growl out, "Send one of your goons to deal with me now. I dare you."

FIFTEEN

Dimitri

"**S**hut down the feed." When the eyes of over a dozen thirsty men who should know better than to look at anything they don't own stray toward my laptop screen, I scream at the top of my lungs, "Shut down the fucking feed!"

Even knowing too well yanking the cord out of my laptop won't stop the camera in Roxanne's room from broadcasting elsewhere, I rip it out before sending my laptop sailing across the room. My plan worked. I forced her to eat. Now she's upped the fucking ante.

"Tell me it's shut down, Smith."

When he hesitates, my jaw works through a hard grind. "It's not an easy fix, Dimi. You wanted the best. The best doesn't crumble for anything. Besides, the feed shouldn't be the sole focus of your concern."

After spinning away from the group of men gawking at

me, annoyed I canceled the provocative show early, I ask, "What should be?"

"Rocco." Smith's simple reply shouldn't agitate me to no end, but it does. "He's heading to Roxanne's room."

"Call him back."

He laughs at me as if I'm an idiot. It's the same chuckle he hit me with when I told him about my plan to force Roxanne to eat. "He isn't wearing an earpiece."

After hitting a pompous prick with a stern finger point, warning him I'm seconds from removing his finger if he dares to tap my shoulder one more time, I ask, "Why not?"

Smith's laugh shifts to a bark. "'Cause you wanted to keep him out of the loop with your plan, that's why."

"Lose the fucking attitude, Smith. My plan worked, didn't it?"

He acts as if my threat doesn't have an ounce of sting to it. "If you consider your girl being eyeballed by men who'd happily hurt her while she's butt-naked, yeah, I'd say it was successful."

I don't know what to take my anger out on first. Roxanne's gall or Smith's fucking shitty attitude. I go for both when I snarl, "She isn't my girl."

"Then you'll have no issues with her and Rocco getting super friendly in ten... nine... eight..."

I spin around to face the procession of money-hungry gangsters so fast I make myself dizzy. "Our meeting has been postponed until next month."

They have the hide to grumble at me under their breath like I don't have the ability to sideswipe their entire existence with my pinkie finger. They did the same thing when I took an intermission in our meeting to authenticate the effectiveness of my ruse with Roxanne. I acted as maniacally back then as I do now.

"You either accept a second interlude in our proceedings, or we permanently part ways." When silence stretches across the room, I get cocky. "That's what I thought. I don't want to work with you pricks any more than you don't want to lick the soles of my shoes for an ounce of my attention. Unfortunately, you don't have a choice. You need me. It'll do you best to remember that the next time we meet."

After ensuring my father absorbed my words along with the rest of our 'family,' I race out of my office and hotfoot it up a set of stairs I've avoided like the plague the past four days.

Smith is no longer counting in my ears, but I mentally tick over two just as I stop outside Roxanne's bedroom door. I'm too worked-up to mull over the fact Rocco could be inside. I just throw open the door and step into a warzone without adequate protection.

Roxanne doesn't just hurl words when she's angry. She tosses out fists as if they are grenades. She whacks them into my back, my stomach, and attempts to collide them with my nuts before I pin her to the wall with my brooding frame.

With her fists immobilized at her sides, she uses the rest of her body to inflict her anguish. She thrashes out her legs, throws her head around, and screams like she's being murdered.

"Stop it!" I shake her hard enough that her brain rattles in her skull. This isn't just about anyone but me seeing her naked anymore. If she doesn't calm down, she will hurt herself. That's as unacceptable as her wish to starve herself to death. "I had to do something to force you to eat. You were fading to nothing."

Her words seethe out of her mouth like lava, "Don't act as if any of this was about me! You tried to destroy the only person I've ever cared about."

"Clover was ordered not to hurt her."

She calls me out as the liar I am. "He's a trained killer! That's all he knows, and you put her on his radar!"

"To protect you!" I scream back, as unhinged as her. "That's why you've been locked in your room. That's why I stayed the fuck away. I was trying to protect you."

To ensure she can't miss the angst eating me alive, I release one of her wrists from my hold before bringing her eyes to mine by a brutal grip on her face. I'm hurting her, but it has nothing on the pain that ripped through me when Smith announced the price on her head was double the ransom they requested for my wife.

"Seven point six million dollars. What do you think they'd want for that amount, Roxanne? Your virginity? A couple of kids?" I press into her deeper, stealing more than the air from her lungs. "Your fucking soul? They have my daughter, my flesh and blood, yet they're still not done fucking me in the ass. They want you, too."

Roxanne's tiptoe to insanity is showcased in the worst light when she snaps out, "Then let them have me!"

I shake her again, hopeful a good rattle of her skull will have her brain switching on. "They don't want you for the trade, Roxanne. They want to torture you for hours on end before killing you like you're a piece of meat—"

I recoil like I've been slapped when she butts in, "Just like you?"

My laugh reveals how close to the edge I am. I'm ready to jump, to freefall into hell, but there's only one reason I can't let go, and for the first time in a long time, it doesn't solely fall on Fien's shoulders.

"I'm nothing like my enemies."

I step back from Roxanne like her eyes are loaded with bullets when she comes at me with more than a mutual attraction. She hits me below the belt with a rarity in this industry. She knocks me out with straight-up honesty. "You've said time and time again that I'm responsible for your wife's death, that if she hadn't been swapped for me, your life would be ten times easier, but we both know that isn't what this is about. You didn't give a shit about Audrey. If she wasn't carrying your child, I doubt you would have paid her ransom. This is about you believing I'm only here because I feel responsible for Fien's captivity. You can't believe someone would help you out of the kindness of their own heart. You refuse to accept that not everyone is out to get you. You see everyone as your enemy... even those closest to you."

As her watering eyes bounce between mine, their wetness doubles. "The spark in the alleyway, that zap so fierce, I put my entire life on the line to seek it for a second time occurred *before* I knew you had a daughter. It was there *before* we discovered how fucked up my parents are, and *before* you realized the extent of your father's evilness. It was there from the very beginning, yet, you're still trying to deny it."

For how red-faced she is, her hand shouldn't feel like ice

when she curls it around my jaw. "You've always believed you were fighting this war alone. Now, I'm willing to let you." She doesn't say she's done with me, but her facial expression most certainly does. "If you want to change that, you know where to find me."

She slips under my arm before making her way to the bathroom. Her steps are extra fast, hopeful she'll make it to safety before the tears brimming in her eyes roll down her face.

Her desire for privacy is awarded with barely a second to spare. However, her retreat to the only room in this compound without a camera has its downfalls. The space is large and covered with tiles, so every painful sob she fails to hold in bounces into the main part of our room. They're as gut-wrenching as the crunch my knuckles make when they pierce through the drywall I had Roxanne pinned against, and just as devastating as my cowardly exit of a room cloaked with hate.

SIXTEEN

Dimitri

My eyes drift from Roxanne nibbling on her breakfast as if she's a mouse to Rocco when he enters my downstairs office without bothering to knock. It's been four days since my exchange with Roxanne, four days since I raced Rocco to her room without realizing I couldn't beat him there without overtaking him since there's only one way in and out of my room, and four days since Roxanne has uttered a syllable to me.

She hasn't spoken to me in days.

Not when I sneak into our bed in the middle of the night.

Not when I deliver the food she's eaten with protest.

Not even when I pull her into my arms so the tears she releases every night can be absorbed by my chest.

She has said nothing, and it's fucking killing me.

I've always thought violence was the only way to voice your anger. Roxanne is showing me otherwise. Her silence is worse than any massacre I've been a part of. It's draining my veins of blood as if she ripped away a part of my soul instead of my enemies.

"Don't bother shutting it down," Rocco says on a laugh as he spins around the chair on the opposite side of my desk to straddle it backward. "Even with you making her feed private, I know you're stalking her like you had me do the months after her hospital stay."

Determined to prove I'm not the soft cock he thinks I am, I switch off the monitor Roxanne's white face is filling before slouching low into my office chair.

I should have realized Rocco wouldn't fall for my tricks. He knows me too well to lap up my bullshit excuses. "Do you really think that will cut it?" Although he's asking a question, he continues talking, stealing my chance to reply. "Hiding her away won't fix shit, Dimi. Acting as if she means nothing to you won't fix shit." He slants his head to the side before arching his brow. "Holding her when she cries won't fix shit… especially when you're the reason she's crying."

Smith's silence reveals he knew Rocco's plan to throw him into the deep end without a life jacket. If he weren't aware, he would have defended himself by now.

I've avoided Rocco's emotional jabs for the past two decades, but I can't do it anymore. "What do you suggest I do, Rocco? Feed her to the wolves?"

I'm anticipating for him to come back with the loved-up shit his mother used to excuse his father for beating her to a pulp, so you can imagine my surprise when he takes our conversation in a direction I never saw coming. "Stop taking it up the ass as if you enjoy it."

My laugh belongs to a maniac. It rolls up my chest as quickly as my fists ball, but it does little to weaken Rocco's campaign. "When we were kids, every fucking game without fail, you played the character less likely to win all because you were determined to prove Princess Peach wasn't a damsel in distress. You didn't give a fuck that you lost time and time again 'cause it wasn't about winning, it was about being the better person." He points to my door as if Roxanne is on the other side. "You finally won, but instead of giving Princess P her time to shine, you locked her away in another fucked-up kingdom."

"To protect her." My words seethe out of my mouth like venom.

Rocco scoffs at me like I'm not seconds from pressing my gun to his temple and blowing his brains out. "You're not protecting her. You are bending over and taking it up the ass like you have the past two years." His words shift to a chuckle when I dive over my desk, remove my gun from the back of my trousers, and use the barrel to smooth the crinkle between his dark brows. "You can't kill me, Dimi. Your enemies haven't ordered you to, and we both know you don't do anything until they tell you to."

Too pissed to think clearly, I flick off the safety on my gun before inching back the trigger. "I'm Dimitri fucking Petretti. I don't answer to anyone."

"Prove it," Rocco mocks, staring straight at me. "Kill me."

His suggestion both shocks and pisses me off, but I play it cool. "You're willing to die for Roxanne?"

He shakes his head, his smile picking up. "Nah, D. This

has nothing to do with Roxie. You, on the other hand, this has everything to do with *you*. If you need to kill me to get your balls back, I'm willing. As you said, you're Dimitri fucking Petretti, so how about you start acting like it? We play to play, we kill to kill, and we——"

"Take down any fucker stupid enough to get in our way."

His smile is smug now instead of mocking. "I can't imagine what's going through your head. I assume it's some fucked-up shit, but you'll never win the war if you're not willing to fire at the opposition."

Although I agree with him, there's one thing I can't discount. "Fien——"

"Is a weakness they're exploiting because they assume you won't fight back." He frees himself from my vicious clutch before scooting to the back of his chair, bringing himself closer to me. "Roxanne is a way of showing them you're not to be messed with. Bring back the fear, Dimi. Bring back the respect." He nudges his head to the monitor I switched off when he arrived. "Bring back the woman willing to die for a little girl she's never met. If you bring those things back, Fien will soon follow. I guarantee you that."

Rocco doesn't make pledges he can't keep. Everyone he has made, he's upheld—including his promise that he'd walk away from our friendship if I married Audrey. He knew it would cause a heap of trouble, though I doubt he ever guessed it would be this bad.

That's why I sent Clover to do Audrey's ransom drop instead of Rocco. We had been out of contact for months. Something about Audrey rubbed him the wrong way. He never told me what, but it was as obvious as the sun hanging in the sky.

Taking my silence as the end of our conversation, Rocco stands to his feet, flips his chair back around, then makes a beeline to the door.

He halts opening it when I ask, "What was it about Audrey that you hated."

He cranks his neck my way. "I didn't hate her, D. She just had nothing in her eyes that proved she deserved you."

"And Roxanne does?"

His lips curl into the corner. "Fuckin' oath she does." He pivots around to face me front on. "The first time I saw her, the thoughts I had when you showed me a photo of Fien rolled through my head. Born in the wrong era, to the wrong family, but so fucking full of life, she'd survive the shittiest of circumstances."

I try to hold back my nod, but my chin bobs before I can. That's almost spot on to what I thought when I saw Roxanne with black smudges smeared on her cheeks. The beauty she tried to hide with goth clothing and black makeup captured my attention but knowing she could leap over the grief holding her down utterly sealed my devotion. She had strength I'd never seen in a woman—not even my mother.

Strength she could have again if I'm willing to loosen the reins.

"Rocco…"

He takes a moment to wipe the hope from his face before answering, "Yeah."

He shouldn't have bothered. It comes back in abundance

when I say, "Have Smith clear my schedule. Unless it directly corresponds with Fien, I don't want to know about it."

He hits me with a frisky wink. "It'll be my pleasure."

He isn't glamouring up because he finally has the chance to run things around here. He's had numerous opportunities to create his own sanction the past decade. It's never been of interest to him. He's just grateful we're once again on the same team. That hasn't been the case the past four days. Roxanne's silence wasn't the only one I was dealing with. Rocco had kept his distance as well.

That's done with now. Rocco is right. I can't be fucked in the ass unless I'm willing to lay down and take it. For too long, I've allowed others to write my story. This is my life and my mistakes, so I refuse to let anyone edit out the parts that need to be shared—even the brutal bits. This is my story, and I'm going to tell it how it's supposed to be told.

SEVENTEEN

Roxanne

My steps out of the bathroom are reduced to half their natural stride when I spot an outfit splayed across the mattress I've shared with Dimitri the past four nights even with us not sharing a word between us. I've climaxed on that bed, laughed on it, and shed tears on it more times than I can count, but this is the first time I've ever had an outfit laid out on it.

It's not a fancy dress like the many in the walk-in closet, nor is it an innocent outfit. It's modest yet sexy if that's possible. The cut of the full-length leather pants assures me they'll hug my butt in all the right places. The shimmery beige material of the strapless crop top adds glitz to the ensemble while the denim jacket promises to keep me warm even if my bosoms spill over the skimpy material that's meant to cover my midsection.

With my gut twisted in confusion, I seek answers from the last person likely to give them to me. "Smith…" He has been as silent as Dimitri and Rocco the past four days, but that doesn't mean he isn't watching me. Other than my thirty-second lapse of judgment days ago, the red light in the corner of the room has continuously blinked.

My eyes snap to the other side of the room when a rough, gravelly tone says, "Smith is no longer in charge of the surveillance for this room." Dimitri doesn't need to say who's helming the watch. His eyes are very telling.

Even with my body showing signs it's missed his voice the past few days, I act as if he isn't in the room with me. I dart for the walk-in closet, eager to switch out my dressing gown with something a little cooler. The heat bouncing between Dimitri and me is too much. It's as fiery as it has always been, but since it is also fueled by anger, it is unbearable.

It is the fight of my life to hold in my scream when my race for the closet reveals it's as empty as my chest feels. All the clothes have been removed—even Dimitri's. I want to say he knows I'm a stubborn ass, so he put steps in place to force me to submit to him, but I won't give him the satisfaction.

"I need you to get dressed and come with me."

I'm torn. With a sudden knowledge that I hate enclosed spaces, I'd donate a kidney to leave these four walls, but if I give in like I did my hunger strike, how bad will my next test be? Perhaps it will be a kidney? I've faced every other injustice in my short twenty years, so why not throw organ trafficking into the mix.

Proof he's as bossy and domineering as ever is showcased in the worst light when Dimitri barks out, "What's our agreement, Roxanne?"

Over him and his stupid mind games, I march to the

mattress, snatch up the leather pants as if I'll skip chaffing from wearing them sans underwear, carefully pry open my dressing gown, then stuff my feet into the opening of my pants.

Once I have them over my butt, which I'm embarrassed to say took longer than two minutes, I snap up the skimpy strapless top Dimitri picked for me to wear before I spin around to face him.

When I nudge my head to the door, requesting privacy, he has the audacity to do his infamous half-smirk. I don't know why. The slightest peek he got of the back of my knees when I tugged the rigid leather up my legs is the *only* piece of my skin he'll ever see. *Again.* I can't do anything about our previous exchanges.

"Fine." He throws his hand into the air to display his annoyance before he pivots to face the door.

Wanting to ensure there's no chance he'll get a sneaky peek later, I face the bathroom door before removing my dressing gown. I could get dressed in the bathroom, but considering my room now has multiple cameras, it wouldn't do me any good.

After ensuring my nipples aren't showing, I slip my feet into the boots at the end of the bed, then join Dimitri by the door. Sensing my approach, he spins around to face me. I won't lie, even pissed, I relish the way he can't help but glide his eyes down my body.

His gaze is so white-hot when he suggests for me to grab my jacket, I shake my head.

A brick lodges in my throat when he says, "It's cold where you're going. I don't want your lips turning a shade of blue." However, he doesn't see my panicked response since he gathers up my jacket on my behalf.

The last time he spoke those words to me, my world was upended.

Although petrified I'm about to meet with my maker, I won't beg. I'm the one who suggested for Dimitri to give me to his enemies, so how can I act shocked by him doing exactly that?

An eerie feeling bombards me when Dimitri guides me down the staircase at the end of the hallway our room is located in. His home isn't silenced by unusual quiet. Energy is bristling in the air, and I'm reasonably sure only some of it is compliments to Dimitri's hand hovering above the unconcealed skin on the lower half of my back.

When we enter a room two spots down from Dimitri's downstairs office, the reason for the hum of chatter is exposed. There are three to four dozen men filling the space. Half are seated around a large oval-size boardroom table, and the rest are standing toward the back.

"Take a good look at this face," Dimitri says when his suffocating aura deprives the room of oxygen as effectively as his next set of words steal the air from my lungs. "I'm sure you've heard the rumors that this face is worth seven point six million dollars." He strays his eyes across the men eyeing him with as much interest as me. "I'm here to tell you this face won't earn you millions if you attempt to cash in the bounty on her head. She will cost you everything. Your life. Your wife. Not even your children will be spared. I'll destroy you and anyone associated with you. If you don't believe me, I'm more than happy to display how foolish you are."

My eyes bounce between Dimitri's narrowed gaze and his ear when the faintest trickle of a unique accent sounds in my ears. Smith is guiding Dimitri's eyes around the room as he did mine weeks ago, honing him in on his targets—which is reduced by one when Dimitri lines up his gun with a man at the back of the room and fires one shot.

The man slumps to the floor in an instant, the bullet wound between his eyes as unforgiving as Dimitri's anger when the cell phone that clatters out of his hand reveals my image on the screen. My outfit proves it was just taken, although it remains unsent in the man's outbox.

"I understand the bounty is impressive, and that you believe it's worth the risk, but is it more valuable than your family?"

My eyes don't know which direction to look when a large screen at the side of the room commences broadcasting a raid in progress. The balaclava-clad faces conducting the raid aren't members of the FBI or local law enforcement office. Their eyes are familiar. I've seen them multiple times the past few weeks, most notably the murky green pair that executes three men kneeling in front of a large brute with a clover tattoo on his cheek.

When Clover lifts one of the deceased man's heads to face the camera, a collective hiss rolls around the room. The victims' matching bullet wounds aren't their only familiarities. If you wiped three decades off the age of the first victim's face, it would be almost identical to the one Clover is holding up.

"I have men at the front of all your houses." There's too

much honesty in Dimitri's tone to discount. "Is anyone else willing to test the authenticity of my threat?"

Most of the men shake their heads. Only one is stupid enough to add words into the mix. "You need to be reasonable, Dimitri. We're only trying to support our families."

Dimitri gives the gray-haired man a look as if to say he isn't as stupid as he's implying. The bounty on my head isn't the only mine these men are drilling. They've got their hands in as many pots as Dimitri.

"I'm well aware what you need money for, Mark. It has nothing to do with that pretty little wife of yours and everything to do with the underaged girls you beat and sodomize once a week." His lack of denial exposes Dimitri is on the money. "As for the rest of you, I'm willing to negotiate more suitable terms. How does fifteen million sound?" The excitement building in the room skyrockets as high as my blood pressure when Dimitri adds, "That's the amount I'll pay when you bring me the people responsible for the bounty on Roxanne's head. If they're brought in alive, I'll double it."

"Dimitri…" I can't say more. I'm too shocked. He's put thirty million dollars on the line for my safety. That's insane. I'm not worth that much.

Before I've worked through half my shock, Dimitri instructs Smith to do a final once-over of the room. Once he's confident his offer is more enticing than that of his enemies, he grips the top of my arm and drags me out of the room. I don't think he means to hurt me. He's just too doped up on adrenaline to realize how strong his grip is. I'm feeling superhuman, and I did nothing but stand at his side with my jaw hanging open.

Halfway down the hallway, Dimitri's brittle tone snaps me out of my shock. "Take them out to the Hole. There are men out there waiting." His comment exposes he knew at least one of the men would test him. "We should arrive in around thirty minutes." During the 'we' part of his statement, his eyes drift to me. "Is everything ready?"

I discover the reason he suggested for me to take a jacket when he throws open the front door of his compound and guides me outside. Although it isn't as cold here as it was in New York, there's a brisk coolness in the air.

The goosebumps coating my skin augment when Dimitri assists me into the front passenger seat of a fierce-looking sports car. It's warm in the cabin of his sleek ride. My body just couldn't help but respond to him leaning across my frozen frame to fasten my seat belt. Even with the smell of a recently fired gun lingering in my nostrils, his scent is scrumptious. It grips my senses for the next several minutes, only relinquishing its hold when Dimitri pulls down a familiar-looking road twenty minutes later.

Although this isn't the most direct route to my grandparents' farm, it's the one people use when they want to be discreet. My mom went this way when she abandoned me, and I used this off-beat track when I snuck back home after my failed meet-up with my father. My nanna told me not to go. I thought I knew better as I do again now.

"Why are we here?"

Dimitri flashes his headlights three times before he drifts his eyes to me. "My enemies think this is friendly territory. They'd never believe I'd shelter anyone here."

"You just put up thirty million dollars to guarantee my safety. You don't need to hide me anymore."

My shock shifts to panic when Dimitri says, "I'm not hiding you, Roxanne. I'm letting you out of our agreement."

"Why? Our agreement was supposed to end once you got your daughter back." I don't know whether to scream or cry when a reason for his unusual bend of the rules smack into me. "Is this a test?"

"No." His curt reply does little to slacken the noose in my stomach, but before I can continue to interrogate him, the quickest flash in the corner of my eye steals my devotion. "Sniper," Dimitri informs like it's an everyday occurrence to have men lying in wake in overgrown fields. "There are two covering the front and back entrances and one on the main gate. They'll remain until the threat has been neutralized."

I've barely gotten over my shock when I'm smacked for the second time. This surprise doesn't come in the form of violence. It's too beautifully sweet to have an ounce of disdain attached to it. Or should I say, *she* is too beautifully sweet.

"Estelle."

I throw open Dimitri's car door before he comes to a stop. Not even the slop of a recently dug-up ground can slow me down. I race Estelle's way, my feet moving as fast as my heart.

The collision of our bodies is as brutal as the rain falling down on us when the heavens open up. Although it has nothing on the wetness that fills my eyes when it dawns on me why Estelle's hair appears as red as my natural hair coloring.

Dimitri's car is no longer rolling toward my grandparents' ranch. It's heading in the opposite direction. His eyes aren't seeking potholes in the sloshy road, though. They stare at me in the side mirror, watching me as adeptly as he did in the alleyway all those months ago. It's a beautiful stare that could only be more appealing if it weren't cloaked with darkness. It feels so final like tonight will be the last time I'll see him.

If the dip of his chin before he pulls onto the main road is anything to go by, I'm reasonably sure it will be.

EIGHTEEN

Dimitri

Dimitri

Paranoia can make the sanest man feel unhinged. It eats away at you worse than low self-esteem, depression, and all that other whacked-up shit therapists toss around when seeking new patients. It sees a once-stable man freeing the only person who's ever made him feel normal, so he can become a creep who crawls into voids above seedy restaurants to spy on his enemies.

When you lose the ability to tell the difference between your rivals and your comrades, you should consider shutting up shop. But since this is me, and nothing ever comes easy for me, I've done the opposite. I opened my doors and invited my enemies inside, aware that a meal shared with a rival is often less disastrous than one shared with family.

My focus shifts back to the present when Rocco's boorish tone sounds down the earpiece lodged in my ear canal.

"Clover's big ass will have you receiving company in five... four..."

The manhole I closed after crawling into a roof of a restaurant that's heydays are long behind it pops open just as Rocco hits three. The lack of concern in his tone weakens the itch of my trigger finger. If he were worried about my pop-in visitor, he wouldn't have announced his arrival only seconds before it was set to occur. He wants us to meet up. For what reason? I don't know. But I will find out. You can put your money on it.

Once my guest squeezes through the tight opening like his shoulders are the width of mine, his identity is immediately unearthed. All agents have the same putrid scent, but Brandon James is more perverse since he attempts to mask the smell with a pricy cologne.

"You need to change your aftershave. I could smell that shit long before you crawled through the vent."

I'm lying, and Brandon fucking knows it. I can feel the arrogance beaming out of him, much less see it on his face when he switches on the torch mounted to his Bureau-issued pistol. "You know I'm well within my right to shoot you, right?"

A *pfft* vibrates my lips. "If you wanted to shoot me, you would have done it the instant I turned my back to you. That's how most agents operate, isn't it?"

Incapable of denying the truth, he houses his gun onto the holster on his hip before he joins me above the hub of the restaurant I've been watching like a hawk the past hour. It isn't every day a booking is made in the name of a notorious gangster, especially in a town he has no right to be in without permission, so I don't need to mention the fact this restaurant is way below Cartel standards. It has me suspicious Theresa's claims about an alleged Russian takeover were gospel. That frustrates me even more than my enemies' belief they can arrive in my town without notice. I'd usually kill a man for less. Alas, some of Roxanne's quirks rubbed off on me—most notably her inquisitiveness.

"He's smarter than he looks," Smith mutters in my ear when Brandon asks, "Who's he meeting with?"

For all he knew, I could have been scoping potential clients for the prostitution conglomerate the Petrettis have mingled in for decades. Only someone in the know understands the boss only gets his hands dirty when the target is top grade.

Albert Sokolov may not be feared as he was once, but his murder count alone ensures his respect remains high enough if he were to be killed, it wouldn't be done by a foot soldier. He's Vladimir Popov's number two, and up until ten minutes ago, I was convinced he was here on behalf of Nikolai. Now I'm eating more than my words.

"An old Russian sanction was here a few years back, but there's been no rumblings from their barracks in almost a decade."

I smirk when Brandon cringes about the cobwebs on his jacket before replying, "He's not meeting with a fellow Russian."

Feeling generous, and a little bit lost on how to absorb what's happening today, I nudge my head to the scope of my gun, offering Brandon the chance to cream his pants. He *thinks* he has a vault-load of weapons at his disposal. He's dead fucking wrong. The guns the Feds are playing with have nothing on my arsenal of toys.

"What the fuck?" Brandon mumbles under his breath a few seconds later, expressing my exact sentiment when I discovered the reason for Albert's visit. He isn't here to stake a claim on Nikolai's birthright, he's here to schmooze Isaac Holt—the very man who ran Russians out of his town only a couple of years ago.

"Party Pooper," Rocco murmurs when Brandon's brief perusal of the room below is quickly chased by him, removing a handkerchief from his pocket so he can scrub his fingerprints from a weapon the Bureau would give anything to log into evidence. "Who the fuck carries around a snot-rag in their pocket these days? What is he? A hundred!"

I have no reason to hold in my chuckles about Rocco's witty comment when Brandon warns, "Unless you want to be stuck up here all night, or better yet, detained in a holding cell, I suggest you leave now. This place is about to be raided." The concern in his voice has me wondering which team he bats for. Right now, the odds aren't swinging in his favor. I don't have anything against gay men, I just can't understand how some of them give up the holy grail without first sampling it.

I guess I can't talk. I've never tasted a cunt as sweet as Roxanne's, and I let her walk away from me. Am I regretting my decision? Ask me again when I'm not stationed outside of her ranch every night, monitoring her every move. I might be in the right headspace then to give you an accurate answer.

After dismantling my customized M-4, I remove a single

sheet of paper out of my duffle bag and thrust it into Brandon's chest. "With the government eager to do some digging on my businesses, I commenced some of my own."

I lower my eyes to the photograph of Isabelle I snapped earlier this week. With Theresa's claims of a takeover ringing in my ears and discovering multiple drawings of Isabelle in Roxanne's sketchpad, I looked a little deeper into Isabelle's connection with the Russian Mafia. It isn't pretty, and it pains me to admit, the controversy isn't coming from Isabelle. She's on my father's radar, and he's making costly mistakes to ensure both she and Isaac know it.

After a quick shake of my head to remove the negativity inside it, I ask, "Do you know who she's related to?"

When Brandon takes in Isabelle's photo, his throat works through a brutal swallow. I didn't have Smith age my photograph. I kept it simple and to the point. Even the date in the far corner remains.

My lips twist when protectiveness vibrates out of Brandon in invisible waves. He looks like he's about to blow his top, and he has everyone, including Rocco, paying careful attention to every expression that crosses his face. A man only projects this level of fearlessness when he either wants to fuck the woman he's protecting, or he's related to her. There's no in-between.

"Ah… so you do know who she is." Even knowing Isabelle isn't causing the ruckus in Hopeton I pretend she is, hopeful it will have Brandon on the back foot. The more Feds I have nibbling out of my hand, the quicker Fien will be returned. "If she is what this is about…" I motion my head to the hole in the wall I used to line up my target, "... we're going to have issues. This isn't Russian territory—"

"She has nothing to do with this. I don't even know if Isaac is aware who her father is." His mortified expression is priceless. It makes me laugh. It isn't a hinged, sane man laugh. It shows just how deeply I've dived down the rabbit hole the past few weeks.

With my mood now hostile, it's an effort to act unaffected by it, but I give it my best shot, mindful Brandon and I aren't on the same team. We weren't when his team helmed the operation that had my daughter's whereabouts unknown for months. We won't be when I fix the injustice of his mistakes. "Bring me everything you have in five days. *If* I find it satisfactory, I'll share some hard truths with you."

"And if it isn't?"

My smile should tell him everything, but just in case it doesn't, I expose exactly what will happen to him if he double-crosses me. With my hand shaped into a gun, and my eyes slitted, I press my fingers to his temple and mimic the sound of me blowing his brains out.

"Five days, Brandon. Don't keep me waiting."

I make it out of the tight opening easier than I did crawling into it. That might have something to do with the deflation of my ego. I stormed up here loaded and ready for carnage. I leave without a single drop of blood being shed. Some may say it's because I'm maturing, and with that comes greater understanding.

My testimony wouldn't be anywhere near as polite as that. I've always been a grumpy, surly bastard, but it's been worse the past few weeks. I don't know why. I'm used to people disappointing me. I just never figured Roxanne would be added to the long list.

"Boy in blue on your nine when you exit."

As I make my way through the narrow corridors of a Chinese restaurant like I own the place, I jerk up my chin, advising Rocco I understand his command. Boy in blue is his nickname for Detective Ryan Carter. He's one of the rare good ones around here.

It doesn't make us friends, though.

While breaking through the rickety back entrance of a restaurant on the outskirts of Hopeton, I put on my game face. I'm weaponed up, ready for war, and heading straight toward a man who won't take bribes no matter how hard I push him. I'd let you call me insane if I wouldn't have to kill you for it. "You know you'd get more action if you placed yourself amongst the riffraff."

Ryan smirks. It's as cool as his blue eyes. "You wouldn't believe the things I've witnessed from sitting back and watching the shit unfold."

"From what I've heard, that isn't your style. Not now, and not when your daddy took his failures out on your momma."

That changes the expression on his face in an instant. He looks seconds from killing me, the only reason he doesn't is because there was nothing but respect in my tone when I spoke. If the rumors are true, if he gunned down his father like Rocco did his, he earned my respect. It takes guts to go against the man who created you—strength I've yet to garner.

"Between me and you, he deserved it." Ryan doesn't deny my claims, assuring me he believes the same thing.

Over our pointless chit-chat, I lift my chin in farewell before making my way to the tank Rocco is camped out in. I'm halfway there when the quickest warning stops me in my tracks. "They're not the only Russians you should be watching."

I have no clue who Ryan is talking about until he inconspicuously nudges his head to my right. A novice would immediately glance in the direction he nudged. I was born for this industry, so you can be guaranteed I won't make a rookie mistake. I've only done that once. It cost me everything.

After slotting into the passenger seat of a prototype vehicle I had customized to withstand war, I instruct for Rocco to take the long route home. He doesn't ask questions. He just strays his eyes to the side mirrors as swiftly as mine, aware I only ever say that when I'm suspicious we have a tail.

We're almost at the end of the street before a vehicle parked a few spaces back from our original location pulls off the curb. From the outside, it appears to be a car an underpaid federal officer would get around in. It's basic, modest, and has tinted windows. Regretfully, the plates aren't government-issued. Smith was quick to run the tags through the system the instant Ryan pointed out I had an admirer. The modest thirty-thousand-dollar ride is straight off the lot. It was purchased with cash.

"Head for the tunnel. It can shelter a body for a couple of days." I'm not in the mood to play games. As Rocco said, we play to play, we kill to kill, and we take down any fucker stupid enough to get in our way. This fucker is in my way.

While Rocco leads our prey to his final resting place, I

remove the tripod and scope from my M4. I could use the weapon stuffed down the back of my trousers, but this will be more fun. An M4 wound shows precision and skill. My gun just blows people's brains out. After the shit few weeks I've had, I need to flex a bit of muscle.

"Pull over here, then continue on."

Although disappointed he will miss most of the action, Rocco does as instructed. He's been a little quiet the past four weeks like Roxanne's silence stung his ego as much as it did mine.

Once the taillights of Rocco's ride are far enough away for our lead to continue the chase, I sink myself into the marshland on the side of the road, unfearful an alligator may be lying in wake. Even prehistoric creatures aren't stupid enough to go against a madman with an M4.

As the blue sedan rolls down the asphalt, I take aim at his front passenger side tire. I don't want the flip to kill him. I want that pleasure to be all mine.

Pop. His tire is taken out with a clean through-and-through, and as predicted, it causes his sedan to cartwheel. It somersaults down the isolated road before it comes to a dead stop mere feet from me.

I'm up and out of the marshland in an instant, my movements replicating those of men born for carnage. I am dripping wet, peering down my gun's barrel, and ready to execute my third foot soldier this week. The only reason I hold back desires greater than anything I've ever experienced is because the man hanging upside down in the cab of his car, aiming his gun at my head, has a highly recognizable face.

Some may say he's the real brother of Nikolai Popov.

I'm the only one who knows that's far from the truth.

If DNA chooses your enemies as it does your family, Rico Popov should be Nikolai's number one enemy. The war between the Popovs and the Perettis has been running longer than both of them have been born, and despite his last name, Nikolai is a Petretti, and I have the DNA evidence to prove it.

NINETEEN

Dimitri

R ico's dark eyes lift to Rocco when he places down a set of keys for a white Range Rover on the desk separating us. Rocco isn't impressed I'm gifting one of our prized fleet to the enemy, but replacing the ride I totaled is the least I can do after all the information Rico unknowingly shared with me the past couple of hours.

It's disappointing when you learn how far your father is willing to stoop for revenge. However, it's also cathartic. My father has never given a shit about anyone but himself.

If it had the possibility of making him rich, he ran with it.

If he had to stomp on his family for it to occur, he still ran with it.

If it came with the risk of killing every single person with his blood, he still fucking ran with it.

Nothing stopped him, not a single thing, so you can imagine my surprise when I learned who his revenge centers around. He didn't bring the law into a war they don't belong in for his own benefit. He did it for Ophelia, the only daughter he ever acknowledged as his own.

His show of chivalry was years too late, but it's better than it not happening at all.

"I'll talk to my father." My words are as bitter as the bile in the back of my throat. I haven't seen hide nor hair of my father since our canceled meeting weeks ago. Usually, I'd relish the silence, but Rico's unexpected trip to this side of the country exposes that would be stupid for me to do. My father is making costly mistakes, blunders that could cost him more than his empire. They may even cause my demise. "But I should warn you, my father's interest in Isabelle isn't the only one you should be paying attention to."

Rico arches a thick brow but remains silent. His respect sees me offering more information than I planned to give.

"Isabelle has been spotted numerous times with Isaac Holt the past couple of weeks." I twist around the tablet Smith uploaded a range of long-range surveillance shots onto while watching Rico's face to see if Isaac's name registers as familiar.

Although his jaw gains an involuntary tick, his expression remains somewhat neutral. "I've heard of Isaac before. He's not of interest to me." His approval is shocking. However, it has nothing on what he says next, "If you heard any of his conversation with Albert this afternoon, you'd know why."

It isn't what he said that shocks me. It's how he said it. It had a protective edge to it. It could be because he believes sheltering Isaac will keep his long-lost sister safe, but I have a feeling that's only part of his reasoning.

"It isn't Isaac I'm warning you about. It's his baggage." The altering of his facial features I was seeking earlier occur this time around. I'm not surprised the shockwaves of a mafia princess's death spread across the globe like wildfire. It's why even without proof of life, I'd still know Fien is okay. Women in this industry are valued as useless until they're being torn between two men. Then it's a free-for-all. Nothing is off-limits.

Deciding it isn't my place to make my sworn enemy's jobs easier, I get back to the reason Rico is surrounded by over a dozen men with body-maiming weapons. "Meet-ups without prior knowledge isn't something I take lightly."

Rico smiles as if my tone didn't have an ounce of bitterness. "We advised of our arrival. Your father suggested for it to occur in Hopeton."

I want to call him out a liar before showing him exactly what happens to men who double-cross me, but there's too much honesty in his eyes to discount. He has the eyes of Satan. They're just minus the pure evilness his father's have.

"What was the business about?" We've talked shop the past two hours, but since Rico's focus was solely on my father's trek across the country to rile Vladimir about having contact with his favorite whore's daughter, Isaac's meeting with Vladimir's number two went unmentioned.

My jaw almost cracks when Rico replies, "Nothing that concerns you." As he stands from his seat, he does up the middle button on his business jacket. "Don't get up. I'll show myself out."

He laughs like his life isn't on the line when Clover forcefully places him back into his seat. His chuckles sound fake, but the mask he's wearing is anything but when he threatens Clover with the edge of a psychotic man. He's young, but this industry has aged him as much as it has me. "If you think Dimitri is the only one who removes fingers when you touch something you shouldn't have, you need to be taught a lesson on how my family operates." He cranks his head back to face Clover. Considering he's seated, and Clover is standing, there should be more distance between them than there is. "But since this isn't my turf, I'll offer leniency. Don't expect another one."

Like the paid soldier he is, Clover continues pinching Rico's shoulder until I advise him otherwise. Several men circling us should take note of his obedience. They're getting thirsty for a bloodbath, which also means they're becoming ignorant of the rules. I'd pull them immediately into line if their disrespect didn't come with benefits. It's amazing the tales men tell when they're coked out of their minds. They are almost as perverse as a mafia man unknowingly dropping information he didn't mean to give.

"Guy's punishment was handled in-house..." I walk around my desk, then prop my backside on the edge. I'm close enough to Rico, I could kill him with barely an effort, but not quite close enough he can smell the annoyance pumping out of me. "So how do you know about it?"

Guy wouldn't be game to go against me, and a majority of the bidders had left before his punishment, so I'm eager to discover exactly who tattled about an in-house operation.

I shouldn't have bothered keeping my distance. Two towns over could smell the putrid scent excreting from my pores when Rico cocks a brow and says, "You don't really believe your sweet ole Pa traveled all the way to Vegas just to rub salt into my father's wound, do you?" Although he's asking a question, he continues talking as if he didn't. "Rumors are there's thirty-million dollars on the table over this side of the country. He only wants ten percent for a finder's fee."

If it were any other man but Rico sitting across from me, I would have taken the humor in his voice as a threat. The only reason I don't is because thirty-million dollars is chump change to him. This kills me to admit, but the Popovs are riding the high of not being saddled down with the shit my father doused our family name in decades ago. It also gives reason for Nikolai's lack of interest in his true birthright.

My voice is almost violent when I switch tactics for the third time today. "Theresa Veneto organized Isabelle's placement in Ravenshoe because she has similarities to my deceased sister." With Smith on the ball, I show Rico a side-by-side comparison of Ophelia and Isabelle. Excluding their hair, eyes, and skin tone, they don't have much in common, but I'm hoping Rico is too bogged down with revenge to notice. "Isabelle was supposed to persuade Isaac into spilling secrets. Instead—"

"She fell in love. You're not telling me anything I haven't already heard," Rico interrupts, his tone bored.

"So you know about Theresa's plan to go after Isabelle?" I'm bluffing. I haven't had contact with Theresa in weeks. I'm just assuming that will be her next move since all vindictive cows operate the same way. "We can only hope things don't end as badly for her as they did your mother."

Now I fucking have him—hook, line, and sinker—

although he tries to deny it. "My mother died of an overdose."

"If you believe that, I guess you also believe your father's claims he's a king." Rico watches me with unease when I move back to my side of the desk to gather a set of documents from the drawer. They're the sworn testimonies the film documentary producer lodged with the Bureau years ago. He swore until he was blue in the face that Felicia wasn't a drug addict. "Your mother didn't have a single track-mark on her arms during filming. The documentary was filmed only months before her death." I show him stills of the footage that proves what I'm saying. "The coroner's report states—"

"Coroner? What fucking coroner? Other than moving her off the kitchen floor days after her fucking death, Vladimir wouldn't let anyone touch her." The violence in his roar exposes his agitation, but it's also proof he's looked into his mother's death before. He wouldn't do that unless he were suspicious his father wasn't telling the truth.

"Your mother was murdered, Rico, and I'm reasonably sure I know who did it." I'm once again stretching the boundaries of truth, but when you are desperate, you're desperate. I'm fucking desperate. "However, I'm not going to tell you a thing until we've reached an agreement."

"Only a fool sides with his enemy."

I brush off his anger as if it doesn't have any sting. "Not when it's for the greater good. This is for the greater good."

The fret on Rocco's face when I laid down my first set of cards weakens as I reveal my final hand. It isn't an image of the person I believe is responsible for Rico's mother's death, it's a photograph of my daughter. If her angelic eyes and face can't prove to him this is bigger than anything we could have ever imagined, nothing will.

"That's my daughter, Fien. She will be two in a little under three months, and I've not yet laid my eyes on her in person." Before he can voice one of the questions I see in his eyes, I add, "Because she was taken by the same man who killed your mother."

It's the fight of my life not to rip Fien's photograph out of Rico's grip when he lifts it off my desk, but I manage—somewhat. I've tried every angle I can the past twenty-two months. I'm running out of options. My desperation could backfire in my face, but would the blow-on effect be any worse than what I'm currently facing? I doubt it, so I'm willing to give it a shot.

After staring at Fien's chubby cheeks for a couple of seconds, Rico raises his dark eyes to me. "What do you need?"

TWENTY

Dimitri

W hile grumbling about the brutal crunch of his gearstick as I shift from second to first, Smith shuts down the equipment he had utilized the two and a half hours of our trip. He isn't a fan of road trips, but when it forces him away from equipment he's rarely without, he fucking hates them.

"You need to update this piece of shit. Your laptops are more valuable than the junk you're carting them around in."

Smith makes a 'duh' face while Rocco gives reason for his lack of class. "That's the idea, D. Who'd suspect a rusty van would be holding half a million dollars' worth of equipment?"

Since he has a point, I quit whining before clambering out of the driver's seat. It's early, but our visit to a maximum-security prison hasn't come without notice. Three red dots highlight my chest a mere second before I'm blinded by a megawatt spotlight.

I don't know whether to be amused or pissed when the voice of Warden Mattue crackles over the speakers of the establishment we're visiting long before visiting hours commence. I'm grateful he requested for the guards to lower their weapons, but the superiority in his tone is too haughty for my liking.

Anyone would think he's running the show around here. I know that's far from the truth. I've had a hold of things for years, and my power will only get stronger now I have Rico on-side. We'll never be classified as friends, but as long as our agreement continues serving both our objectives, it will continue without bloodshed.

I stop smirking like a pompous prick when a man who walks like he has a stick shoved up his ass greets me with a wonky smile. His lopsided grin reminds me of the one Brandon gave me when he arrived at my office on precisely day five of my threat. The information he shared about Isabelle wasn't anything Smith hadn't already unearthed, but it felt good knowing I could tell Brandon to jump, and he'd ask how high.

"Dimitri, good morning," stutters Warden Mattue. "To what do we owe the pleasure?"

Ignoring the hand he's holding out, I slant my head and arch a brow. "Do I need a reason to visit?"

He gives it his best shot to hide the quiver my tone caused his thighs. His efforts are pointless. I can smell his fear, much less taste it. "No, not at all. We're pleased to have you."

When he waves his hand across his body, inviting us in, I drift my eyes to Smith.

"One sec…" While chewing on the corner of his lower lip, he taps on a silicon keyboard stuck to the hood of his old van. In quicker than I can snap my fingers, the spotlight Rocco is shielding his eyes from with his forearm switches off, once again shrouding the parking lot into darkness. "Okay, you're good to go."

After lifting my chin in thanks, I shift my focus back to Warden Mattue. "We wouldn't want news of my visit getting out, would we?"

"Not at all," he parrots again when he hears the threat in my voice.

With Smith taking care of the cameras inside and outside of the prison we're about to visit, the only way my tour will reach my father's ear is if Warden Mattue tattles. That will end badly for him. Very *very* badly, although not quite as graphic as the punishment I handed down to a group of my father's associates when they stupidly decided to test my patience last week.

They sought vengeance for the slaughter of Mikoloff and his family six weeks ago. The insolence caused their family's downfall. They're not just dead, they are buried in unmarked graves no one will ever find, and their legacy was struck from the record.

Their punishment was so brutal, no man will be game to test me again. Everything is operating like clockwork. Roxanne is safe, my bank accounts all remain in the seven figures, and Fien's last ransom was received without the slightest delay.

All I need now is an outlet for the frustration keeping my body temperature in the scalding range the past six weeks.

Whores won't come close to scratching it, so I don't bother. A bloody massacre barely skimmed off the surface, and I refuse to let another drug-fueled bender curtail my life. That only leaves one thing capable of taking the edge off, and even she isn't at my disposal right now.

With my blood already bubbling with anger, you can picture my struggle to maintain a rational head when a bitch from my past shouts my name. Theresa Veneto smiles like the badge on her hip will save her brain from being pierced with a bullet from my gun. She's dead fucking wrong. This prison is home to America's deadliest criminals, which means it's located miles from the nearest town. Many people have gotten lost out here the past six years, even Federal agents who don't know how to back the fuck up when asked.

Before I can voice my annoyance about my unexpected guest, Rocco takes up my slack. "I thought only vampires roamed the planet at dusk. Who knew witches got around, too? Do you fly above the houses to avoid collisions with your sister witches, or do you prefer the sewer network?"

While Theresa hisses at Rocco, I shift my eyes to Smith, curious to discover how Theresa's movements slipped past us without notice. We've been scrutinizing her as closely as Rico has my father the past two weeks.

When Smith shrugs, as pissed as me, I return my focus to Theresa. "Are you here to cover your tracks? Or are you hoping to lead me away from them?"

The past two weeks weren't solely gobbled up embedding Rico deeply into my father's operation. My team put both the time and the snippets of information Rico has discovered in an embarrassingly short amount of time to good use.

Little threads are coming undone everywhere. It will only be a matter of time before my father's outfit is unraveled, and considering Theresa seems to be very much a part of his ensemble, she'll come undone right along with him.

Theresa's laugh agitates me to no end. "Cover what tracks, Dimi?"

Her use of my nickname pisses me off. Only my friends get to call me Dimi. She most certainly isn't one of them. "Oh, I don't know. How about putting a man away for a murder he didn't commit? Or falsifying police records to conjure up a fake victim? Then we also have the fact you left an unstable woman to defend for herself."

I don't know what's more frustrating, Theresa's cocky smirk or what she says next, "The fact your focus centers around me shows how far off the mark you are." She steps closer to me, switching out Warden Mattue's feared scent with an over-priced perfume. "I was merely upholding my end of our agreement."

"*Our* agreement?" I query, too interested in the honesty in her eyes to act nonchalant.

"You're a Petretti, aren't you?"

When she attempts to hand me a stack of papers, Smith snatches them out of her grip. I don't mind. They're official-looking documents he'll have a better chance of deciphering than me.

Seemingly believing we work for her instead of the other way around, Theresa explains, "They're transcripts of conversations I've had with your father. Their seal should prove their legitimacy, but in case they don't, I forwarded links to the original files to your email."

Smith logs into my email server before I can gesture for him to, and even quicker than that, he authenticates Theresa's claims. "Imagery is shit, but the audio is first-class. Your father approached Theresa." He listens for a couple of seconds before his brows draw together. "He didn't want Megan killed. He had her admitted for a psych workup. That kept her under lock and key for over a year."

"Why?" My question isn't for Smith. It's for Theresa, who looks way too fucking smug for my liking. "What possible benefit would my father get from keeping her alive? Why wouldn't he just kill her?"

She shrugs. "I didn't ask questions. That isn't the way I operate."

I smirk before hitting her with one-tenth of the attitude she's smacking me with. "That's right. I forgot the only time you exert any kind of normalcy is when you're flat on your back being served a healthy dose of dick. Is that why you keep showing up? Does the big gaping hole between your legs still need filling?"

Rocco's snicker annoys her, but it has nothing on the rage that fills her eyes when her body responds to the faintest touch of my finger as I drag it up her arm. She doesn't hate me, even though she really wants to.

With a huff, she folds her arms in front of her chest to hide the budding of her nipples. "I'm here to cash in the favor your father is refusing to bequeath."

I *tsk* at her, disappointed she believes I'm stupid enough to fall for the oldest trick in the book. "As I've told you before, if your favor was issued by my father, he's the only one who can grant it."

"He's refusing!" she shouts in my face.

I bite my lip to half my smile before asking, "And how is that my problem?"

I swear steam almost billows out of her ears when she stifles her scream with a growl. "Because everyone knows you clean up your father's messes. It's what you do! You've done it for years."

"For clients I deem worthy. Dried-up old hags who should have gotten out of the game years ago don't count." I catch her hand before it gets close to my face. Then I use it to bring her within an inch of my snarling lips. "You might have Isaac on the back foot with your tricks, but I don't play by those rules. When you are no longer of use in this industry, you're as good as dead."

Her minty fresh breath hits my lips when she gabbles out, "Are you threatening me?"

I drag my index finger down her white cheek before trekking it across her lips. "No, baby. If I were threatening you, you'd already be on your knees, saying your final farewell." Her cheeks will feel my nails for days when I grip her face with everything I have. "Now get the fuck out of my face before I send Clover over for a visit. He's been waiting years to mess up that pretty little face of yours."

I push her away from me, smirking when she almost loses her footing on the loose gravel. As she straightens out her jacket like it's the only thing my grip creased, her eyes bounce between Smith, Rocco, and me. She doesn't bother with Warden Mattue because even someone as fucked in the head as her knows the only pull he has around here is getting his dick sucked by one of the female prisoners.

Did I forget to mention this prison is mixed gender? My bad.

"This won't be the last of this," Theresa warns before she makes a beeline to a Fed-issued car at the back of the lot.

She's right. This won't end until one of us is dead. You can be assured my name won't be on a headstone anytime soon. I can't make the same guarantee for Theresa.

I'm almost made out to be a liar when my silent thoughts are interrupted for the second time this morning. This time, the female's call of my name doesn't send me into a fit of rage. It sees me issuing a threat so fucking firm, Satan will hear it. "If I find out your guards' fingers got within an inch of their triggers, I'll gut you where you stand."

Warden Mattue's eyes snap to Roxanne frozen at our right for the quickest second before they jackknife back to me. He drinks in the fury the red dots highlighting Roxanne's chest caused my face before he frantically waves his hand through the air, demanding for his men to stand down.

The eagerness of his request is appreciated, but it's too late for him now. He's a dead man walking. He knows it. I know it, and so the fuck does Roxanne. My ruling six weeks ago wasn't just that she wasn't to be touched. She can't be threatened either. Lighting up her chest with a dozen assault weapons is a threat, and I refuse to let the injustice off lightly.

"Go..." When Warden Mattue steps closer to me with his hands held up in a non-defensive manner, my souring mood the past six weeks steamrolls back into me. "Go!"

I want to follow through with my threat, I want to pull

his insides out of his belly button before stabbing a knife in his eye, but since Roxanne is too close not to see me as the monster I am, I maintain my cool—barely.

After watching the warden's terrified scuttle, I shift on my feet to face Roxanne. I haven't seen her in the flesh in weeks. Just like Petretti's restaurant, I kept her family's ranch without surveillance. A system can't be hacked if it doesn't exist.

I want to say Roxanne has put back on the pounds she lost during her hunger strike, that she looks well-rested and healthy. Regretfully, I can't. She looks as tired as I feel like the past six weeks were as painful for her as they were for me. Don't misconstrue. She looks good—*she will always look good*—she's just a smidge below the woman my thoughts drift to every night when I succumb to the tiredness overwhelming me.

"What are you doing here, Roxanne?"

Although my question is for Roxanne, my narrowed gaze is for Smith. This is his second slip-up today. That isn't just a new record, it's also unacceptable. He can't watch Roxanne for every hour of every day, but he *is* supposed to log her movements. The last report my eyes skimmed this morning was about the light in her bedroom being switched off a little after midnight, so how the fuck did she get here by five?

"This isn't Smith's fault." Roxanne skips across the dusty lot as if she isn't placing herself in the firing line for the second time this morning. "Infrareds have their faults." She presses a kiss to Smith's cheek before she throws her arms around Rocco's neck to hug him fiercely. "Is this new?" she asks while teasingly dragging her index finger across Rocco's pecs, lingering longer than I care to admit. "I don't recall seeing it on you before. It's cute and body-hugging. I like it."

I know what's she's doing, and I don't fucking like it. She saw my altercation with Theresa, but instead of working out why it annoyed her, she's serving the jealousy our exchange hit her with back to me one bitter pill at a time.

With my mood not knowing which way to swing, I take the easy route. "Get your ass in the van, Roxanne. Smith will take you home."

She whips around so fast, her recently colored hair slaps her in the face. "No."

"I beg your pardon?" I'm reasonably sure half the block hears me. That's how loud my roar is. "I wasn't asking."

"It wouldn't make a difference if you were. You can't boss me around anymore, Dimitri." She spits out my name as if it's trash. "You lost the chance when you abandoned me."

My jaw falls open like a fish out of water. "Abandoned you? I didn't abandon you. I set you free."

She folds her arms in front of her chest all prissy like. "In the house my uncle, aunt, and quite possibly my grandfather were murdered in, with three snipers outside the door, and shitty-ass cell reception inside it! You may as well cut off my wings."

"Where the fuck are you going?" I ask when she pulls away from me. "I'm not done with you yet."

Roxanne shrugs out of my hold before I can dig my nails into her arm. "We came here to visit my friend. Since you seem to have pull with the warden, I guess we don't have to wait for visiting hours anymore."

Her friend she nudged her head to during the first half of her comment isn't eager to join her campaign. She looks on the verge of pooping her pants. I understand her concern. I'm five seconds from killing someone. I just have no clue if that someone is Roxanne or me. I love her feistiness. It thickens my cock as quickly as it fills my mind with immoral thoughts. A girl has to have spunk to be fingered in an alleyway with a stranger watching, much less go against a man as powerful as me. But her spunk also drives me nuts. Furthermore, I wouldn't have let her out of our agreement if I knew she was going to march straight back into it.

I shouldn't be surprised. She's always there, in every frame, causing trouble.

It's one of the things I like about her the most.

When Roxanne disappears into the entrance of the prison, I jerk my head in the direction she went. "Go with her. Make sure she sees who she came here to see, then load her into my car."

"What car, D?" Rocco asks as he struggles not to laugh about the rage on my face. "Do you wanna drive your girl home from your first date in Smith's beat-up van?"

I talk through a tightened jaw. "The car Smith is going to get here A-S-A-fucking-P if he wants to keep his job."

Smith holds his hands in the air, knowing he did wrong before he puts them to good use. He will build a car if he can't get one here within the next thirty minutes.

"All right." While rubbing his hands together like he's choosing a whore for the night, Rocco takes off in the direction Roxanne just went. Her friend reluctantly follows them.

Although I'm pissed at Smith, I am too confused about

my exchange with Theresa to discount it for a second longer. "Did Theresa's information sway your opinion at all?"

We only arrived here on the cusp of dawn for one reason —to unearth if Maddox is aware the woman he's serving a life sentence for isn't dead. It's obvious from what Rico and Smith have discovered the past couple of weeks that Megan is alive and well, so why the fuck is Maddox keeping his mouth shut about it? If you had an out for a lifetime sentence, would you continue serving it? I fucking wouldn't.

Smith twists his lips, a sign he's confused. "From what I heard, your father is aware Megan is alive. I'm just struggling to understand why."

"You're not the only one," I breathe out before I can stop myself.

When they were alive, my father chewed up and spat out his daughters as if they were tobacco, so why would he give a shit about a random woman, let alone one who's batshit crazy? He kept Megan alive for a reason, I've just got to find out why.

"While I talk with Maddox, look a little deeper into the files Theresa handed over. She said she did this for a favor, but we both know she doesn't do shit without some type of payment upfront."

Air whizzes from Smith's nose when he hums in agreement. "I'll do that as soon as I organize a car. Any particular brand?"

"Something fast and noisy..." I almost add, *just like Roxanne*, but hold back the urge. I don't need to brag. Roxanne's moans could be heard two towns over. Smith and Rocco live on the same block as me.

Smith's smirk reveals he heard my inner monologue. It's as cocky as the heat that roars through me when Roxanne can't help but watch my entrance to Wallens Ridge State Prison. She keeps her gawk on the down-low with lowered lashes, but I don't need to see her eyes to know she's watching me. I can feel it in my bones. It thickens my cock in an instant, which doubles the heat of her stare.

"Prisoner 9429 is waiting for you in my office."

I shift my eyes from Roxanne to Warden Mattue. It's a fucking hard feat, only done because I'm curious to learn how he knew which prisoner I wanted to visit. This is my first time at this establishment since Rocco was an inmate.

When he catches my imprudent stare, the Warden's throat works hard to swallow. "I assumed he was who you were wanting to see, considering you've seen him once a month since his conviction."

He shows me a visitor ledger with a barely eligible D Petretti scribbled in the log once a month for the past year. It's not close to my signature, but I'm reasonably sure I know who it belongs to.

"You can wait here." When the Warden attempts a rebuttal, I slice my hand through the air. "Did I sound like I was asking permission?"

I don't watch the bob of his head. I'm too fascinated by the faintest hint of a smile under locks of red hair to pay his mundane submissiveness any attention. Even with her veins bubbling with anger, Roxanne can't help but respond to my surly personality. She seems to get off on it like she's obsessed with the thought I can protect her unlike anyone else.

It instantly proves my reason for sending her away was

the most stupid idea I've ever had. As I've said before, she doesn't want a man to take care of her. She wants a bastard, a monster, a man so evil, even when he has the blood of her mother on his face, she'll still crawl onto his lap and snuggle in.

If Fien weren't on my mind, I'd show Roxanne right now that I can give her all of that and so much more. Instead, I return her steely stare for a couple more seconds before I make my way to the Warden's office.

Once again, it's a fucking hard feat.

TWENTY-ONE

Dimitri

I could never be accused of being tiny, especially when my chest is swollen with smugness, but I feel a couple of inches shorter when Maddox notices my entrance into the Warden's office. The Walsh brothers don't have the notoriety the Petrettis do, but they're well known amongst the locals. Their mixed-race background makes them a little bulkier than their counterparts, and Maddox has taken it one step further by adding a good twenty pounds of muscle to his frame during his first stint in lock-up.

He has tatted up since the last time I saw him as well. His artwork almost looks as extensive as mine. If the quality of the work is anything to go by, he got a majority of them done outside of these walls, which is interesting considering he barely had a sleeve when he was arrested at Demi's place of employment.

"If I knew it was you, I would have gotten dressed up for the occasion." Don't misconstrue his words. They were laced with so much sarcasm, they left a bad taste in my mouth, so I'd hate to experience what Maddox's throat is going through. "What the fuck are you doing here, Dimitri?"

I take his brusque attitude in my stride. "I thought we were friends. Isn't this what friends do? Visit the other while they're locked up."

He looks like he wants to spit at my feet.

The feeling is mutual.

"We ain't friends."

I smirk, grateful he walked straight into the trap I was setting. After pressing my palms on the Warden's desk, I peer him dead-set in the eyes. "That's right. We're not. You just used my contacts to line your pockets with money, and then you wonder why we're not friends."

He's got nothing. Not a single fucking thing.

"Sit down, Maddox, and for once in your fucking life, listen. If you had done that from the get-go, you wouldn't be here."

His sneer would make most men shake in their boots. It doesn't cut the mustard with me. I was raised by a man who thought a fire stoke was a tool to keep his children in line. The hotter it was, the harder he struck me with it.

Don't feel sorry for me. My father's ways ensured I don't feel pain. As you can imagine, the ability made me a cold-hearted man. I'm not worried. Love and hate are on par when it comes to emotions. Both take everything you have and give nothing in return.

I'm hopeful my thoughts will change when I meet my daughter in the flesh for the first time, but it's hard to change the views of a skeptic. Audrey attempted to chip at the decay.

She barely made an indent. Roxanne, on the other hand, had me acting as if I had a heart in my chest. I would have taken a thirty-million-dollar hit for her—I still would.

My thoughts snap back to the present when Maddox's chuckles ring through my ears. "He was right. You're so fucking gone."

He doesn't need to spell out the name of the man he's referencing for me to understand our conversation is no longer between us.

Maddox refers to everyone by name—except my father.

"I'm gone? Ha! I'm not the one in cahoots with the man who marked up my sister with a mangy mutt." That shuts up his chuckles in an instant. Fucking good as I was tempted to use my fists. "What did he tell you, Ox? That I ordered for her to be punished?"

His silence is extremely telling. It isn't just my father whispering in his ear, it's someone he'd pay careful attention to.

Confident I know which way to take our conversation, I ask, "What's he got on her?"

He blows off the concern in my voice as if it's fake before he takes a seat as requested earlier.

"If my father has a noose around Demi's throat, I can help."

Maddox slants his head to make sure his glare has the effect he's aiming for. "Like you did Justine?"

I growl, baring teeth. "She's alive, isn't she?"

He slams his fist down on the desk separating us. "And crying every week on the phone. You fucked her over good, D. I don't know if she'll ever come back from this."

His words are a kick to the gut, but they push our conversation in the direction I need it to go. "So, you're gonna let him do the same to Demi?" When he scoffs, I hit him with straight-up facts. "You kept my daughter's existence a secret. You didn't do that for no reason, Ox. I'm here to find out why, and I ain't leaving until I do."

His tongue peeks between his teeth when I roll back the Warden's chair, take a seat, then hook my boots onto his desk. This is the first time in my life I wish I had trod in dog shit. I'd loved nothing more than to see the Warden's face when he rocked up to his office to find a big, dirty piece of shit on his spotless desk.

With Maddox as stubborn as me, our conversation soon hits a stalemate. This kills me to admit, but I have to break the silence. I don't have time to sit around and twiddle my thumbs. I'm juggling balls, many of them. If I don't want them to fall, I need to move our exchange along.

"With Megan Shroud being alive and well, your debt has *not* been fulfilled. Since you're an inmate in a maximum-security prison, I have no choice but to transfer that debt back to its original owner."

I'm all but threatening his sister, and he knows it. "You wouldn't fucking dare."

"Try me, Maddox. I've got a heap of anger and no one to take it out on." My words aren't lies. They're as gospel as my pledge to bring Fien home.

Spit seethes between Maddox's clenched teeth. "My debt is with your father."

I shrug before shaking my head. "Not according to you. I punished your sister, that means her debt falls on me."

He's speechless, truly and utterly speechless.

"I'm willing to negotiate—"

"With what? I gave your father everything I have. I have nothing left to give." The angst in his tone is more telling than the worry on his face. I don't know what my father is holding over his head, but it's more than his sister's life.

I remove my feet from the desk before balancing my elbows on the chipped surface. "Give me information—"

"I don't know anything."

I continue talking as if he never interrupted me. "And in good faith, I'll repay the favor. Special perks, hours outside these walls…" I watch his face to gauge any response to if my offers have already been brought forward. When his expression remains neutral, I continue, "I could even organize some additional conjugal visits."

He seems conflicted. I understand why when he asks, "Can you get Demi out?"

I'm reasonably sure I know what he's asking, but I'd rather he spell it out for me, then we both know *exactly* what he's asking of me. This isn't a standard favor. It will cost him more than a couple of years in county jail. "Out of what, exactly?"

He doesn't speak a word. He doesn't need to. I can see the fear in his eyes. Smell it on his skin. His debt with my father has nothing to do with his sister and everything to do with his girl.

"If she's out, she can't come here anymore, Ox. When you are out, you're out. You can never get back in. Are you willing to face that?" He takes a moment to deliberate before jerking up his chin. The worry in his eyes should see me granting him a few more minutes to consider his options, but as I said earlier, I don't have time to waste. "All right. But I'm going to need to know *everything*."

The panic on his face recedes in an instant. "Have you got a pen and a piece of paper? You're gonna need it."

Smith's eyes lift to mine when I race across the dusty lot like a bat out of hell. He's working from the hood of a brand-spanking-new Mercedes Benz G class. It looks like a tank, so it suits the terrain. The same can't be said of the feisty redhead in the front passenger seat. I don't know what Rocco said to get Roxanne in my car in one piece. It must have been something good because not only is she strapped in, ready to go, she's only glaring at me with half the intensity of her earlier stare.

"Did you get that?" Just because Smith switched off surveillance doesn't mean he didn't have eyes and ears in the room with me. Feds aren't the only ones familiar with button cameras.

Smith lifts his chin. "I'm hacking into the hospital servers now."

When Roxanne slips out of the passenger seat of the Mercedes Benz to peer at Smith's screen with Rocco and me, I don't request for the feed to be shut down like I usually would. She has said all along that the organizer of Fien's captivity is a woman, so it's only fair she watches us hone in on one.

"There." I point to a female with mousy brown hair and

a skittish demeanor. Even with the footage being a couple of months old, she looks similar to the child in the images I've pursued of Megan the past few weeks.

"Is that her?" I ask when Smith zooms in.

"Give me a sec…" He takes a screenshot of her profile before he uploads it to his state-of-the-art facial recognition system. It brings up a match in under three seconds. "Bingo. We have a match."

Aware he's now tracking the right person, he traces Megan's movements back several months, dragging the timeline back to the day Maddox said she was admitted to a mental hospital for a ninety-six-hour hold. It was well over a year ago. Maddox doesn't know why she was admitted. All he knew was that my father wanted her alive no matter the cost—something about her having information he couldn't get elsewhere.

"There," Roxanne parrots a few seconds later, pointing to a reflection bouncing off the admission glass mounted to protect the staff from the crazies.

The brightness of the woman's hair reveals she's blonde, but we can't see her face.

"Do you think it's the woman you were talking to earlier?" Roxanne asks after drifting her eyes to me.

I want to say yes, it would make things a shit ton easier if Theresa were the only villain in this story, but my gut is cautioning me to remain wary, so I shrug instead. "Can you clean up the footage?"

Smith screws up his nose. "I'd have a better chance with wired equipment. The upload speed is as slow as fuck out here."

"Then head back to the compound." I take a quick snapshot of Megan's up-to-date picture before gathering up his equipment and stuffing it into the passenger seat of his van. "Forward anything you find directly to me."

Rocco cocks a dark brow as mirth hardens his features. "Are you not heading back to the compound?"

His face appears a mix of jeering and confusion when I answer, "I've got to take Roxanne home first," before it switches to straight-up anarchy.

"I can do that for you. You don't have to go out of your way."

Needing to leave before I knock his teeth out, I grip the top of Roxanne's arm before placing her into the passenger seat of the Mercedes with less aggression than I did Smith's equipment. I'm not known for being gentle, but Smith's laptop is only worth a little over half a million dollars. Roxanne's price tag is closer to thirty—*if not priceless.*

"We need to find out what information Megan has that makes her invaluable to my father. If we can do that out without needing to travel to her, I'd much appreciate it."

The last thing I want is a cross-country adventure when solid intel of a Russian invasion just landed in my inbox. Since the information came from a man with nothing to lose, I'm paying it more attention than I did when Theresa suggested the same thing.

I stop leaning across Roxanne's body to fasten her seat belt when Smith says, "Megan could come to us."

"How?" Roxanne asks before I get the chance.

I scrub at my jaw to hide my grin when Smith's eyes lift from his prototype phone. He's never without an electronic device. "She's all-types of crazy... but not enough for a permanent placement. She could be signed out to a guardian."

My eyes snap to Roxanne's. I have no fucking clue why I'm seeking her advice. I am just relaying to you what's happening. It could be the fact that I've spent the past few weeks going through the files she compiled while I was flat on my back. Or it could be her perfume. Whatever it is, a gleam in her eyes exposes she appreciates me seeking her opinion.

While bouncing her eyes between mine, she hesitantly shrugs. "She could lead us to the people we're seeking." The fact she says 'us' messes with my head even more than all the shit Maddox just bombarded it with. "It's a risk, but if the reward could potentially exceed the danger, we have to take a chance."

Because I agree with her, I give Smith the go-ahead, but with added stipulations. "Tag her before she's released. We don't want her location falling through the cracks."

Smith's hard swallow reveals he heard the words I didn't speak, and the narrowing of Roxanne's eyes exposes she's just as telepathic. "You can't microchip her like she's a dog."

"I can't? Since when?"

The huff she does while crossing her arms under her chest is cute. I can't wait to see how she responds when I order Smith to do the same to her. Then, there'll be no more sneaking up on me. I'll know where she is at all times of the day and night.

TWENTY-TWO

Roxanne

For how pricy this car is, it has shit ventilation. I've done everything imaginable to lessen the intensity of Dimitri's unique scent—I've rolled down the window, cranked up the air conditioning, and removed my boots with the hope stinky socks would eradicate it—nothing has worked! It's still there, lingering in my nostrils as often as his infamous half-smirk has trickled into my mind the past six weeks. And don't get me started on other wondrous parts of his body, or you'll book me in for more than a lobotomy.

Ugh! Why do I continue tormenting myself like this? He killed my boyfriend, tortured my parents, then sent a killer to my best friend's apartment. I should have been glad to see the backend of him. I just wasn't.

It's for Claudia, I remind myself. *I agreed to a ride I didn't need for her.*

With that in mind, I pull up my big girl panties, glide up the window I've been dangerously balancing out of the past hour, then shift my focus to Dimitri. Just like the first seventy miles of our trip, he stares straight at me. It should be impossible to watch both the road and me, but he makes it look easy.

"How much pull do you have with the warden at Wallens Ridge?"

He wrings the steering wheel two times before replying, "Depends who's asking."

"Me. I'm asking." His grip on the steering wheel turns deadly. It makes his knuckles go white, but I push on, determined to have an injustice rectified. "Claudia was unfairly convicted—"

Dimitri cuts me off with a brittle laugh. "That's what all criminals say."

Even though his tone is brimming with mirth, I still narrow my eyes at him. "She *is* innocent. Her boyfriend was an abusive ass. Witness statements prove his hand was on the steering wheel when they veered off the road, yet she's still serving time. How is that fair?"

He waits a beat to absorb what I said before he asks, "Who prosecuted her case?"

Although I'm a little lost to where he's going with this, I answer, "A DA more interested in looking at her tits than compiling legitimate evidence."

I thought my description would match a thousand district attorneys. I was clearly wrong. "Luca Marco?"

After picking up my jaw from the floor, I ask, "Have you heard of him?"

When Dimitri dips his chin, the scent I've been struggling to ignore the past hour doubles. I think the full beard he doesn't usually wear is responsible for the increase of his scent. It seems capable of soaking in everything around him, and considering that everything seems to only be him, it's as intoxicating as the fact he didn't replace me with the first blonde to cross his path.

"Do you have anything on him we could use to have Claudia's conviction overturned?" There I go again, using the infamous 'we' on him. "*I'm* willing to get *my* hands dirty."

"Although *I* appreciate the offer *you're* making…" I poke my tongue out at him, stuffing his exaggerated words down his throat with a bucket load of attitude. "It's not as simple as getting dirt on someone. His rulings are out of my jurisdiction." When confusion crosses my features, he smirks, making a mess of my panties. "Marco is Ravenshoe's DA. I don't have jurisdiction there."

"How? Why?" I shouldn't sound as appalled as I do. I'm just stunned. Ravenshoe skirts Hopeton, and from the information Estelle and I have gathered the past six weeks, they've had a stronghold on that town for decades.

Dimitri appreciates my disgust. "Don't worry, I was as shocked as you." He indicates to take a left before shifting his focus back to me. "I've considered a takeover a couple of times, but I can't bring myself to do it." The reasoning behind his decision makes sense when he adds, "Isaac threw himself into that town when Ophelia died. It's his way of coping." This isn't the first time I've heard of his sister, but it's the first time it came directly from the source.

"Would he help?"

"Isaac?" Dimitri asks through crimped lips.

"Uh-huh."

His hair that's a little overdue for a trim falls into his eyes when he shakes his head. "That bridge was burned a long time ago. Besides, we're set to become enemies even more than we already are."

Now it's my turn to be confused. "Why?"

I wish he didn't need to pause to consider if he can trust me, but I understand why he does. Trust doesn't come easy for most people, much less the son of a Cartel hierarchy. "The man I was just visiting—"

"Maddox."

Dimitri's tightened jaw reveals he's going to have a talk with Rocco about his waggling tongue the instant he returns to the compound. "Yes, Maddox advised a Russian sanction is endeavoring to set up shop in Ravenshoe."

"Shouldn't that be Isaac's problem?" I'm not being bitchy. I am genuinely curious.

"If it were anyone but this man, I wouldn't have an issue with it. Since that isn't the case, I'll be keeping a close eye on the proceedings."

Dimitri wets his lips when I ask, "Bad blood?"

"It's been stale for years but turned potent a couple of years back." He doesn't need to spell out the details for me. I know what happens when you steal from the Cartel. I saw it firsthand only a couple of months ago. "Have you ever heard of Katie Bryne?"

The name freezes me for a couple of seconds. It's a common name, but I swear I've heard it before.

When the truth smacks into me, my jaw drops. "She was abducted a few years back, right?" I give myself a mental pat on the back when Dimitri lifts his chin, then almost vomit when past conversations smack into me. "She wasn't abducted for the baby-farming trade, was she?"

I gulp down a breath like I haven't breathed the past three minutes when Dimitri shakes his head. "She was taken by Russians." I nod, suddenly recalling that. The gossip spread through the local schools like wildfire, making it mighty uncomfortable for any foreign students with a Russian accent. "However, she was sold by my father years later to a Russian."

Oh. That can't be good. Even a mafia novice could understand that this isn't kosher.

"Do you think Fien's abduction has anything to do with Katie?"

Dimitri's pause this time around isn't to contemplate what he's going to tell me. He's deliberating as to why he has never considered this angle before.

My palms flatten on the roof of Dimitri's recently-purchased ride when he yanks it off the road. Since his phone isn't linked to the state-of-the-art Bluetooth system, he has to yank his cell phone out of his pocket to make a call. Usually, he conducts his calls in private, so you can imagine my pleasure when he hits the speaker button on his phone a mere second after dialing a frequently-called number.

Smith answers a few seconds later. "What's up?"

"Did we ever find out what caused the delay between Katie's abduction and her sale?" Dimitri's question divulges he's been looking into Katie's case a little more than a standard case. Nowhere near as much effort as I've put into his family history, but still noticeable.

Smith grunts before the whoosh of a headshake sounds out of Dimitri's phone. "We figured it was training."

"What if it wasn't? What if it was something more than that?" When Smith takes a moment to deliberate, Dimitri fills in the silence. "She was taken when she was fourteen. Underage or not, her training shouldn't have taken as long as it did."

I don't want to know what training he's referencing, nor am I going to ask him about it. Sometimes it's better to have your head stuck in the sand—kind of like mine was when news of my aunt's death reached my ears.

I thought Dimitri's reluctance to let me attend the search of my family ranch was because he was being an ass. I had no clue it was because my mother told her drug counselor there was at least one corpse buried near the home where she grew up.

Curious, I ask, "Could Katie have been placed into the baby-farming trade before being sold?"

Dimitri shakes his head. "We had considered that, but Kirill only ever purchases virgins, and he doesn't take anyone's word for it, either."

I'm glad Dimitri pulled over to make his call. It saves the leather interior of his new ride being coated in my vomit.

"Is she all right?" I hear Smith ask while Dimitri's hand circles my back in a soothing motion. I told Estelle eggs aren't supposed to smell fishy. She didn't believe me.

Dimitri's eyes flick between me and the minute bit of vomit on the edge of the road surface for several long seconds before he mutters, "She will be." After switching off the speaker feature on his phone, he squashes it against his ear. "Send Rocco to correspond with Megan's release. I need you to share the information Maddox disclosed with Rico before looking more closely at Katie's sale." His eyes float to me before he says, "We'll find Demi *after* I've ensured Roxanne has eaten."

"I've eaten," I mumble, denying the accusation in his eyes with words. "Not a lot, but enough." My last comment is barely a whisper, but Dimitri still hears them. His jaw stiffens a mere second before it works through a stern grind.

He has no right to be angry. He dumped me in a house with groceries older than dirt, and his goons weren't overly friendly when we suggested for them to get us supplies. They thought we were trying to play them. In reality, we were endeavoring not to starve to death.

When I say that to Dimitri, his face reddens to the color of my favorite crayon when I was a kid—blistering red. "Send Clover extermination orders for Roxanne's ranch." He waits for panic to make itself known with my face before he adds, "Warn him if he so much as rustles a hair on Ms. Armstead's head, the next rodent I exterminate will be him."

I don't know whether to be turned on by his threat or spooked. I love that he's protecting Estelle as fiercely as he protected me weeks ago, but not only is it after he put her life at risk, so it's a little too late to act chivalrous, his reply exposes he knows Estelle's last name. That can only mean one thing. He's been looking into her past as much as he did mine at the start of our arrangement. I don't know if that's a good thing or a bad thing. Estelle has always been the more attractive one of our duo. That's why I bring the spunk. I thought it would even things between us. I'm not so confident now, though.

I'm so deep in my pitiful thought process, I don't realize Dimitri ended his call and recommenced our trip until he asks, "When was the last time you ate?"

"Other than regurgitated slop I just threw up?" I relish his lowered lids for a second before putting him out of his misery. "I ate last night." I cringe, hating my inability to lie. "If you class three in the afternoon as nighttime."

"You last ate yesterday afternoon?" When I nod, his eyes lock with the dashboard of his swanky new ride. "It's now ten in the morning." I can't work out a single thing he says after this. It's all grumbled and spaced by a heap of swear words. They make me smile until he says more clearly, "You won't be smiling when I tan your ass for thinking this is funny."

Once again, I don't know how to respond. Should I be turned on or scared by his threat?

I lose the chance to deliberate when Dimitri pulls into the first gas station he finds. It's skanky, stinky, and looks like it hasn't been updated since the nineties. "I'd rather drink water out of a toilet bowl than eat here."

Ignoring me, he throws open his door, clambers out, then locks his eyes with mine. Not a word seeps from his lips. He doesn't need to voice his commands when his eyes can take up the slack. I either follow him inside willingly, or he'll drag me in there and tie me to my seat.

"Considering you released me from our contract..." I stop my climb out of his car to air quote my last word, "... you're a little too possessive for my liking."

The brutal closure of my door should gobble up his reply. It doesn't. I hear every painstaking word. "Uncaging a bird doesn't mean you're done with her. It can be quite the opposite, actually. What's that saying? *Set her free. If she comes back, she's yours. If she doesn't, she never was.*"

On that note, he enters the restaurant, leaving me standing in the dusty lot with my jaw hanging open and my heart in tatters.

I thought he let me go to save me from the madness. I had no clue he did it to save himself from a lunacy not even someone as strong as him can survive.

TWENTY-THREE

Dimitri

—————

My hand stops creeping for my gun when Roxanne soundlessly begs for me not to respond to an insolent man's overfriendly approach. Things have been different between us the past hour and a half—I fucked up by speaking before thinking—but one thing hasn't changed. Roxanne's ability to look a madman in the eyes and see the good in them.

This beggar has been watching her from afar since we arrived. He doesn't want the money I tossed at his feet, nor the scraps of our meals. He wants Roxanne to dance with him, knowing having her in his arms for a second will make up for a lifetime of injustices.

I'd rather he fuck off, but Roxanne is refusing to let me send him away. She finds him endearing. Why? I have no fucking clue. He stinks, his clothes are four sizes too big, and his toes are peeking out of his shoes, yet Roxanne looks at him as if he's a man who's just a little down on his luck.

My jaw almost cracks when Roxanne holds her index finger in the air. "One dance."

"Roxanne."

The gravelly deliverance of her name snaps her eyes to mine in an instant. Even though she's panicked, she holds her ground. "It's one dance." I'm about to tell her I don't give a fuck if he was going to pay her a million dollars for thirty seconds worth of work but lose the chance when her next comment stuns me as much as my earlier one did her. "If you let me go this one last time, I promise I'll come back."

I'm too shocked to talk. This has never happened before. Usually, I go in guns blazing. I don't want to do that this time around. So instead, I let her stretch her wings.

With a smile that makes me regret every decision I've ever made, Roxanne mouths, "*Thank you,*" before she accepts the hand the man is holding out in offering.

While he whizzes her around a shoddy restaurant, I watch them like a hawk, uncaring if I look like a deranged stalker. If his hands move within an inch of an area I deem unacceptable, the guests at this establishment will be eating mutton for the next six months.

Disappointment is the first thing I feel when the man keeps his hands high on Roxanne's back for their entire dance. His unusual gallantry stays with me long after I've bundled Roxanne back into my car and recommenced our trip. It played in my mind when I stopped for gas and lingered well into the three hours it took us to arrive at my cousin's last known address. It only clears when the reason for the sparkle in his eyes finally dawns on me.

"Who did he think you were?"

Roxanne's smiles compete with the low-hanging sun. "His daughter."

She adds a giggle to her grin when my lip furls. The man would have been well into his seventies, and I'm being kind considering most homeless people age quicker than their sheltered counterparts.

"His head is a little muddled," Roxanne explains when I pull into the driveway of a standard house in the middle of the burbs. "He still thinks he's serving in Vietnam."

"You learned all that by looking in his eyes?"

She shakes her head. "It was a little more complicated than that." When I wave my hand through the air, encouraging her to reveal the secrets I see in her eyes, she says, "He had a squadron tattoo on his hand. The research I did for the one I saw at Joop revealed it was from a combat unit that was deployed to Vietnam in the early seventies. His boots, although holey, were from his infantry days, and although it was badly faded, the photograph he keeps safe in his bootstrap had the faintest red coloring on the edges. It could have been a dress, but I took a chance on it being the color of his daughter's hair." She twists to face me like it's an everyday occurrence for a two-hundred-thousand-dollar car to be parked in the driveway of a house worth half the price. "How did you know he mistook me for someone?"

Untrusting of my mouth not to make the mistake it did earlier, I hit her with a frisky wink before exiting a car that will be sold for parts by the end of the week. If you think Smith secured our ride the legitimate way, you still have a lot to learn about my operation.

"Whose house is this?" Roxanne asks after joining me on the footpath. The confusion in her tone is understandable. Not only does she comprehend the reason for my silence, Demi is blood-related. You wouldn't know it from how rundown and derelict her house is.

This property has been in the Petrettis' vault of arsenal for the past two decades. I've never seen it this derelict. The gutters are paint peeled and hanging on by a single screw, several roof shingles need replacing, and the outside looks like it hasn't been touched with a paintbrush or a lawn-mower in years.

"Stay behind me."

Although peeved I didn't answer her question, Roxanne does as instructed. The removal of my gun already has her on edge, much less the faintest creep of a shadow across the front living room window.

"Demi…" We walk up the cracked, overgrown footpath slowly. The shadow was larger than Demi's svelte frame, but that doesn't necessarily mean it isn't her. We're not on good terms. The fact I let her boyfriend be put away for life means we haven't spoken in over a year. "Ox sent me."

I feel Roxanne's curiosity rising. The hand she's gripping the waistband of my trouser with is very indicating, let alone the increase in her breaths. Although only a handful of people call Maddox 'Ox,' I'm confident Roxanne has heard of him before.

Our cautious approach sends my nerves into a tailspin. I'm not used to taking things slow. Just like I fuck, I approach danger with the same fierceness—hard and fast. I can't do that this time around. I put up an impressive capital to keep

Roxanne safe, so you sure as hell can guarantee I won't put her life on the line for anything.

When my knock on Demi's door goes unanswered, I scoop down to gather the pistol strapped to my ankle. Some may say I'm a fool to hand Roxanne a loaded weapon—things have been tense between us today—but I'd rather have her weaponed-up and ready to fire than be a sitting duck.

Roxanne peers at me with wide apprehensive eyes when I say, "There's no safety. Just aim and fire."

She looks as if she wants to drop my gun like it's a hot potato when I place it in her palm. Then she swallows, puts on her game face, and raises her gun like I forced her to do to her mother.

Her kick-ass fighter stance crumbles when I kick open Demi's door with my boot. It isn't my unexpected show of strength that has her knees knocking. It's the horrendous smell vaping out of Demi's house. If she thought her daddy stunk up my compound while building the courage to blow his brains out, she had no idea. This place fucking reeks.

"Stay behind me," I instruct again when Roxanne's morbid curiosity gets the best of her. She isn't moving for the window we saw the shadow creep across. She's heading for the bedroom responsible for the smell.

Although pissed at her inability to do as she's told, her mix-up saves me from making a fatal mistake. The shadow didn't belong to Demi. It was from the big black beast standing over her beaten body, protecting her with fangs bared and a vicious growl. It's her Doberman—Max.

TWENTY-FOUR

Roxanne

D emi's one blue eye not hidden by a smattering of bruises across her face peeks up at me when I place down a mug of coffee in front of her. Even with the fireplace of my grandparents' ranch over stacked with wood, she's still shuddering like she's in the middle of Antarctica. Her jitters are understandable. I'm still hyped up with adrenaline, and all I did was view the man she gunned down in self-defense from a distance.

I can imagine what she's been through the past three days. It's clear from the extent of her bruises that she fought with everything she had before she resorted to the gun her boyfriend made her hide under her pillow. It was horrendous holding a gun to someone's head. I couldn't imagine firing it while they're squashed on top of you. Just the thought of crawling out from beneath a dead body sends shivers rolling through me. They have Dimitri watching me even closer than he has the past three hours.

He's been endeavoring to find out what happened to Demi without being insensitive, but with her shock too high for her cousin to break through, Dimitri has been left to handle his inquiries alone. Considering those investigations are taking place here, at my family's ranch of all places, exposes who his lead suspect is. If your relationship with your son is disgruntled enough he doubts your participation in the captivity of your only grandchild, why would he think a niece would fare a better chance, especially one who seems out of the loop on all things Cartel.

"Are you sure you don't want anything to eat?" Demi would have to be hungry. From what I picked up between keeping Estelle up to date on our unexpected guests and making sure Dimitri's crew has everything they need, it appears as if she shot her intruder three days ago. If she's been as closed off the past three days as she has the past three hours, not all the grumbles I've heard seep from her mouth have been whimpers. Some may be from her hungry tummy. "I can whip up a batch of mean pancakes. Ask Dimi, he ate them and survived."

My heart flutters in my chest when the briefest smile creeps out from behind locks of dark hair. It's only faint, but her smile reminds me that the world does spin.

"If you change your mind, my kitchen is open twenty-four-seven."

Before she can thank me for an offer she shouldn't class as friendly, a much more dangerous situation than my horrific cooking skills confronts us. A fleet of five police cruisers is blazing down the driveway. Their brutal speed kicks up as much dust as my feet when I race toward Dimitri to tell him the quickest and safest exit.

I'm not the only one moving fast. Max is on his feet in an instant, growling and barking at the procession of cars as if they're the enemy. It's weird to see him acting so violent. He's been fine with Dimitri and over a dozen of his armored goons the past three hours, so why is he acting so irritated by men sworn to protect?

"It's okay," Dimitri assures me before he quiets Max's ruckus with the swiftest lift of his hand.

Although his vicious gaze remains locked on the fleet of vehicles coming to a stop at the front of the ranch, Max licks the dribble his vicious growl instigated before he returns to his protective post by Demi's feet.

Confident he has one disaster diverted, Dimitri shifts his focus back to me. "They're not here for me." I choke on my spit when he nudges his head to Demi and says, "They are here for her."

From the corner of the room, I watch the scene unfold. The dozen or more police officers don't approach my home. They maintain their stalk from outside when a man with blondish brown hair exits the convoy from the final vehicle. Although the stranger is dressed differently than the prisoner I saw in the wee hours of this morning, I'm confident he's one and the same. Not only does he have a distinct set of tattoos, when I was ushered past the Warden's office, I watched him like a hawk when he went toe to toe with Dimitri. Excluding Rocco, I had never seen a man stupid enough to go against Dimitri.

I was fascinated by their exchange and somewhat

worried. Don't misunderstand. I wasn't worried Maddox would hurt Dimitri. I was panicked how turned on I was watching Dimitri in his element. He was as bossy and domineering as he was in the parking lot, but for once, his annoyance wasn't focused on me.

"Who's Maddox to Demi?"

Dimitri doesn't need to answer my question. Maddox's dart across the room tells me everything I need to know, much less Max's blasé response to his quick approach. Furthermore, Demi responds to Maddox as if he's the only man in the room, so I won't mention the loving way Maddox cups her bruised cheeks, or you'll think I'm a creeper.

I can't help but watch. The fireworks sparking between them is out of this world. It's almost as explosive as the ones that forever bristle between Dimitri and me.

"Is there somewhere they can go… for privacy?"

I glance up at Dimitri with playful mocking beaming from my eyes, adoring the unease of his question. I didn't think he knew what awkwardness was, let alone have the ability to display it. "We don't have any sex pods here. My nanna was miles ahead of her time, but she wasn't *that* advanced."

When his lips furl at the ends, I suck in a relieved breath. Even with his smile being as ghost-like as Demi's, it's better than the downward trend his lips have been wearing the past three hours. I still have a lot of anger to work through for how we departed, and why, but seeing how he coerced Demi from her hiding spot has me seeing him in an entirely different light. His naturally engrained protectiveness already makes him a great father, not to mention his ability to nurture when required.

"Perhaps my grandparents' room would work?"

After jerking up his chin, Dimitri runs his hand down my arm in thanks, then makes his way to Demi and Maddox's side of the room. I want to continue soaking up their tear-producing display of affection but lose the chance when the heat of a gaze captures my attention.

I'm assuming Estelle has noticed my body's response to Dimitri's briefest touch, so you can picture my shock when I realize her stare isn't directed at me. She's peering past me, eyeballing the last person I ever anticipated for her to watch. She's gawking at Clover, and if the fizzle of their stares going to war is anything to go by, he's watching her just as closely.

"That's not a good idea," I warn after joining her on the couch.

The hiss zapping in the air weakens when Estelle drags her eyes to me. "What isn't a good idea?" She's been super quiet this afternoon like visiting prisoners and being surrounded by gangsters isn't an everyday occurrence for her. She works at an establishment owned by no other than Mr. Monroe. He's as well-known amongst the locals of Erkinsvale as the Petrettis are to Hopeton inhabitants, so she can't play the innocent card.

"Giving gaga eyes to a paid hitman."

Estelle rolls her eyes like I didn't hit the bullseye. "*Puhleaze.* I was warning him to stay away."

I wiggle my finger around her flushed cheeks. "If this is your threatening face, what was the one I saw when you and Brayden went to town Thanksgiving weekend?"

"Don't you dare judge me." The humor on her face weakens the intensity of her snapped tone. "You were all, *'good riddance, I can't stand him, how dare he treat me the way he did'* to, *'hey there, good-looking, can I get you a cup of coffee? One clump or two?'*"

I sock her in the arm, doubling her smile. "I was trying to be helpful."

"You were trying to take the focus off your pressing thighs." When the truth of her statement lowers my shoulders, she jabs her elbow into my ribs. "I can't blame you. He's fucking hot, they all are, but…"

When she fails to find a reason for my insanity, I help a girl out. "It's crazy to think *this* is any type of normal?"

After breathing out of her nose, she nods.

"Would it make you feel any better if I said it's not close to being normal because it's not meant to be? There's bad and good in every person. You've just got to find the one who makes your flaws less obvious."

"What are you saying, Roxie? You're the concealer for Dimitri's blemishes?"

I shake my head before I can stop myself. "He's not the one with the marks, Estelle. I am."

Before the shock of my confession can register, the man we're talking about steals my focus from across the room. The briefest glance Dimitri awards me under hooded lashes isn't responsible for my utmost devotion. It's the tick of his jaw when he stares down at a tablet Smith shoves under his nose.

My brows spike as quickly as my heart rate when Dimitri instructs Rocco to take me to my room. He only ever does that when he's going to hurt someone I love or punish me. With his narrowed eyes locked on a group of officers mingling on the front porch, I doubt the latter is a contender. He's so worked up, Smith's tablet barely dings before he races across the room like a bullet being fired from a gun.

I sidestep Rocco just as quickly, certain the cause of Dimitri's aggression has something to do with me. The image Smith showed him was blurry from a distance, but several parts of it were distinct—the most obvious, my recently dyed flaming red hair.

"Roxie…" Don't misconstrue the annoyance in Rocco's tone. If he didn't want me to sidestep him, he wouldn't have let it happen. From what I've overheard the past couple of hours, he encouraged Dimitri to let me stretch my wings, unaware Dimitri's growth would come in the form of his possessiveness. He feels somewhat responsible for the six-week gap in whatever the fuck you consider my relationship with Dimitri to be. I assured him he has nothing to feel guilty about. He disregarded my offer on the basis I didn't know all the facts. Supposedly, the bender Dimitri went on weeks ago wasn't his lowest low. The past six weeks were.

"Dimitri!" I shout when he pole drives an officer in the middle of the group. The man he's assaulting is in uniform, his colleagues are surrounding him. I don't see him coming out of this with anything less than an extremely long rap sheet.

When the group of twenty-plus officers part to watch the charade unfold, I'm given an uninterrupted view of Dimitri clambering off the unnamed officer. He isn't satisfied he beat his face to within an inch of recognition with only a handful of swings. He's moving for the old rope swing in the front tree.

He doesn't yank it out of the tree. He merely curls the frayed end around the officer's throat before he hauls him onto his feet with inhumane strength. The dark-haired man's feet dangle an inch from the soggy ground within seconds, and his friends do nothing but stare when he clutches at the rope burning his throat.

His imminent death already looks painful, but I realize it's about to get worse when Dimitri knots the rope so that the officer is suspended mid-air without Dimitri needing to maintain his grip on the pulley. It isn't just the wet patch on the front of the man's pants responsible for my beliefs, it's the deadly gleam in Dimitri's eyes when he removes his suit jacket and commences rolling up the sleeves of his dress shirt. He's set to punish this man, his endeavor only thwarted when he spots my watch.

"Get her out of here!" he yells at Rocco, his voice unlike anything I've ever heard.

Rocco doesn't ignore his command this time around. He wraps his arm around my waist and hoists me away just as Dimitri hits the officer's ribs with a punishing left-right-left combination.

As the officer slowly asphyxiates, his eyes protrude out of his head. It has nothing on the bulge mine do when I see Smith's tablet screen head-on. The man who swore to uphold the law wasn't tempted by the bounty on my head. He put my license on a rape-play site. The address of the apartment I share with Estelle is on a website specifically designed for men to connect with women who fantasize about being raped, clear as day for all to see.

It isn't the only identification card on display either. There are several beneath me. One I recognize almost as immediately as I did mine. It's a photo identification from what appears to be Demi's place of employment. It states she enjoys being taken unaware, and the rougher her unknown john is, the better.

Oh. My. God. Is that why Demi was assaulted? Because the man Dimitri is killing made out she fantasizes about being raped? If that's the case, what would have happened to me if Smith hadn't found his disturbing website? I don't have a dog nor a gun to keep me safe.

I only have Dimitri.

In all honesty, that's all I need. It doesn't make my anger any less violent, though. What if I weren't home when the men came looking? What if they hurt Estelle believing she was me?

As the anger inside of me evolves, I fight with everything I have. "Let me go," I seethe through clenched teeth when Rocco refuses to relinquish his grip around my waist. "I'm gonna pull his insides out of his nostrils."

"You're too late, Princess P," he informs on a laugh. "He's already met with his maker."

My eyes jackknife back in just enough time to take in the fatal flop of the officer's head. Although he's still hanging from the tree I climbed as a child, I don't believe he died from strangulation. There's too much blood oozing from the many nicks and cuts on his body for the coroner to place anything but torture down as his cause of death.

TWENTY-FIVE

Dimitri

M y blood is boiling hot. I'm pissed, frustrated as fuck, and reasonably sure one kill won't cut it. I want to murder Officer Daniel's entire precinct. Do you truly expect my anger to be any less? He didn't arrive with Maddox's fleet. He's been here since the start, standing mere feet from Roxanne for hours, drinking her coffee, and nibbling on the only morsel of food she had left in her cupboards. But instead of thanking her for her generosity, he put her information on a rape fantasy site. *All* her information—date of birth, height, weight, and exactly how you can sneak into her apartment via the fire escape ladder on the west side of her building. He even made out she likes being sodomized with household equipment.

Why, you ask? Because Officer Daniel Packwood works for the special victims' unit branched under Ravenshoe PD's umbrella, meaning he wouldn't just be in charge of Roxanne's case if one of the sick fucks on that site believed her kink was rape, he'd hear every sickening detail of her assault directly from the source—just like he did with Demi.

That's his kink. He isn't a rapist. He just wants to hear the fear in the woman's voice when she recalls her nightmare firsthand, then he'd go home to spank one out before climbing into bed with his wife—a rape victim and advocator for women's rights.

And you thought I was sick.

"Has the site been taken down?"

Smith waits for me to remove some of Officer Packwood's blood from my hands with the towel Clover tossed at me before jerking up his chin. "A new one will be back up by tomorrow. That's how these sites operate."

"His wife?" I question through a tight jaw.

"Had no fucking clue why her hosting server was being hit with a million views per week," Rocco answers on Smith's behalf. "She isn't in the wrong here, Dimi. There's no need to punish her, too."

Even confident he's right doesn't weaken my agitation. It will take Smith hours to comb through the website's visitors to see who screenshot Roxanne's information. That's hours he will be off Fien's case, but hours I can't refuse to give. Roxanne hasn't been to her apartment building in months, but that doesn't mean she's safe. You won't believe the lengths men go when they're on the hunt. Nothing is off-limits. If they want to find her, they will. No fear.

"Send two guys to watch out front. Officer Packwood wasn't working alone, so he'll have a visitor or two show up when he fails to arrive for duty Monday morning."

"And them?" Clover asks, peering at the officers who did

nothing to help their boy in blue, too grateful it wasn't them to risk punishment by intervening.

He stops rubbing his hands together like a kid in a toyshop when I say, "They're on payroll, so they'll keep their mouths shut. If they don't..." When he spots the murderous gleam darting through my eyes, he recommences rubbing his hands. "When another site pops up, what are the chances of tracing the source of the server?"

Smith pulls a face I'd rather not see when I'm itching to kill for the second time. "Not good."

"Why not? You traced that one." This question didn't come from me. It came from Rocco, who's just as pissed as me. Men like Officer Packwood are the worst of the worst to him. If he didn't need to keep Roxanne contained in her room, I'm reasonably sure he would have joined me in punishing him.

"I followed a ping off Daniel's phone. If I hadn't, I would have never found the site he was posting to. It was buried too deeply in the dark web for standard searches."

Smith doesn't say it, but I felt his underhanded jab that he's struggling to do every task I'm assigning him on the mobile equipment he only uses when we're on the road. His hub was built on my compound for a reason. I get the best from him when he's in an area specially created for him.

With that in mind, I nudge my head to the door. "Head back to the compound. Roxanne and I will join you there shortly."

I can see on Rocco's face how badly he wants to rib me for backpedaling on the decision I made six weeks ago, but since he knows better than to annoy me when I'm fuming mad, he keeps his mouth shut. It's for the best. I'm so fucking angry right now, I can't guarantee I won't take it out on the wrong person—Roxanne and my second-in-charge included.

I'm about to head for the room I hear running water coming from when an earlier incident pops back into my head. I crank my neck to peer at Rocco so quickly, I give myself whiplash. "Why are you here? You were meant to sign Megan out."

His face whitens as his panicked eyes shift to Smith. "You didn't tell him?"

"Tell me what?" I ask when Smith shrugs, my temper short-fused.

"Fuck, douchebag. I thought you were on the ball." Rocco whacks Smith in the gut before giving him and Clover their marching orders, and then he walks away from a group of men acting as if they didn't just witness a murder. "Megan skipped bail. From what I coerced out of a medical team accepting no liability whatsoever for her misdiagnosis, it occurred a couple of weeks ago. She knocked a guard out cold. Chair straight over the fucking head." He scoots in even closer. "We're not the only ones hunting her." He glances toward the corrupt cops without moving his head. "They even brought in sniffer dogs."

"Who ordered the search?" Rocco's stern facial expression answers my question on his behalf. "So Theresa's act this morning was a ploy." I'm not seeking clarity. I'm stating a fact. "She isn't worried about Maddox—"

"Because she already knows she has that boy in check."

Since I agree with him, I don't voice annoyance about

his interruption. I merely continue as if he never butted in. "She's petrified we're getting close to the truth."

Rocco whistles out an agreeing tune. "That's why we need to squeeze her a little harder."

"Or I could just kill her. Get the inevitable over and done with." My tone is as flat and bothersome as I'd feel knowing Theresa was lying in the bottom of the ocean, held down by bricks. That's how inconsequential her life is. No one would care if she were dead, not even the little boy she's trying to palm off as Isaac's.

"You could," Rocco agrees, smiling, "But you won't... because at the end of the day, you know the only time that bitch shares secrets is when she's on her back, being fed a healthy dose of your dick. Considering your girl looked set to murder when you traced your finger down her cheek this morning, I wouldn't recommend it. She's more than ready to bring the bat to the game for you, so why not have her swinging at the big hitters instead of the small fry like Theresa."

His comment switches the heat of my blood from chaos to yearning in under a second. Even with my blood pressure almost bursting my eardrums, I heard Roxanne's fight when she endeavored to free herself from Rocco's clutch. She wasn't fighting to save Officer Packwood's life. She wanted to witness the monster inside of me roar to life firsthand, to drink him in, in all his glory, and I'm about ready to grant her wish.

TWENTY-SIX

Roxanne

The soap doesn't have a chance in hell of remaining in my grip when the stern and clipped voice of Dimitri rolls across my bathroom. "Eyes to the wall."

My bathroom is tiny. It has the standard square upright shower, one vanity that's missing the cupboards beneath it, and a toilet's peach coloring shows how long ago it was installed. However, I still knew about Dimitri's arrival before he announced it. The aura that beamed out of him while he used the unnamed officer's body as a boxing bag hissed in the air, heating my skin as effectively as the boiling hot water pumping out of the showerhead.

"Don't make me ask you again, Roxanne," he growls out when my shock at his request has me desperate to peer over my shoulder.

I want to drink in the energy I've been in awe of for over a year before doubling it. I love his arrogance. It's what mesmerized me when he stood outside the alleyway watching me be fingered by a man well below my league, and it's what kept my feet grounded when Estelle used the distraction to make a break for it.

She begged me to go with her, but I couldn't. Dimitri was only on a murderous rampage because a man tried to hurt me. I can't be angry at him for that. I've been seeking this level of protection since I was a child, so it'll take more than the occasional death of a stupid man for me to give it up.

"Keep them there," Dimitri demands when my eyes finally submit to the prompts of my overworked brain.

My heart rages out of control when the steam inside my little bubble is released from Dimitri opening the glass door. After stepping into the space, which feels ten times smaller with his brooding frame taking up a majority of the tiled floor, in the corner of my eye, I watch him cup a generous serving of water in his bruised and battered hands. When he throws the water over his face, I realize what he is doing. He's cleaning himself up for me, afraid the gore and violence his life is shrouded in will scare me away.

"Goddammit, Roxanne! Do you ever do as you're told?" Dimitri grinds out with a roar when I spin around to face him.

I want to shake my head but can't. The view is too wondrous for me to move, much less garner a half-assed reply to his accurate statement. Our contrasting heights and widths are obvious when we're dressed, so you can imagine how conflicting they are when we're in a tiny space, butt naked. Add that to the fact Dimitri's muscles are strained from their earlier un-koshered workout, and you've got the ultimate recipe of lust, intrigue, and mystery.

I'm a part of this story, and I'm still dying to read what happens next.

My hands rattle when I raise them to Dimitri's face. I'm not worried he will reject me. The pulsating rod of flesh stealing my smarts assures me that won't happen. I'm simply disappointed I can't nurture him without removing the blood of another man from his face.

Shockwaves roll down my spine when Dimitri catches my hand before it gets near his face. His hold isn't painful, but it's most definitely aggressive. "You don't want to act like a lady any more than I want to pretend to be a gentleman."

As I wiggle to break free from his hold, I fight not to moan. His voice was as hot as honey, warm and inviting but so bitterly sweet, it will give me a toothache for days.

"You want a monster, a bastard." His grip on my wrist firms, along with the tightness of my womb. "You want me."

There's no point resisting what he's saying. Every word he speaks is true. So, instead, I nod. It commences an avalanche of groping hands and lust-blistering kisses. While he pins the lower half of my body to the tiled shower wall with his impressive crotch, he attacks my mouth with a blurring mix of licks, bites, and moans. It's a hurried, frantic exchange full of passionate touches, wandering hands, and moans my nanna would have killed me for only two years ago.

My noisy moans can't be helped. My pussy, tits, and ass are being lavished by Dimitri's big hands while his mouth encourages mine to defeat logic. It shouldn't be possible to be this noisy when my lungs are breathless, but somehow, I pull off the inevitable.

My head lowers to take in Dimitri biting a trail of love bites down my stomach. He licks, bites, then kisses me until his mouth is an inch from my aching sex, and I'm hoisted up the tiled wall as if I'm weightless. The small confines of the shower mean he can't kneel to devour his feast, so he brings his meal to himself, instead.

I tremble with the breath he releases when he instructs me to watch him. "I like your eyes on me…" Half of his face disappears between my splayed thighs before he does one controlled lick up my soaked slit. "Especially when I'm doing this…" He licks, tugs, and makes me come undone in an embarrassing quick eight seconds. "And even more so when you do that."

He holds nothing back for the next several minutes, not even when his accidental bump of the faucet switches the temperature of the water from roasting to freezing. The change-up is nice. I'm hot all over, so excluding my initial yelp about the rapid change in my core body temperature, I relish the refreshing change.

"Oh…" I'm close to climax again. It's building inside of me like a tsunami, encouraged by the short, powerful flicks Dimitri hits my clit with. He toys with the bundle of nerves between my legs until the moans seeping from my mouth can wake the dead. "I'm… I'm…" Fucking insane if I ever believed things between us were over. Something so explosive is indestructible. Unbreakable. *Everlasting.*

An orgasm washes through me when the possibility of forever hits me. I can't do anything but pant and scream.

The intensity of my climax is insane. It rushes over me again and again and again until the feverish moans bouncing off the bathroom walls switch to a pained grunt from Dimitri's cock's sudden entrance to my clenching sex.

With one of my legs curled around his waist and the other hooked around his elbow, Dimitri drives into me on repeat. The pain of taking him for only the third time shouldn't have me close to detonation again, but it does. It builds inside of me, chasing its next release right along with Dimitri's bid to find his own.

He fucks the living hell out of me, screwing me so hard, I'm confident the spasms hitting my uterus are no longer associated with my looming period. He pounds and pounds and pounds into me until I'm screaming his name as if I am possessed.

"It feels so good. You feel so good," I grunt through the tremors overwhelming me. "Don't stop. Please don't ever stop. I'll die without this, without you."

Dimitri does the exact opposite of my moaned requests. He lowers the swings of his hips before he rests his forehead on mine. I don't mind. The change-up in speed will allow him to drink in the alteration of the light in my eyes, the transferal only he can instigate.

"Do you have any idea how many times I've dreamed about this?" he asks a few seconds later. "I blanket every inch of you as envisioned. Your entire ass fits in my palm."

As his eyes bounce between mine, they replicate the variation in color mine underwent minutes ago, except they appear more painted with anger than euphoria. I discover why when he adds, "I could have squashed you like a bug, but all I wanted to do was cocoon you until your wings were fully grown."

It feels like his cock is about to poke out of my stomach when he adds a roll to his hips. He's more deeply seated now, almost fully immersed. He isn't just ensuring I'll feel him for days, he's reminding me of exactly what I gave up six weeks ago.

"But do you know what happens when a butterfly gets her wings?"

I kiss him with everything I have, hopeful my tongue will ram his hurtful words down his throat before he can express them. I understand I stuffed up. I realize I should have fought harder. I don't need him to teach me a lesson while reminding me just how explosive we are.

Although my kiss doubles the heat bristling between us, it doesn't stop his words. "She flies away."

"I didn't."

He responds to my lie with both his cock and his eyes. He pounds into me, bringing me to the very edge of insanity before he freezes like his thighs are as lifeless as my heart felt the past six weeks. "Yes. You. Did."

Even aware I'm digging my hole deeper, I continue to fight. "No." Water flings off my cheeks when I shake my head. "You dropped me off. You let me out of our agreement—"

Dimitri's roar shudders my heart straight out of my chest. "Because I wanted to see if you'd come back! I wanted proof you were there for me and not because you were in fear for your life."

"You had armed men on every corner, Dimi."

For how hard his hips are now thrusting, his words shouldn't be as smooth as silk. "Men you had no trouble bypassing when it suited you. Hair dye, trips to visit a state prison inmate… if you fucking wanted it, you found a way to get it."

Even with it being true, I hate everything he's saying. If I wanted his attention, I merely needed to walk out the front door any time after dusk because despite what Rocco says, I know Dimitri was outside the first twenty-eight days of my incarceration. I could feel him there, I was just too stubborn to succumb to the pressure eating me alive. Then I thought I was too late. Excluding earlier today, I hadn't sensed his presence in over two weeks.

"I was angry. You threatened my friend. You sent a murderer to her house. I wanted to get back at you." I try to hold in the truth, but just like I can't stop my tears once they start, there's no stopping my honesty, either. "I wanted you to beg me for a second chance, and to understand how pathetic I felt pinning for you when you seemed to hate me."

My confession punishes me more than Dimitri. He fucks the living hell out of me, pounding, grunting, and thrusting until my orgasm peaks, then he once again freezes like a statue.

"Don't do this. Don't punish me because I wanted to be first for a change."

My drenched hair flops against my cheeks when Dimitri forces my eyes to his. "You wanted to be first? That's the excuse you're running with?"

"It's not an excuse. Wanting to be someone's everything isn't an excuse," I reply before I realize how stupid I'm being.

I got angry about him not giving me his undivided attention *after* pledging not to take more of his time than he's able to give me.

How foolish am I?

Not only am I in love with a gangster who's threatened to kill me more than once, I'm hoping he'll replicate feelings he doesn't understand.

I need my head examined.

My sigh has two meanings when Dimitri shuts off the faucet and carries me out of the bathroom. Because he's still inside of me, thick and heavy, I don't advise him fresh towels are hanging on the back of the door he left wide open as if we're the only two people in the room. It's clear he isn't done with my punishment just yet. The unrecognizable mask he's wearing is sure-fire proof of this, much less the way he dismounts me from his cock and dumps me onto my bed.

In a quick snag, flip, and lift maneuver, my ass is perched high in the air, and Dimitri's big cock pokes at my puckered hole.

"Don't fucking tempt me," he growls when my back instinctively arches, seeking firmer contact. "I don't have any lubricant, and if I find out you do, your ass won't be pounded with my cock. It will wear my handprint for days."

As warmth spreads through me, I tremble.

"I knew I'd need more than an hour to work through your kinks." As he rubs his erection against a region of my body I didn't realize had its own pulse, his hand slithers around my jittery stomach. I almost vault off my bed when he finds my clit without the stumbling hands Eddie used.

The quickest recollection of Eddie's golden eyes should

cause the excitement flooding my insides to dampen. It doesn't. If anything, it makes it more perverse. I suspected Dimitri killed him because of what he had done to me. The officer's murder earlier this evening reveals that was the case. Dimitri is a monster who can fly off the hinges at any moment, but I don't believe that makes him hideously ugly. He's dark, yet undeniably beautiful. Deranged, yet somehow sane. And he can love, he just hasn't been shown how to yet.

"Let me make it up to you."

"No," Dimitri immediately answers like he knows what I'm talking about.

Considering I've orgasmed multiple times tonight, he could mistake my offer as a wish to reciprocate the favor, but I know that isn't the case. Even when he's knee-deep in filth, Dimitri's thoughts are always with his daughter.

"I can help, Dimi. Dr. Bates isn't as smart as his credentials—"

"No!" he screams with a brutal thrust of his hips.

The way he enters me should have me screaming just as loudly, but my target is locked and loaded, and I'm not giving him up for anything. "He walks around with dollar signs in his eyes—"

"For fuck's sake, Roxanne, shut up before I force you to be quiet."

His threat doesn't penetrate my mind in the slightest. "He'd be an easy man for you to fool. Force his hand, Dimitri. Show him you're not to be messed with. Gut him like you did Eddie, then do the same to your father."

I'm panting now, full-on moaning, overcome by the vicious fucking Dimitri is bombarding me with. He pounds into me so hard, my insides feel like they're being shifted to accommodate his massive dick. It's painful yet beautiful— just like him.

"You have nothing to lose and everything to gain. You've just got to show the people who have your back that you believe in them by accepting their help."

There's nothing romantic about our fuck. Dimitri takes all the control, leaving nothing in his wake until I freefall into an uprising of warmth and comfort. It's a ferociously stunning few minutes that only grows more striking when Dimitri withdraws his magnificent cock, brings it to my lips, then grunts, "Reciprocate."

A normal person would mistake his command as him wanting head.

As I've said time and time again, I'm nothing close to ordinary.

After nodding, wordlessly advising him I understand his request, I take his dick between my lips and swallow down, smug as hell I guided a man as powerful as him through the fog before his cock got anywhere near my mouth.

TWENTY-SEVEN

Roxanne

I grimace when the quickest hiss darts through my ears. Smith numbed the area he's inserting a micro tracker into, so I don't feel an ounce of pain. It's just realizing I'll have a foreign device in my arm for the rest of my life that has me grimacing.

Although I would have preferred not to be microchipped like a dog, I didn't have much choice. If I denied Dimitri's request, he would have reneged on the agreement we made last night. I couldn't let that happen. Our ruse is his first solid chance to get his daughter back. It should come before anything—even my freedom.

Fien is a captive because my mother begged my father to swap Dimitri's wife with me, so it's my responsibility to do everything in my power to help Dimitri get her back. I'm scared, but I'm also hopeful. It's clear Dimitri loves his daughter. Once she's back, perhaps he will realize love comes in many forms.

"Does that feel okay?"

I raise my eyes to Smith, the querier of my question. "It feels a little weird."

"The device or your head?" Rocco asks on a laugh, shocked by the slur of my words. I don't know what Smith used to numb my arm, but it has my head convinced I guzzled a fifth of vodka with my dinner.

"A teeny bit of both."

"Your dizziness will settle soon." Smith rubs an alcohol swap over the nick in my arm before he places a Band-Aid over it. "If it doesn't, I'll give you another dose. It will have you sleeping like a baby within an hour."

I want to sock him in the stomach but hold back the urge when I notice Dimitri's narrowed gaze. He looks five seconds from killing Smith, and his oxygen-depriving protectiveness doubles the wooziness bombarding me.

"Thank you."

Smith lifts his chin, acknowledging my thanks before he moves to clean up the mess he made in his makeshift hospital room. We're still at my family's ranch, conscious my booking for Dr. Bates's clinic may have eyes placed on me earlier than my appointment. The shutters are closed, a beat-up Honda is in the driveway, and Smith has numerous jammers scattered amongst the dated furniture. To anyone outside of these walls, it appears as if Dimitri is still done with me. Only those in the know are experiencing his panic firsthand.

He's been more reserved than usual today. He agrees our plan is smart, but he's still cautious he's making the wrong decision. I'll do my best to assure him otherwise between now and my appointment tomorrow morning. By remaining fearless, he'll soon realize just how much faith I have in him. He will keep me safe no matter what. I've never had more confidence in anything in my life but that.

After a lengthy debate this morning, we decided the go with the ploy Smith and I discussed while Dimitri was unconscious from a combined drug overdose and exhaustion. According to our plan, I called the private cell phone Dr. Bates scribbled across his business card when he endeavored to buy me outright, panicked out of my mind that my period was late and how Dimitri would kill me if he found out.

By staying on script, we learned that Dr. Bates is knowledgeable on parts of Dimitri's life not many people know about. His voice didn't waver in the slightest when I said Dimitri would be mad as hell if I fell pregnant at the start of our relationship like his wife did. It was as if he already knew their story. I wasn't sharing anything new with him.

After ensuring me I'd be okay, Dr. Bates offered to clear his schedule so I could immediately come in. That threw me out of the loop for a couple of seconds. I hadn't expected him to react so quickly. Although I was eager to get our ruse started—the quicker it occurs, the faster Fien will be returned—I knew Dimitri's team needed more than twenty minutes to put steps into play to ensure Dr. Bates's every move was being scrutinized.

I also perhaps needed more than a measly twenty minutes with Dimitri before his life is upended for the second time. We haven't had a moment of quiet since he agreed to my offer. It's been full steam ahead since then.

"Still nothing?" I ask after stopping at Dimitri's side. I

don't know who he's been trying to call the past six hours, but the tension on his face grows more obvious the longer his calls remain unanswered. I'm confident his worry doesn't stem from his cousin. She left here earlier today with an armored fleet as impressive as the one they used to bring Maddox here for the night, but it's clear he's noticing their absence.

"He must be somewhere without cell phone service as he's never not taken my call."

As he slides his phone into the pocket of his trousers, I spot the name of the man he's endeavoring to reach on its screen. Rico. He must be new to Dimitri's sanction because it isn't a name I've heard the past several weeks.

"Ask Smith to track his cell. If it's turned on, he should be able to find it." Keen to soothe the heavy groove between his brows, I add, "Even without a trendy microchip installed in your arm, it's almost impossible to remain incognito these days."

His smirk is only half what I was hoping for, but it's better than nothing.

After a few more minutes soaking up his handsome face, I say, "I'm going to go lay down for a couple of minutes. My head is a little woozy." I peer up at him with hopeful eyes. "Would you care to join me?"

Only weeks ago, I wouldn't have been game to assume he wants to sleep with me. Now, it feels as natural as breathing. Even with his quiet taking up a majority of my focus today, I've noticed his heated gaze directed at me multiple times. He finally believes I'm on his side, and I'm more than willing to continue convincing him, especially if that can only occur while he's naked. I've always been the more daring one of my friends, and now that I've discovered just how powerful sex can make you feel, I want to flex my muscles.

Either mishearing the innuendo in my tone or too worried to sleep, Dimitri replies, "I've got a few things to take care of first. I'll join you once they're finalized." The drop of my bottom lip isn't as noticeable when he lowers his voice to ensure his next set of words is only for my ears. "Sleep naked. I don't want anything between us when I come to bed."

"Okay." Considering I only spoke one word, it shouldn't be as breathy as it is.

After squeezing his hand, wordlessly assuring him he has nothing to worry about, I skip to my room, confident it's the perfect location to ease his panic.

Many, many hours later, the creak of an old set of hinges wakes me from my slumber. My head is still a little woozy, but it's more compliments to Dimitri's delicious scent than the sedative Smith gave me. He strips beside the bed like he did every night we shared the same room before he slips between the sheets.

Unlike our last night together at his compound, I don't cry into his chest when he pulls me into his arms. I moan. He's thick, warm, and he smells like me since the only shower he's had the past twenty-four hours is the one we shared.

A husky moan fills my ears when he curls my leg around his waist. For once, I'm confident it didn't come from me. Dimitri is responding to my submissiveness in a way that ensures it will occur more often from here on out. I'm naked as he requested, and his scent alone has me the wettest I've ever been.

"Grip my shoulders like your cunt does my cock. If I go too fast, dig your nails in deep." He bites my bottom lip, drags his tongue across the welt, then tastes the minty flavor of my toothpaste before he adds, "I don't want to hurt you."

"You won't."

A stretch of silence follows my promise. It's a tense, beautiful moment occupied by Dimitri slowly sinking inside of me. I fist the sheets as big, extended breaths seep from my mouth. The feeling of being stretched so wide is wondrous, but it has nothing on the sensation that overwhelms me when our eyes collide. His earlier panic has receded. Now, nothing but pleasing me is on his mind.

When shudders commence rolling through me, I freeze. I can't possibly be coming already. He's barely rocked his hips four times.

The thought he can bring me to climax so fast turns me on more than I could ever explain. It doubles the tingles in my womb and ramps up my moans to an embarrassing level.

"Come hard for me, Roxie. Coat my cock with your juices, then I can try and stuff my cock all the way in."

His tongue laps at my lips as he rocks in and out of me, prolonging my orgasm to the point I'm considering classing it as two. The wetness soaking the sheets should have me blushing. However, it doesn't. I'm drenched front to back, moaning like we're the only two people in the world and clenching around Dimitri's fat cock with every plunge he does.

We're not brutally fucking as we did last night, proving I don't need violence nor an audience to get off. The perfect rolls of his hips and the dirty words he whispers in my ear is everything I need.

It's perfect.

Mind-blowing.

Fireworks producing.

It has me stuttering out a warning I'm about to come again before the first one has fully dissipated. It's a brilliant exchange that verifies every crazy decision I've made the past nine weeks was for the best.

"I knew you'd be like this. Explosive and un-fucking-relentless." Dimitri rolls me onto my back before he curls my legs around his sweaty back. "How many times did you dream about this after that dweeb's attempt to get you off in the alleyway?"

"More times than I can count," I answer truthfully, unconcerned by his name-calling. You can't be expected to think morally when you're in a situation like this. Even the most solid principles burn when the fire is out of control. "But it's better than I could have ever comprehended. No one can predict explosions like this. They're unpredictable..." I lock my eyes with Dimitri's, meowing when I notice how clear of trouble they are, "... kind of like you."

He thrusts into me deeper, faster, and harder, turned on by my words. It's crazy, but within seconds, I feel another powerful, all-encompassing orgasm building inside of me, and I'm not the only one noticing.

As he demands the attention of my dripping sex with quick, powerful strokes, Dimitri raises his hand to one of my breasts. He pinches my nipple, growling when the sharpness of his touch sends me freefalling over the edge.

A shudder rips through me from my head to my toes as Dimitri's name leaves my throat in a grunted moan. My climax is violent. It takes everything I have and then some. I feel incapable of breathing. I'm hot everywhere and screaming oh so loudly. I can't control it. It's uncontrollable. It pummels into me over and over again like a violent ocean refusing to leave a single victim. I'd let it take me if it promised every night would be as exquisite as this one.

"There you are," Dimitri mutters against my lips, God knows how long later. I'm dazed like I zoned out for longer than a couple of minutes, the prompts of my body no longer mine. They've been relinquished to Dimitri, along with my heart.

"I love…" I freeze, fretful I'm about to make a horrendous mistake.

I don't know this man. We were strangers only months ago, but that doesn't mean I can't also love him, does it? He forced me to share information I've never wanted to give anyone, but that isn't necessarily a bad thing. I may have very well fallen in love with him that morning in the plane. He didn't judge me as I thought he would. He held me in his arms and wiped away my tears. He was there for me like no one ever was.

Whether in fear or euphoria, he makes my heart beat like

no one else can. Its patters will never be matched for anyone who isn't him.

That, in itself, is worthy of recognition.

That deserves acknowledgment.

Confident this will be by far the least stupid thing I've done, I return my eyes to Dimitri's face, gulping when I notice his watch. The speed of his pumps hasn't slackened in the slightest despite him noticing my thirty seconds of deliberation. He stares straight at me, the altering of the light in his eyes as fascinating as his infamous half-smirk when I say, "I love you, Dimitri Petretti. Your fierceness, your cockiness, I love everything about you."

TWENTY-EIGHT

Dimitri

oing everything I can to weaken the knot in my gut, I pace the room. I didn't know I was walking into a trap when I offered to chauffeur Audrey to her baby shower. If I'd known, I would have put actions into place to protect her and keep our daughter safe. I would have had every eye of my team on her as they are now on Roxanne. However, no matter what I did twenty-two months ago, my panic would still be valid today.

If my enemies hadn't taken Audrey, they would have taken Roxanne, and then I wouldn't have heard the words she spoke to me as clear as day last night.

I killed her boyfriend, tortured her family, and have threatened to kill her more times than I've showed her an ounce of affection, yet, she still loves me.

She. *Loves*. Me.

The thought blows my mind. It also had cum rushing out of my cock last night like I hadn't had sex in years. I filled

Roxanne to the brim before displaying exactly what her words meant to me with my body. We fucked for hours. It was glorious, the best sex I've ever had, but it feels like a thing of the past now as I watch Roxanne prepare for her appointment with Dr. Bates.

The beat-up Honda Rocco purchased from a used-car dealer three towns over is wired to the hilt. It has a tracker, multiple microphones, and almost as many cameras as Roxanne's clothing. We have every angle covered, yet I still feel like I should call off the whole thing.

I wouldn't hesitate if Fien's ransom hadn't landed in my inbox this morning. It was short, snarky, and requesting a year's payout for only one month, proving Roxanne's chat with Dr. Bates yesterday morning has circulated amongst my enemies.

It also has me confident Roxanne is right. The instigator of Fien's captivity is a woman. I can smell bullshit from a mile out. Jealousy extends to five. The scent that streamed through my nose while reading Fien's ransom request was fucking rank. The person responsible for the hell I've lived in the past two years is a female—a dead one when I find out who she is.

"Is that everything?" I ask Roxanne when she ties up the final lace of her boots.

Alice picked a casual look for Roxanne today with a free-flowing dress, a cropped jacket, tights, and boots that are more than capable of removing a guy's nuts if he gets out of line.

I requested for her to wear the boots.

Rocco was adamant they needed to be steel caps.

Nodding, Roxanne licks her lips. She won't say she's scared because she knows I'd call off our ruse in an instant. Little threads are unraveling everywhere, so it will only be a matter of time before Fien's captives are brought to justice, but Roxanne is also mindful that every hour I'm without Fien feels like a lifetime of punishment. For some insane reason, she wants to save me from the nightmare, and her motives have nothing to do with the fact she was swapped for Audrey. She's so under my thumb, even if her parents had nothing to do with Audrey's murder, she'd still offer to place her life on the line for Fien. No fear.

That thought alone has me doing something my crew would never expect to see me do. I don't bid Roxanne farewell with a dip of my chin. I kiss her with everything I have. Teeth, lips, tongue, they all get in on the action. I pass on my appreciation for what she's doing and the words she shared last night, then I promise her loyalty won't go unnoticed.

I *will* protect her better than I did Audrey.

I *will* keep her safe.

She has my guarantee I won't let anything happen to her.

By the time I pull back, Roxanne's knees are wobbling, and Rocco is clapping. "I didn't think you had it in you, D, but I was wrong. You can *totally* make me hard."

I cut off the grab of his crotch with a stern sideways glance. I appreciate he's trying to bring down the tension in the room with a little bit of humor, but now isn't the time. I'm five seconds from throwing in the towel on an operation that could get me my daughter back. That's unacceptable even to consider. However, it's straight-up honest. I've never felt as conflicted as I do now. It feels as if I have Roxanne's life in one hand and Fien's in the other with no possibility of them both making it out of the carnage unscathed.

I've just got to try what Roxanne suggested. I have to put my faith in the people who have never given me any reason to doubt their loyalty. I won't lie. The track is bumpy, but I'm giving it my best shot.

I return Roxanne's focus to me by running my index finger down the little bump in her arm. The implant site of her tracker is still sensitive to touch, but since the tracker is the size of a grain of rice, it's barely noticeable to the human eye. "If at any time you feel something is off, signal for us to move in. Rocco will be in the pharmacy next door. Clover and a team are one block over. I've got as many men on this as possible—"

"I know, Dimi," she interrupts, smiling to assure me she got the gist of what my kiss was about. "We've got every base covered. Now we just need to get your daughter back." She wipes off her sticky lip gloss from my mouth before she pivots to face Rocco. "Ready?"

Rocco's face is well-known to our enemies, so he can't drive Roxanne to her appointment, but he will tail her two-town trip. My enemies would expect her to have a constant shadow since I'm as neurotic as I am wealthy.

"I was born ready." After gathering up a set of keys, Rocco heads for the back entrance, so he can be in his truck before Roxanne departs the main entrance, patting my shoulder on the way by. "She's got this, D. She was run over *twice*. She can handle anything."

Once Smith gives Roxanne a final rundown on each camera button in her dress, she glances my way for the quickest second, waves like her heart isn't thudding in her chest, then slips out the front door.

My brain switches from personal to business just as quickly. "Bring up the surveillance cameras in Dr. Bates's office."

One of the techies Smith brings in when he gets snowed under jumps to my command. I can't recall his name. It starts with an H, I think.

Once Dr. Bates's office is displayed on multiple screens in front of me, I shift on my feet to face Smith. "Are all communication methods hacked?"

He jerks up his chin. "We've got eyes and ears in each location and frequencies scanning remotely. Even if he uses a burner phone, we'll know exactly what he sends and who he sends it to."

"Will it give us a location?"

My jaw tightens when he shakes his head. "But that will come with time."

It's an effort not to sigh as I have no patience whatsoever. That's why our plan today is slowly killing me. We have every intention to let Roxanne be kidnapped this morning, confident the group Dr. Bates is working with will take her straight to Rimi Castro. Then we'll use the tracker in Roxanne's arm to pinpoint her location, go in hard, then come out victorious.

Sounds easy enough, but very rarely does it pan out that way. And I'm not going to mention my intuition warning me to pull back on the reins, or I'll instruct Smith to overtake the controls of Roxanne's car she's steering toward Hopeton.

We have control of everything except the one thing I want to control the most. I can slay my enemies, I can gut them until they're spineless, worthless men, but I can't seem to outrun them lately. I'm always one step behind, and more times than not, that minute gap is filled with the biggest chunk of anarchy.

It kills me to admit that. I'd give anything to change it. But I can't. That isn't the way things work in this industry. If you're not giving it to someone up the ass, you're taking it. I'm so fucking over it, but I have no choice but to play the game as it's meant to be played. I can mix up the pieces as I did by bringing Rico onto my side of the board, I can strategize to ensure the princess is protected above the king, but I can't alter the rules to suit myself. If I did, it wouldn't just be me paying the penalty. Fien would, and so would Roxanne.

With that in mind, I get back to business. "How many patients does Dr. Bates have coming in today?"

"According to his schedule, over half a dozen."

Sensing some unease in Smith's reply, I ask, "And according to you?"

He takes a moment to deliberate before locking his brown eyes with mine. "He's organized to have lunch with his wife today. They're planning to eat in Ravenshoe."

"Is that out of the ordinary for them?"

He nods. "The last time they ate together was Thanksgiving four years ago. To say things are strained would be an understatement, so why would he go out of his way to wine and dine her today?"

He has a point—regretfully. "Send someone to the restaurant he's planning to dine at. It could be a waste of resources, but I'd rather be cautious."

While he attends to that, I request the techie whose name I still can't remember to bring up the main camera in Roxanne's car, praying like fuck the last time I see her face won't be through a computer monitor.

TWENTY-NINE

Roxanne

I breathe out the nerves making me a jittery mess before making my way to the reception desk at Dr. Bates's OBGYN office for the second time this morning. The foyer is inviting with music playing softly in the background and scented candles wafting in the air, but the feeling of dread refuses to leave me. Dr. Bates was the least creepy of my suitors when I was put up for auction. He was well-spoken, dressed nicely, and excluding when he tried to un-cut Dimitri's profit by offering to pay me directly for my virginity, he seemed pleasant.

Fool me once, shame on me.

He won't fool me again.

The information Smith shared about him when we discussed a way to bring him down for drugging Dimitri had me rechewing food I had earlier eaten. He has bounced his practice state to state, had more than a dozen affairs on his wife, and is linked to the disappearance of at least three women. All were in their final weeks of pregnancy, and all of them were blonde—his seemingly preferred choice.

His knowable likes are the reason I kept my hair red. We're not here to entice him into locking me up in his playroom of kinks. We want him to pass me onto the men Dimitri believes are responsible for his daughter's captivity.

Just the thought of being in the room with such men gives me the heebie-jeebies. Fortunately, the tingles I still feel buzzing on my lips from Dimitri's awe-inspiring kiss is much more potent. It would encourage a saint to walk through Hell's gates with a smile on her face and a wish for Satan to bring everything he has to the party.

"You can go straight in, Ms. Grace," informs the receptionist when I place down the clipboard she requested me to fill in on arrival.

"Are you sure?" I scan the room brimming with patients, certain almost all of them were here before I arrived.

"Yes," she responds with a smile, drawing my focus back to her. "Dr. Bates is waiting for you."

"Okay." I sound as uneased as I feel. The overflowing waiting room would make most women feel safe. There's a weird comfort you get with numbers, but I'm not experiencing that. There is less chance of me being kidnapped since it's the middle of the day, so my chances are even lower with a heap of spectators. I hope today's charade isn't utterly pointless. "Which way?"

The receptionist hands me a gown and a small jar with a yellow lid before pointing to a hall on our right. "Bathrooms are through the second door on the left. Dr. Bates is the one just after that."

Nodding, I slowly make my way to Dr. Bates's office. I could get changed as per the receptionist's underhanded demand, but that would make the camera buttons in my dress futile. Considering it took Smith almost all night to fit them, I'd rather keep them in operation.

After breathing out my nerves, I push open the door with Dr. Bates tacked on the front. "Dr. Bates, hi." My greeting is ridiculously sweet, my role of knocked-up virgin played to perfection. "The bathrooms were occupied, so I hope you don't mind me skipping that part of my appointment." I bite on the inside of my cheek, hopeful a rush of blood from my gnaw will have Dr. Bates believing I'm blushing. "I don't feel comfortable doing *that...*" I wave my hand over the ultrasound equipment next to a bed with obvious stirrups.

He swivels around to face me, blocking the images of multiple blonde females on the screen of his computer with his wide shoulders. Since he dyes his hair, it's hard to guess his age, but if forced, I'd say mid-forties. "That's fine, Roxanne. I don't need to examine you today." As he drags his eyes over my fire-engine red hair, he stands to his feet. He's dressed more casually than he was at my auction, which is shocking considering this is his place of occupation. "Is that new?"

I sheepishly balance my chin on my chest as if I'm ashamed. "Dimitri preferred redheads."

It's the fight of my life not to seek out one of the many hidden cameras Smith advised me about this morning when Dr. Bates replies, "I have heard that." While smiling at my flushed cheeks, he gestures his hand to the examination table. "Why don't you put down your things and take a seat."

I begin to wonder if we've misjudged him when my jump to his command is quickly chased by him checking my vitals. He takes my blood pressure, checks my pulse, and flashes a light into my eyes before asking a set of personal questions, such as, when did I last have my period.

"Umm…" His question legitimately stumps me. With my last thirty-six hours spent ensuring Dimitri has made the right decision to trust me, I didn't have time to sit down and calculate a date that would have me six or so weeks along. "Around eight weeks ago."

I touch his arm like I'm embarrassed to admit I had no reason to keep an eye on things like that only months ago. I'm honestly ashamed, so it's an easy act for me to pull off.

An unpleasant glint darts through Dr. Bates's eyes as he asks, "Have you had unprotected sex since your last period?"

The heat on my cheeks is real this time around. Not only is Dimitri eavesdropping on our conversation, almost every member of his team is as well. "Yes. Multiple times."

I almost choke on my last two words, stunned I've not once cited an objection to Dimitri's inability to sheath his cock with protection. I shouldn't be surprised. I barely keep a rational head when he looks at me, so I don't see me having the power to bark out a set of orders when his head is between my legs.

Dr. Bates drops his eyes to the monitor of his computer before asking, "Have you had sexual intercourse in the last twenty-four hours?" He didn't need to hide his eyes for me to sense his annoyance. I can feel it radiating out of him.

I almost nod before recalling why I left my grandparents' ranch this morning. As far as Dimitri's enemies are concerned, we're over and done with, his annoyance about my 'supposed' pregnancy the cause of our breakup. "No, I haven't."

"Great!" Dr. Bates's shouted word startles me. "So, there shouldn't be any issues with your test."

Panic and fear roll through me at the same time. "Test? I thought you didn't need to examine me today?"

You could class Dr. Bates's smile as cute if he didn't have the markings of a psychopath. "Not a physical test. A pregnancy test."

I gulp back my sigh when he stands from his chair to gather the jar the receptionist handed me five minutes ago. "You can use my private restroom." He presses his palm against a wooden panel next to his desk before moving to stand in front of the doorway leading to the hall, blocking my only exit. "Then you won't have any worries about stage fright."

"I don't really need to go." When the humor on his face evaporates, I switch tactics. "But I guess there's no harm in trying."

After snatching the jar out of his hand, I make a beeline for his private washroom, ensuring the door latches shut behind me.

"I'm so sorry," I apologize to my reflection in the mirror. "I didn't think he would do a test."

My lack of knowledge can easily be excused. Up until a few weeks ago, I was a virgin. It doesn't make me naïve, but it most certainly has me on the back foot when it comes to things like babies and pregnancy tests.

"Please tell me you're not going to watch me pee."

Dimitri can't answer me. The radio frequency Smith needed to track any calls coming in and out of Dr. Bates's office means I couldn't use the fancy bead-like listening device I did when my virginity was auctioned.

Confident Dimitri is too possessive to let anyone see me in a vulnerable state, I walk to the toilet, hook up my dress, yank down my panties and tights, then pee into the jar Dr. Bates was kind enough to open for me.

With my knees shaking in disappointment, half my pee lands on my hand instead of the jar. It frustrates me, but it has nothing on how annoyed I'll be when my ruse backfires in my face in a couple of minutes. When my test comes back negative, Dr. Bates may become suspicious we're onto him. If that happens, he may shut up shop for the fifth time this decade. Then our chances of finding Fien will be even lower than they already are.

Once my hands are scrubbed clean, and the panic is washed from my face, I exit the bathroom. Dr. Bates appears as if he hasn't moved. I know that isn't the case. He not only has a pregnancy test in his hand, but there's also an outline of a cell phone in his pocket.

Sorry, buddy. Your bank accounts aren't about to become overloaded with funds, I mumble in my head while handing him a jar of pee.

While Dr. Bates dips the end of the pregnancy test into the jar, I conjure up an excuse to leave. "How long do these things take? Should I wait outside while you do your magic?"

Light hair falls into his eyes when he peers at me over his shoulder. "No, that isn't necessary. They only take a minute at the most."

Knowing what the results will be, I gather my belongings from the examination table before hovering near the door. My nervous bob shifts to a shake when Dr. Bates says, "Or in your case, only thirty seconds."

I feel my pupils dilate to the size of saucers when he lifts a positive pregnancy test in the air a mere second before he peers into an obvious camera in the corner of the room. Then, not even a second later, I feel someone creeping up on me.

THIRTY

Dimitri

"Get her out." I leap up from my chair, too bristling with unease to sit for a second longer. "Get her out now!"

I'm stunned I can talk. My brain is fried from taking in Roxanne's positive pregnancy test. It makes the ruse I was certain was just about to bust more authentic, but I'll be fucked if I let my enemies get another one of my children.

I also don't want Roxanne to go through what Audrey went through. I could barely stomach it when it happened to my wife. I won't handle it occurring to a woman I love.

As Rocco leaps into action, I dart my eyes between the many monitors in front of me. Roxanne appears as shocked by the results as me. She stares at the now-blue stick with her mouth hanging open and her eyes bulged. Her expression is the same shocked one Audrey wore when her test came back positive. However, she isn't being subjected to the verbal tirade I spat out upon discovering the news I was about to be a father.

Back then, I thought my world was crumbling.

Now I know it most definitely is.

Even with my wish to kill the highest it's ever been, I keep a rational head. Flying off the hinges won't help anyone right now. It won't help me, it won't help Fien, and it most certainly won't help Roxanne.

"What was that?" I point to the monitor, the quickest flurry of black darted past. It could have been the shadow of one of the many pregnant women mingling in the hallway, but it seemed wider, more deviant.

It feels like the world caves in on me when the dozen monitors surrounding me suddenly plunge into blackness. It's a total communication blackout, leaving Roxanne utterly defenseless.

"Move!"

Smith forcefully plucks one of the techies from his chair so he can take over the controls. He taps on a gel keyboard like a madman, bringing up one camera at a time. He's working as fast as he can, but to me, it isn't fast enough. My worst nightmare is coming true for the second time, except this time, I'm knee-deep in the controversy.

I agreed to Roxanne's suggestion.

I put her in danger.

Once again, nothing happening is her fault.

"Where is she?" I ask fearfully when the return of the live feed to Dr. Bates's office comes up empty. As my eyes dart from screen to screen to screen seeking the feeblest snippet of red, my blood boils. She has to be there. The cameras were down for barely twenty seconds. No one can move that fast—not even me.

"There!" shouts a blond-haired techy who's pointing to a screen on my left.

Relief engulfs me when my eyes drink in Roxanne's svelte frame and beautiful face. It doesn't linger for long. She's no longer on her feet. She's been carried down an isolated corridor in the arms of a man wearing all black, their brisk walk shadowed by Dr. Bates. She is also without clothing.

"Their taking her out the hidden entrance," I advise Rocco via the comms server I'm praying is still in function.

When my demand is followed by a painful stretch of silence, I shout, "Get him on his cell."

Smith's voice makes it seem as if his throat is being shredded with the same razor blades cutting up mine. "On it."

I rip my fingers through my hair when the buzz of Rocco's cell phone rings out of the speakers of Smith's computer over and over again. He isn't in any of the frames, he's nowhere to be found, and Roxanne's unconscious body is being thrown into the back of an unmarked van.

"Prepare to commence trace." I watch in feared awe as Smith takes hold of the reins like he was born to do it. He activates the chip in Roxanne's arm and advises Clover coordinates are on their way before he raises his eyes to mine. "Are you sure you want Clover to move in now? This was the plan, Dimi. Roxie could lead us straight to Fien."

I'm so fucking torn. It truly feels like this decision will tear me in two. If I don't move now, I could lose Roxanne. If

I hold off, I could bring both her and my daughter home—but what happens if that occurs *after* Roxanne has already been hurt. What if I'm too late for the second time?

I'm convinced my enemies are wired-tapped into my inner-workings when the decision is taken out of my hands. Just as quickly as the surveillance devices shutdown in Dr. Bates's office, we lose our connection with Roxanne's tracker.

Fury boils beneath my skin as I stare at an unmoving blue dot on a map of the town I should have owned years ago. "What happened?"

Smith shrugs. Anger is written all over his face. As he strives to find answers, he punishes his keyboard. I struggle not to do the same to his face when he sinks into his chair with a groan a few seconds later. "They removed her fucking tracker."

"What do you mean?" I ask, my voice unlike anything I've ever heard before. "No one knows she was wearing a tracker, so how do you know they've removed it."

My confusion is alleviated in the worst way possible when Smith hooks his thumb to the screen of his laptop. Rocco is in the middle of the monitor. He's bleeding, red-faced, and holding up the tiniest little microchip to a security camera in the back alleyway of a Publix Supermarket chain.

I played with more than I could afford to lose, and I fucking lost—*again*.

The end...

Dimitri and Roxanne's story continues in the next explosive part of the Italian Cartel Series. **Reign** will release November 11, you can preorder it here: books2read. com/u/47XWZN

If you want to hear updates on the next books in this crazy world I've created, be sure to join my **readers group**: Shandi's Book Babes

Or my **Facebook Page**: www.facebook.com/authorshandi

Rico, Asher, Isaac, Brandon, Ryan, Cormack, Enrique & Brax stories have already been released, but Grayson, Rocco, Clover, and all the other great characters of Ravenshoe/Hopeton will be getting their own stories at some point during 2020/2021.

If you enjoyed this book please leave a review.

Acknowledgments

To all the peeps who make this happen, a huge thank you.

To my editor, Nicki @ Swish Design and Editing, my mom, the alpha readers, beta readers, and the people who download my books without even reading the blurb. Thank you, thank you, thank you. I truly appreciate you from the bottom of my heart.

You rock!

I can't do an acknowledgement page without mentioning the man who makes this all possible. To my husband, Chris. Thank you for being you, and for being my number one fan before I had written a single word.

I love you, boo.

Today, tomorrow, and forever.

Shandi xx

Facebook: facebook.com/authorshandi

Instagram: instagram.com/authorshandi

Email: authorshandi@gmail.com

Reader's Group: bit.ly/ShandiBookBabes

Website: authorshandi.com

Newsletter: https://www.subscribepage.com/AuthorShandi

Also by Shandi Boyes

Perception Series

Saving Noah (Noah & Emily)

Fighting Jacob (Jacob & Lola)

Taming Nick (Nick & Jenni)

Redeeming Slater (Slater and Kylie)

Saving Emily (Noah & Emily - Novella)

Wrapped Up with Rise Up (Perception Novella - should be read after the Bound Series)

Enigma

Enigma (Isaac & Isabelle #1)

Unraveling an Enigma (Isaac & Isabelle #2)

Enigma The Mystery Unmasked (Isaac & Isabelle #3)

Enigma: The Final Chapter (Isaac & Isabelle #4)

Beneath The Secrets (Hugo & Ava #1)

Beneath The Sheets(Hugo & Ava #2)

Spy Thy Neighbor (Hunter & Paige)

The Opposite Effect (Brax & Clara)

I Married a Mob Boss(Rico & Blaire)

Second Shot(Hawke & Gemma)

The Way We Are(Ryan & Savannah #1)

The Way We Were(Ryan & Savannah #2)

Sugar and Spice (Cormack & Harlow)

Lady In Waiting (Regan & Alex #1)

Man in Queue (Regan & Alex #2)

Couple on Hold(Regan & Alex #3)

Enigma: The Wedding (Isaac and Isabelle)

Silent Vigilante (Brandon and Melody #1)

Hushed Guardian (Brandon & Melody #2)

Quiet Protector (Brandon & Melody #3)

Bound Series

Chains (Marcus & Cleo #1)

Links(Marcus & Cleo #2)

Bound(Marcus & Cleo #3)

Restrain(Marcus & Cleo #4)

Psycho (Dexter & ??)

Russian Mob Chronicles

Nikolai: A Mafia Prince Romance (Nikolai & Justine #1)

Nikolai: Taking Back What's Mine (Nikolai & Justine #2)

Nikolai: What's Left of Me(Nikolai & Justine #3)

Nikolai: Mine to Protect(Nikolai & Justine #4)

Asher: My Russian Revenge (Asher & Zariah)

Nikolai: Through the Devil's Eyes(Nikolai & Justine #5)

Trey (Trey & K)

The Italian Cartel

Dimitri

Roxanne

Reign

Maddox

Rocco

RomCom Standalones

Just Playin' (Elvis & Willow)

The Drop Zone (Colby & Jamie)

Ain't Happenin'(Lorenzo & Skylar)

Short Stories

Christmas Trio (Wesley, Andrew & Mallory -- short story)

Falling For A Stranger (Short Story)

K (A Trey Sequel)

Coming Soon

Skitzo

Made in United States
North Haven, CT
13 January 2025

64389858R10153